It ha

Out of

In deserted corners of an

unsuspecting city...

THE WOLFEN

There is no defense.

There is no escape.

There is nowhere to hide.

Avon Books are available at special quantity discounts for bulk
purchases for sales promotions, premiums, fund raising or educa-
tional use. Special books, or book excerpts, can also be created to
fit specific needs.

For details write or telephone the office of the Director of Special
Markets, Avon Books, Dept. FP, 105 Madison Avenue, New York,
New York 10016, 212-481-5653.

THE
WOLFEN

WHITLEY STRIEBER

◆ **AVON**
PUBLISHERS OF BARD, CAMELOT, DISCUS AND FLARE BOOKS

AVON BOOKS
A division of
The Hearst Corporation
105 Madison Avenue
New York, New York 10016

Copyright © 1978 by Whitley Strieber
Published by arrangement with William Morrow and Company, Inc.
ISBN: 0-380-70440-4

First Avon Books Printing: March 1988

AVON TRADEMARK REG. U.S. PAT. OFF. AND IN OTHER COUNTRIES, MARCA
REGISTRADA, HECHO EN U.S.A.

Printed in the U.S.A.

K-R 10 9 8 7 6 5 4 3 2 1

For Anne

Since all is well, keep it so:
Wake not the sleeping wolf.

—SHAKESPEARE
Henry IV, Part 2

THE WOLFEN

Chapter 1

In Brooklyn they take abandoned cars to the Fountain
Avenue Automobile Pound adjacent to the Fountain
Avenue Dump. The pound and the dump occupy land
shown on maps as "Spring Creek Park (Proposed)."
There is no spring, no creek, and no park.

Normally the pound is silent, its peace disturbed
only by an occasional fight among the packs of wild
dogs that roam there, or perhaps the cries of the sea
gulls that hover over the stinking, smoldering dump
nearby.

The members of the Police Auto Squad who visit
the pound to mark derelicts for the crusher do not
consider the place dangerous. Once in a while the
foot-long rats will get aggressive and become the victims of target practice. The scruffy little wild dogs will
also attack every so often, but they can usually be
dealt with by a shot into the ground. Auto-pound duty
consists of marking big white X's on the worst of the

1

derelicts and taking Polaroids of them to prove that they were beyond salvage in case any owners turn up.

It isn't the kind of job that the men associate with danger, much less getting killed, so Hugo DiFalco and Dennis Houlihan would have laughed in your face if you told them they had only three minutes to live when they heard the first sound behind them.

"What was that?" Houlihan asked. He was bored and wouldn't have minded getting a couple of shots off at a rat.

"A noise."

"Brilliant. That's what I thought it was too."

They both laughed. Then there was another sound, a staccato growl that ended on a murmuring high note. The two men looked at one another. "That sounds like my brother singing in the shower," DiFalco said.

From ahead of them came further sounds—rustlings and more of the unusual growls. DiFalco and Houlihan stopped. They weren't joking anymore, but they also weren't afraid, only curious. The wet, ruined cars just didn't seem to hold any danger on this dripping autumn afternoon. But there was something out there.

They were now in the center of a circle of half-heard rustling movement. As both men realized that something had surrounded them, they had their first twinge of concern. They now had less than one minute of life remaining. Both of them lived with the central truth of police work—it could happen anytime. But what the hell was happening now?

Then something stepped gingerly from between two derelicts and stood facing the victims.

The men were not frightened, but they sensed danger. As it had before in moments of peril, Hugo

DiFalco's mind turned to a brief thought of his wife, of how she liked to say "We're an us." Dennis Houlihan felt a shiver of prickles come over him as if the hair all over his body was standing up.

"Don't move, man," DiFalco said.

It snarled at the voice. "There's more of 'em behind us, buddy." Their voices were low and controlled, the tone of professionals in trouble. They moved closer together; their shoulders touched. Both men knew that one of them had to turn around, the other keep facing this way. But they didn't need to talk about it; they had worked together too long to have to plan their moves.

DiFalco started to make the turn and draw his pistol. That was the mistake.

Ten seconds later their throats were being torn out. Twenty seconds later the last life was pulsing out of their bodies. Thirty seconds later they were being systematically consumed.

Neither man had made a sound. Houlihan had seen the one in front of them twitch its eyes, but before he could follow the movement there was a searing pain in his throat and he was suddenly, desperately struggling for air through the bubbling torrent of his own blood.

DiFalco's hand had just gripped the familiar checkered wooden butt of his service revolver when it was yanked violently aside. The impression of impossibly fast-moving shapes entered his astonished mind, then something slammed into his chest and he too was bleeding, in his imagination protecting his throat as in reality his body slumped to the ground and his mind sank into darkness.

The attackers moved almost too quickly, their speed born of nervousness at the youth of their victims. The shirts were torn open, the white chests exposed, the entrails tugged out and taken away, the precious organs swallowed. The rest was left behind.

In less than five more minutes it was over. The hollow, ravaged corpses lay there in the mud, two ended lives now food for the wild scavengers of the area.

For a long time nothing more moved at the Fountain Avenue Automobile Pound. The cries of gulls echoed among the rustling hulks of the cars. Around the corpses the blood coagulated and blackened. As the afternoon drew on, the autumn mist became rain, covering the dead policemen with droplets of water and making the blood run again.

Night fell.

Rats worried the corpses until dawn.

The two men had been listed AWOL for fourteen hours. Most unusual for these guys. They were both family types, steady and reliable. AWOL wasn't their style. But still, what could happen to two experienced policemen on marking duty at the auto pound? That was a question nobody would even try to answer until a search was made for the men.

Police work might be dangerous, but nobody seriously believed that DiFalco and Houlihan were in any real trouble. Maybe there had been a family emergency and the two had failed to check in. Maybe a lot of things. And maybe there *was* some trouble. Nobody realized that the world had just become a much more dangerous place, and they wouldn't understand that for quite some time. Right now they were just looking for a couple of missing policemen. Right now the mystery began and ended with four cops poking through the auto pound for signs of their buddies.

"They better not be sleeping in some damn car." Secretly all four men hoped that the two AWOL officers were off on a bender or something. You'd rather see that than the other possibility.

A cop screamed. The sound stunned the other three to silence because it was one they rarely heard.

"Over here," the rookie called in a choking voice.

"Hold on, man." The other three converged on the spot as the rookie's cries sounded again and again. When the older men got there he slumped against a car.

The three older cops cursed.

"Call the hell in. Get Homicide out here. Seal the area. Jesus Christ!"

They covered the remains with their rainslickers. They put their hats where the faces had been.

The police communications network responded fast; fellow officers were dead, nobody wasted time. Ten minutes after the initial alarms had gone out the phone was ringing in the half-empty ready-room of the Brooklyn Homicide Division. Detective Becky Neff picked it up. "Neff," the gruff voice of the Inspector said, "you and Wilson're assigned to a case in the Seventy-fifth Precinct."

"The what?"

"It's the Fountain Avenue Dump. Got a double cop killing, mutilation, probable sex assault, cannibalism. Get the hell out there fast." The line clicked.

"Wake up, George, we've got a case," Neff growled. "We've got a bad one." She had hardly absorbed what the Inspector had said—mutilation and cannibalism? What in the name of God had happened out there? "Somebody killed two cops and cannibalized them."

Wilson, who had been resting in a tilted-back chair after a grueling four-hour paperwork session, leaned forward and got to his feet.

"Let's go. Where's the scene?"

"Fountain Avenue Dump. Seventy-fifth Precinct."

"Goddamn out-of-the-way place." He shook his head. "Guys must have gotten themselves jumped."

They went down to Becky Neff's old blue Pontiac and set the flasher up on the dashboard. She pulled the car out of its parking place and edged into the dense traffic of downtown Brooklyn. Wilson flipped on the radio and reported to the dispatcher. "Siren's working," Wilson commented as he flipped the toggle switch. The siren responded with an electronic warble, and he grunted with satisfaction; it had been on the blink for over a month, and there had been no response from the repair unit. Budget cuts had reduced this once-efficient team to exactly twelve men for the entire fleet of police vehicles. Unmarked cars were low on the list of precedence for flasher and siren repairs.

"I fixed it," Becky Neff said, "and I'm damn glad now." The ride to the car pound would be made much easier by the siren, and time could not be wasted.

Wilson raised his eyebrows. "*You* fixed it?"

"I borrowed the manual and fixed it. Nothing to it." Actually she had gotten a neighborhood electronics freak to do the job, a guy with a computer in his living room. But there was no reason to let Wilson know that.

"*You* fixed it," Wilson said again.

"You're repeating yourself."

He shook his head.

As the car swung onto the Brooklyn-Queens Expressway he used the siren, flipping the toggle to generate a series of startling whoops that cleared something of a path for them. But traffic was even worse as they approached the Battery Tunnel interchange, and the siren did little good in the confusion of trucks and buses. "Step on it, Becky."

"I'm stepping. You're working the siren."

"I don't care what you do, but move!"

His outburst made her want to snap back at him, but she understood how he felt. She shared his emotions and knew his anger was directed at the road. Cop killings made you hate the world, and the damn city in particular.

Wilson leaned out of his window and shouted at the driver of a truck stuck in the middle of the lane. "Police! Get that damn thing moving or you're under arrest!"

The driver shot the finger but moved the vehicle. Becky Neff jammed her accelerator to the floor, skidding around more slowly moving traffic, at times breaking into the clear, at times stuck again.

As the dashboard clock moved through the better part of an hour they approached their destination. They got off the B-Q-E and went straight out Flatbush Avenue, into the sometimes seedy, sometimes neat residential areas beyond. The precincts rolled by, the 78th, the 77th, the 73rd. Finally they entered the 75th and turned onto Flatlands Avenue, a street of nondescript shops in a racially mixed lower- and middle-income neighborhood. The 75th was as average a precinct as there was in New York. About a hundred thousand people lived there, not many poor and not many rich, and about evenly divided between black, white, and Hispanic.

The 75th was the kind of precinct you never read about in the papers, the kind of place where policemen lived out good solid careers without ever shooting a man—not the kind of place where they got killed, much less mutilated and cannibalized.

Finally they turned onto Fountain Avenue. In the distance a little clutch of flashers could be seen in the dismal autumn light—that must mark the official ve-

hicles pulled up to the entrance of the Automobile
Pound. The scene of the crime. And judging from the
news cars careening down the street, the 75th Precinct
wasn't going to be an obscure place much longer.

"Who's Precinct Captain?" Neff asked her superior officer. Wilson was senior man on the team, a fact
which he was careful to make sure she never forgot.
He also had a terrific memory for details.

"Gerardi, I think, something Gerardi. Good
enough cop. The place is tight s'far as I know. Nothin'
much going on. It's not Midtown South, if you know
what I mean."

"Yeah." What Wilson meant was that this precinct
was clean—no bad cops, no mob connections, no serious graft. Unlike Midtown South there wasn't even the
opportunity.

"Sounds like it's a psycho case to me," Neff said.
She was always careful to pick her words when she
theorized around Wilson. He was scathing when he
heard poorly thought out ideas and had no tolerance
for people with less skill than he himself possessed.
Which was to say, he was intolerant of almost the
entire police force. He was probably the best detective
in Homicide, maybe the best on the force. He was
also lazy, venal, inclined toward a Victorian view of
women, and a profound slob. Except for their abilities
in the craft of police detection, Becky liked to think
they had nothing in common. Where Wilson was a
slob, Becky tended to be orderly. She was always the
one who kept at the paperwork when Wilson gave up,
and who kept the dreary minutiae of their professional
lives organized.

She and Wilson didn't exactly dislike one another
—it was more than that, it was pure hate laced with
grudging respect. Neff thought that Wilson was a
Stone Age chauvinist and was revolted by the clerical

role he often forced her to play—and he considered her a female upstart in a profession where women were at best a mistake.

But they were both exceptional detectives, and that kept them together. Neff couldn't help but admire her partner's work, and he had been forced to admit that she was one of the few officers he had encountered who could keep up with him.

The fact that Becky Neff was also not a bad-looking thirty-four had helped as well. Wilson was a bachelor, over fifty and not much more appealing physically than a busted refrigerator (which he resembled in shape and height). Becky saw from the first that she was attractive to him, and she played it up a little, believing that her progress in her career was more important than whether or not she let Wilson flirt with her. But it went no further than that. Becky's husband Dick was also on the force, a captain in Narcotics, and Wilson wouldn't mess around with another cop's wife.

The idea of Wilson messing around with anybody was ridiculous anyway; he had remained a bachelor partly out of choice and partly because few women would tolerate his arrogance and his sloppy indifference to even the most fundamental social graces, like taking the meat out of a hamburger and eating it separately, which was one of his nicer table manners.

"Let's just go blank on this one, sweetheart," Wilson rumbled. "We don't know what the hell happened out there."

"Cannibalism would indicate—"

"We don't know. Guys are excited, maybe it was something else. Let's just find what we find."

Becky pulled the car in among the official vehicles and snapped her folding umbrella out of her purse. She opened it against the rain and was annoyed to see

Wilson go trudging off into the mud, pointedly ignoring his own comfort. "Let the bastard catch pneumonia," she thought as she huddled forward beneath the umbrella. Wilson was a great one for appearances —he gets to the scene wet, indifferent to his own comfort, concerned only with the problem at hand, while his dainty little partner follows along behind with her umbrella, carefully mincing over the puddles. Ignoring him as best she could, she set off toward the kliegs that now lit the scene of the murders some fifty yards into the area.

As soon as she saw the mess she knew that this was no normal case. Something that made you break out in a sweat even in this weather had happened to these men. She glanced at Wilson, surprised to see that even old super-pro's eyes were opened wide with surprise. "Jesus," he said, "I mean . . . what?"

The Precinct Captain came forward. "We don't know, sir," he said to Wilson, acknowledging the other man's seniority and fame on the force. And he also eyed Becky Neff, well-known enough in her own right as one of the most visible female officers in New York. Her picture had appeared in the *Daily News* more than once in connection with some of her and Wilson's more spectacular cases. Wilson shunned the photographers himself—or they shunned him, it was hard to say which. But Becky welcomed them, highly conscious of her role as living and visible proof that female officers could work the front lines as well as their male counterparts.

Taking a deep breath she knelt down beside the corpses while Wilson was still registering his shock. Every fiber of her body wanted to run, to get away from the unspeakable horror before her—but instead she looked closely, peering at the broken, gristle-covered bones and the dark lumps of flesh that seemed almost to glow beneath the lights that had been set up by the Forensics officers.

"Where the hell's the Medical Examiner?" Wilson said behind her. A voice answered. Wilson did not come any closer; she knew that he wasn't going to because he couldn't stomach this sort of thing. Clenching her teeth against her own disgust, she stared at the bodies, noting the most unusual thing about them —the long scrape marks on the exposed bones and the general evidence of gnawing. She stood up and looked around the desolate spot. About a quarter of a mile away the dump could be seen with huge flocks of sea gulls hovering over the mounds of garbage. Even over the hubbub of voices you could hear the gulls screaming. From here to the dump was an ocean of old cars and trucks of every imaginable description, most of them worthless, stripped hulks. A few nearby had white X's on the windshields or hoods, evidence of the work DiFalco and Houlihan had been doing when the attack occurred.

"They were gnawed by rats," Becky said in as level a tone as she could manage, "but those larger marks indicate something else—dogs?"

"The wild dogs around here are just scrawny little mutts," the Precinct Captain said.

"How long were these men missing before you instituted a search, Captain?" Wilson asked.

The Captain glanced sharply at him. Neff was amazed; nobody below the rank of Inspector had the right to ask a captain a question like that, and even then not outside of a Board of Inquiry. It was a question that belonged in a dereliction of duty hearing, not at the scene of a crime.

"We need to know," Wilson added a little too loudly.

"Then ask the M. E. how long they've been dead.

We found them two hours ago. Figure the rest out for yourself." The Captain turned away, and Becky Neff followed his gaze out over the distant Atlantic, where a helicopter could be seen growing rapidly larger. It was a police chopper and it was soon above them, its rotor clattering as it swung around looking for a likely spot to land.

"That's the Commissioner and the Chief," Wilson said. "They must have smelled newsmen." In January a new mayor would take office, and senior city officials were all scrambling to keep their jobs. So these normally anonymous men now jumped at the possibility of getting their faces on the eleven o'clock news. But this time they would be disappointed—because of the unusually hideous nature of the crime, the press was being kept as far away as possible. No pictures allowed until the scene was cleared of the bodies.

At the same time that the Chief of Detectives and the Commissioner were getting out of their helicopter, the Medical Examiner was hurrying across the muddy ground with a newspaper folded up and held over his head against the rain. "It's Evans himself," Wilson said. "I haven't seen that man outdoors in twenty years."

"I'm glad he's here."

Evans was the city's Chief Medical Examiner, a man renowned for his ingenious feats of forensic detection. He rolled along, shabby, tiny, looking very old behind his thick glasses.

He had worked with Wilson and Neff often and greeted them both with a nod. "What's your idea?" he said even before examining the bodies. Most policemen he treated politely enough; these two he respected.

"We're going to have a problem finding the cause

of death," Wilson said, "because of the shape they're in."

Evans nodded. "Is Forensics finished with the bodies?" The Forensics team was finished, which meant that the corpses could be touched. Dr. Evans rolled on his black rubber gloves and bent down. So absorbed did he become that he didn't even acknowledge the approach of the brass.

The group watched Evans as he probed gingerly at the bodies. Later he would do a much more thorough autopsy in his lab, but these first impressions were important and would be his only on-site inspection of the victims.

When he backed away from the bodies, his face was registering confusion. "I don't understand this at all," he said slowly. "These men have been killed by . . . something with claws, teeth. Animals of some kind. But what doesn't make sense is—why didn't they defend themselves?"

"Their guns aren't even drawn," Becky said through dry lips. It was the first thing she had noticed.

"Maybe that wasn't the mode of death, Doctor," Wilson said. "I mean, maybe they were killed first and then eaten by the animals around here. There's rats, gulls, also some wild dogs, the precinct boys say."

The doctor pursed his lips. He nodded. "We'll find out when we do the autopsy. Maybe you're right, but on the surface I'd say we're looking at the fatal wounds."

The Forensics team was photographing and marking the site, picking up scattered remains and vacuuming the area as well as possible considering the mud. They also took impressions of the multitude of pawprints that surrounded the bodies.

The Precinct Captain finally broke the silence. "You're saying that these guys were killed by wild dogs, and they didn't even draw their guns? That can't be right. Those dogs are just little things— they're not even a nuisance." He looked around. "Anybody ever hear of a death from wild dogs in the city? Anybody?"

The Chief and the Commissioner were now standing nearby swathed in heavy coats, shrouded by their umbrellas. Nobody spoke or shook hands. "We'll give you whatever you need to solve this case," the Commissioner said to nobody in particular. Up close his face was almost lifeless, the skin hanging loosely on the bones. He had a reputation for long hours and honest work; unlike many of his predecessors he had attained the respect of the department by his interest in police affairs and his disinterest in politics. For that reason his job was now on the line. He was under criticism for allegedly allowing corruption, for taking cops off the street, for ignoring black and Hispanic neighborhoods, for all the things that usually get police commissioners in trouble. By contrast Chief of Detectives Underwood was pink, fat and rather merry. He was a born politician and was ready to redecorate the Commissioner's office to his own taste. His eyes were watery and he had a nervous cough. He stamped his feet and glanced quickly around, barely even seeing the bodies; it was obvious that he wanted to get back to the comfort of headquarters as soon as he could. "Any leads?" he said, looking at Wilson.

"Nothing."

"Right now it looks like their throats were torn out," the Medical Examiner said, "but we'll reserve judgment until the autopsy."

"A dog theory won't make it," Wilson muttered.

"I never said that," the M. E. flared. "All I said

was the probable cause of death is massive insult to the throat caused by teeth and claws. I don't know about dogs and I don't care to speculate about dogs."

"Thank you, Doctor Evans," Wilson said in a staccato voice. Evans was not numbered among Wilson's few friends despite the professional respect.

The Commissioner stared a long time at the corpses. "Cover 'em up," he said at last, "get 'em out of here. Come on, Herb, let's let these men do their jobs."

The two officials trudged back to their helicopter.

"Morale," the Precinct Captain said as the chopper began to start. "A visit from those two sure charges you up."

The Medical Examiner was still fuming over his run-in with Wilson. "If it was dogs," he said carefully, "they'd have to be seventy, eighty pounds or more. And fast, they'd have to be fast."

"Why so fast?" Becky asked.

"Look at DiFalco's right wrist. Torn. He was going for his pistol when something with teeth hit his arm hard. That means whatever it was, it was damn fast."

Becky Neff thought immediately of the dogs her husband Dick often worked with on the Narcotics Squad. "Attack dogs," she said, "you're describing the work of attack dogs."

The Medical Examiner shrugged. "I'm describing the condition of the bodies. How they got that way is your business, Becky—yours and His Excellency's."

"Screw you too, Evans."

Becky tried to ignore Wilson—she was used to his sour disposition. As long as people like Evans kept working with him it didn't really matter. Sometimes, though, it was nice to see that others disliked him as much as she did.

"If we can establish that attack dogs did this," she said, "then we can narrow our search considerably. Most attack dogs don't kill."

"If the good doctor says they were able to do . . . that, then you might have a point. Let's talk to Tom Rilker, get ourselves a little education on the subject." Rilker trained dogs for the department.

Becky nodded. As usual when they got going, she and Wilson started thinking together. They headed back toward their car. The first step was now clear— they had to find out if attack dogs were involved. If they were, then this was a first—policemen had never been murdered with dogs before. In fact, dogs were an uncommon weapon because it took the work of a skilled professional to train them to kill human beings. And skilled professionals didn't train up dogs for just anybody. If you had gotten a dog trained into a killer, the man who did it would remember you for sure. Most so-called "attack dogs" are nothing more than a loud bark and maybe a bite. The ones that actually go for the throat are not very common. A dog like that is never completely controllable, always a liability unless it is absolutely and essentially needed.

Back in the car, Wilson began to recite what he remembered about cases involving killer dogs. "October, 1966, a pedestrian killed by a dog in Queens. Dog was untrained, believed to have been an accident. I worked that case, I always thought it was fishy but I never got a decent lead. July, 1970, an attack dog escaped from the Willerton Drug Company warehouse in Long Island City and killed a seventeen-year-old boy. Another accident. April, 1973—our only proved murder by dog. A hood named Big Roy Gurner was torn apart by three dogs, later traced to the Thomas Shoe Company, which was a front for the Carlo Midi family. I got close to netting Midi in that one, but the brass removed me from the case. Corrupt bastards. That's my inventory on dogs. You got anything?"

"Well, I don't remember any dog cases since I've been a detective. I've heard about the Gurner thing of course. But the scuttlebutt was you got paid off the case." She watched him pull his chin into his neck at that—it was his characteristic gesture of anger.

And she realized that she shouldn't have goaded him; Wilson was one honest cop, that much was certain. He hated corruption in others and certainly would never bend himself. It was a nasty crack, and she was sorry for it. She tried to apologize, but he wouldn't acknowledge. She had made her mistake; there was no point in continuing to talk about it. "My husband works with dogs all the time," she said to change the subject. "Some attack dogs, but mostly just sniffers. They're his best weapon, so he says."

"I hear about his dogs. All of them are supposedly trained to kill despite that 'sniffer' bullshit. I've heard the stories about those dogs."

She frowned. "What stories?"

"Oh, nothing much really. Just that those dogs sometimes get so excited when they sniff out a little dope that they just happen to kill the jerk they find it on . . . sometimes. But I guess you husband's told you all about that."

"Let's drop it, Wilson. We don't need to go at each other like this. My husband hasn't told me anything about dogs that kill suspects. It sounds pretty outlandish if you ask me."

Wilson snorted, said nothing more. But Becky had heard the rumors he was referring to, that Dick's team sometimes used dogs on difficult suspects. "At least he's not on the take," Becky thought. "I hope to God he's not." Then she thought of a certain problem they used to have paying for his father's nursing home, a problem that seemed to have disappeared—but she refused to think about it.

Corruption was the one thing about police work she hated. Many officers considered the money part of the job, rationalizing it with the idea that their victims were criminals anyway and the payoffs were nothing more than a richly deserved fine. But as far as Becky Neff was concerned, that was crap. You did your job and got your pay, that ought to be enough. She forced herself not to rise to Wilson's bait about her husband, it would probably start a shouting argument.

"Stories aside, I've heard a lot about Tom Rilker. Dick thinks damn highly of him. Says he could train a dog to walk a tightrope if he wanted to." Thomas D. Rilker was a civilian who worked closely with the NYPD, the FBI, and U. S. Customs training the dogs they used in their work. He also did private contract work. He was good, probably the best in the city, maybe the best in the world. His specialty was training dogs to sniff. He had dope dogs, fire dogs, tobacco dogs, booze dogs, you name it. They worked mostly for the Narcotics Squad and the customs agents. They had revolutionized the technique of investigation in these areas and greatly reduced the amount of drugs moving through the port of New York. Becky knew that Dick thought the world of Tom Rilker.

"Keep this damn car moving, sweetheart. You ain't in a parade!"

"You drive, Wilson."

"*Me?* I'm the damn boss. Oughta sit in back."

She pulled over to the curb. "You don't like my driving, you do it yourself."

"I can't, dearest—my license lapsed last year."

"When you teamed up with me, dip."

"Thank you, I'll make a note of that."

Becky swung the car out into traffic and jammed

the accelerator to the floor. She wasn't going to let him get to her. Part of the reason he was like this was because she had forced herself on him. Between her husband Dick and her uncle Bob she had exerted plenty of pull to get herself into Homicide and to land a partner once she got there. It took the pull of her husband's captaincy and her uncle's inspectorship to move her out of the secretary syndrome and onto the street. She had done well as a patrolman and gotten herself promoted to Detective Sergeant when she deserved it. Most of the women she knew on the force got their promotions at least two or three years late, and then had to fight to avoid ending up on some rotten squad like Missing Persons, where the only action you ever saw was an occasional flat tire on an unmaintained squad oar.

So here came Becky Neff just when George Wilson's most recent partner had punched him in the face and transferred to Safes and Locks. Wilson had to take what he could get, and in this situation it was a rookie detective and, worse, a woman.

He had looked at her as if she had contagious leprosy. For the first six weeks together he had said no more than a word a week to her—six words in six weeks, all of them four letter. He had schemed to get her out of the division, even started dark rumors about a Board of Inquiry when she missed an important lead in what should have been an easy case.

But gradually she had become better at the work, until even he had been forced to acknowledge it. Soon they were making collars pretty often. In fact they were getting a reputation.

"Women are mostly awful cops," were his final words on the subject, "but you're unique. Instead of being awful, you're just bad."

Coming from Wilson that was a compliment, perhaps the highest he had ever paid a fellow officer. After that his grumbling became inarticulate and he let the partnership roll along under its own considerable steam.

They worked like two parts of the same person, constantly completing each other's thoughts. People like the Chief Medical Examiner started requesting their help on troublesome cases. But when their work started to reach the papers, it was invariably the attractive, unusual lady cop Becky Neff who ended up in the *Daily News* centerfold. Wilson was only another skilled policeman; Becky was interesting news. Wilson, of course, claimed to hate publicity. But she knew he hated even more the fact that he didn't get any.

"You're making a wrong turn, Becky. We're supposed to be stopping at the Seventy-fifth to get pictures of the bodies and pawprints for Rilker. Give him something to work with."

She wheeled the car around and turned up Flatlands Avenue toward the station house. "Also we ought to call ahead," she said, "let him know we're coming."

"You're sure we trust him? I mean, what if he's doing a little work on the side, like for somebody bad. Calling ahead'll give him time to think."

"Rilker's not working for the Mafia. I don't think that's even worthy of consideration."

"Then I won't consider it." He slumped down in the seat, pushing his knees up against the glove compartment and letting his head lean forward against his chest. It looked like agony, but he closed his eyes. Becky lit a cigarette and drove on in silence, mentally reviewing the case. Despite the fact that it looked like they were on a good lead she could not dismiss the feeling that something was wrong with it. Some element didn't fit. Again and again she reviewed the facts but she couldn't come up with the answer. The one thing that worried her was the lack of resistance. It had happened so fast that they hadn't appeared dangerous until the very last moment.

Did attack dogs lay ambushes? Could they move fast enough to kill two healthy policemen before they even had time to unholster their pistols?

She double-parked the car in front of the 75th Precinct.

Leaving Wilson snoring lightly she hurried up the worn concrete steps of the dingy red-brick building and introduced herself to the desk sergeant. He called Lieutenant Ruiz, who was responsible for the material she needed. He was a six-footer with a trim black mustache and a subdued smile. "Pleased to make your acquaintance, Detective Neff," he said with great formality.

"We need pictures and copies of the prints you took."

"No problem, we've got everything you could want. It's a rotten mess."

A leading statement, but Becky didn't pick up on it. That part of the investigation would come later. Before they identified a motive for the murders they had to have a mode of death.

Sergeant Ruiz produced eleven glossies of the scene, plus a box of plasticasts of the pawprints that had been found surrounding the bodies. "There isn't a single clear print in that box," he said, "just a jumble. If you ask me those prints haven't got a thing to do with it. Just the wild dogs doing a little scavenging. They sure as hell couldn't be responsible for killing those guys, they just came and got their share after the real work was done."

"Why do you say that?" She was examining the photographs as she talked. Why had he handed her one of the less grisly shots?

"The dogs—I've seen them. They're little, like cockers or something, and they're shy as hell. And by the way, I wonder if you could autograph that picture for my daughter." He paused, then added shyly, "She thinks the world of you."

Becky was so pleased by his admiration that she didn't notice Wilson standing behind her.

"I thought we weren't going to give out any more autographs," he said curtly.

"When did we decide not to? I don't remember that."

"Right now. I just decided. This isn't some kind of a game." His hand moved toward the picture but Ruiz's was quicker.

"Thanks, Miss Neff," he said, still smiling. "My daughter'll be thrilled."

Becky gathered the rest of the photographs and picked up the box of prints to lug to the car. She knew without asking that Wilson wouldn't touch it, and she wasn't sure she wanted him to.

"By the way, it's Sergeant Neff," she said over her shoulder to Ruiz, who was still standing there staring.

"Let me help you," he said.

Becky was already out the door and putting the box into the back seat of the car. Wilson followed, got in, and slammed his door. Becky settled herself into the driver's seat and turned on the ignition.

"I just don't want this to be a circus," he said as they headed toward Manhattan. "This case is going to be the most sensational thing we've ever worked on. Reporters are gonna be crawling out of your nightgown in the morning."

"I don't wear a nightgown."

"Whatever, we're gonna have 'em all over us. The point is, it's a serious case and we want to treat it serious."

Wilson could be sententious, but this was ridiculous. She forced herself not to say she knew how serious the case was. If she did he would then launch into a tirade about lady cops, probably ending with a question about her competence or some new criticism of her work. She decided to ignore him and make him shut up as well. To do this she drove like a madwoman, careening down the streets, making hairpin turns, weaving in and out of the traffic at fifty miles an hour. Wilson at first sat with his shoulders hunched and his hands twisted together in his lap, then started using the siren.

"Rilker give you some kind of deadline?"

"No." She had forgotten to call Rilker, dammit. If he wasn't there she'd have to suffer more flak from Wilson.

She lit another cigarette. Smoking was one pleasure that she had really begun to enjoy since the doctor had made Wilson stop.

His response was prompt. "You're polluting."

"Draw an oxygen mask if you don't like it. I've told you that before."

"Thanks for the reminder."

She wished that she smoked cigars.

Chapter 2

Tom Rilker stared at the pictures the two detectives showed him. His face registered disbelief and what looked to Becky Neff like fear. She had never met him before and was surprised to discover that he was old, maybe seventy-five. From her husband's description she had assumed he was a young man. Rilker's hair was white and springy like frayed wool; his right hand shook a little and made the pictures rustle together; his brows knit, the salt-and-pepper eyebrows coming close together, heightening the expression now on his face. "This is impossible," he finally said. The moment he spoke Becky knew why Dick always portrayed him as young—he sounded like a much younger man. "It's completely incredible."

"Why is that?" Wilson asked.

"Well, a dog wouldn't do this. You'd have to train it. These men have been *gutted,* for God's sake. You can train a dog to kill, but if you wanted it to do this to its victims, you'd have to train it very, very well."

"But it could be done."

"Maybe, with the right breed and the right dog. But it wouldn't be easy. You'd need . . . human models for the dog to work on if you wanted it to be reliable."

"What if you just starved the dog?"

"A dog would eat muscle tissue—ma'am, if this bothers you—"

"No," Becky snapped. "You were saying, a dog would eat muscle tissue?"

"Yes, but it wouldn't actually—gut somebody. That isn't the way they feed, not even in the wild state." He picked up the pawprints and shook his head. "These all the prints?"

"How big a dog would it have taken?" Wilson asked. Becky noticed that his questions were becoming gentle but insistent; he must sense that the sight of the pictures had put Rilker under a considerable strain. The man's face was indeed getting flushed, and a band of sweat was appearing on his forehead. He kept giving his head a little toss as if to knock a wisp of hair back. The hand was shaking harder.

"A monster. Something big and fast and mean enough to accept this kind of training. Not all breeds would."

"What breeds?"

"Close to the wild, huskies, German shepherds. Not many. And I've got to tell you, in all my years I've never seen anything like this done by dogs. I think it's—"

He grabbed a cast of some of the pawprints and peered at it, then fumbled with the lamp on his desk and looked closely in the light.

"These are not dog prints."

"What are they then?"

"I don't know. Something very strange."

"Why so?"

Tom Rilker paused, then spoke with exaggerated calm. "These prints have circules, like human hands and feet. But they are clearly pawprints."

"Some kind of animal, other than a dog?"

"I'm sorry to tell you that no animal has prints like this. In fact nothing does. Nothing that I have ever heard of, that is, in fifty years of working with animals."

Becky had to say it: "Werewolves?" She resigned herself to the inevitable scoffing that would come from Wilson later.

Surprisingly, Rilker took some time to dismiss the question. "I don't think such things are possible," he said carofully.

"Well—are they or aren't they?"

Rilker smiled sheepishly. Becky realized that he was being kind. She could see the glee in Wilson's eyes. It was all her partner could do not to whoop with laughter, damn him.

"I don't believe in werewolves either, Mr. Rilker," Becky said. "Frankly, I wanted to know if you did."

"Why?"

"Because if you had, we wouldn't have to trust the rest of what you're saying. As it is, you look like a creditable expert who's just given us a very nasty problem."

"A nasty problem in what way?"

Now Wilson did scoff—but at Rilker. "Well, for one thing, we must proceed under the assumption that these two fully armed police officers were killed by animals. OK, that's not so good. But we've also got to assume that the animals are of an unknown species. That's pretty bad. And now, to cap it all off, we've got to believe that this unknown species of man-killing animals is running free in Brooklyn and nobody knows about it. That I cannot accept."

Becky's mind was racing—this new theory plugged holes but it also had some great big ones of its own. "If it's true, we've got to move fast. Brooklyn's a crowded place."

"Come on, Becky, stop it. Let's get out of here. We've got real work to do."

"Wait a minute, Detective, I'm not sure I like your tone." Rilker stood up and thrust one of the casts in Wilson's face. "Those pawprints were not made by anything that I have ever heard of. By nothing whatsoever. Not even by a species of monkey—I already thought of that." He fumbled for his phone. "I'll call a friend up at the Museum of Natural History. He'll tell you these prints weren't made by any known animal. You're dealing with something highly unusual, that's for damn sure."

Becky felt her heart sink. Wilson had angered Rilker. Rilker's voice rose as his fingers fumbled at the telephone. "Maybe my word isn't good enough for you sharpie cops—but this guy up at the museum's a real expert. He'll tell you bastards I'm right!"

Wilson jerked his head in the direction of the door. "We don't need any help from a museum," he muttered. Becky followed him out, carrying the pictures but leaving the pawprints behind because Rilker seemed to have taken possession of the box. The door to his office slammed behind them with an ear-shattering jolt. His voice rose to a frustrated screech and abruptly ended.

"I hope we didn't give him a coronary," Becky said as they returned to the street.

"You did good, kid," Wilson said. "If you hadn't asked him about the werewolves he would have pulled it off."

"I can hardly believe that was the Tom Rilker I've heard Dick talk about. But I guess he must be a little senile."

"I guess so. Where are the casts?"

"Still in his office. You want them?" Becky dropped her purse in through the window of the car.

"Yeah. We might need them."

"Fine, you go up and get them."

Wilson snorted. "We'll get more from the Seventy-fifth Precinct. You know something?"

"What?"

"You're losing your mascara. You're sweating."

She laughed as she started the car. "I've got to hand it to you, George, you really know how to set a girl up. That's the nicest thing you've said to me in a year."

"Well . . . you're . . . you know, when your stuff gets messed up I notice."

"Good for you. That's the first sign you're becoming human." She pulled out into traffic, heading automatically for what she knew would be their next stop, the office of the Chief Medical Examiner. The autopsies were due to start in half an hour and it was now all the more important to be there. Unless a cause of death came out in autopsy they were going to be forced to conclude the impossible—that the killings had been done by dogs. And that is a very unlikely way for a policeman to die.

Becky could not dispel the growing feeling of sick fear that this case was giving her. She kept imagining the two cops out there in the drizzle, facing whatever in the name of God they had faced . . . and dying with the secret. At times like this she wished she and Dick worked more closely together. He would understand the source of her feeling in a way Wilson never could. She took her cases very personally, it was one of her worst failings (and also the reason she was often so successful, she felt), and each case affected her differently. This one, with its overtones of horror, was going to be unusually hard on her. What had happened to those two cops was the stuff of nightmares. . . .

"You're muttering."

"I am not."

"You're muttering, you're getting crazy."

"I am not! You better keep your mouth shut."

"All right, but I'm telling you that this case is going to eat away at you." He suddenly turned to face her. The movement made her swerve the car—she had the absurd notion that he was going to kiss her. But his face was twisted into a look almost of pain. "It's eating at *me* is the reason I say that. I mean, I don't know what happened out there but it's really getting to me."

"You mean you're pissed off about it, scared of it—what?"

He considered for a moment, then said very quietly, "It scares me." Never before had Wilson said such a thing. Becky kept her eyes on the traffic, her face without expression.

"Me too," she said, "if you want to know. It's a weird case." Extreme caution was called for in this conversation—Wilson could be telling the truth or he could be egging her on, trying to get her to reveal her inner emotions, to force her to admit that she was overinvolved in her work in an unprofessional way. Although she felt secure enough in their partnership she could never be certain that Wilson hadn't concocted some plot to get rid of her. Not that it mattered —nowadays they were waiting in line to work with her, but somehow she wanted to keep the partnership going. Wilson was hard to take but the two of them were so good together it was worth preserving.

"It's hard but it's good," he said suddenly.

"What're you talking about?"

"Us. You're thinking about us, aren't you?"

The way he sounded they might as well have been lovers. "Yes, I am."

"See, that's why it's good. If it wasn't so good, I never would have known."

She took a deep breath. "We're here. Maybe we'll find out they were poisoned and this'll turn into a normal case again."

"We won't."

"Why not? I don't think we can assume—oh, of course, the dogs ate the organs and there are no dead dogs, therefore there was no poison in the organs, therefore et cetera."

"You got it, sweetheart. Let's go up and watch old prickface pretend to be a master sleuth."

"Oh, Wilson, why don't you let the poor man alone. He's just as good at what he does as we are at what we do. Your whole thing with him is personalities."

"Can't be. He hasn't got one."

The Chief Medical Examiner's office was housed in a gleaming modern building across the street from Bellevue Hospital. This "office" was really a factory of forensic pathology, equipped with every conceivable piece of equipment and chemical that could be of use in an autopsy. Literally everything there was to know about a corpse could be discovered in this building. And the Medical Examiner had been responsible for solving many a murder with his equipment and his most considerable skill. Bits of hair, flecks of saliva, fingernail-polish fragments—all had figured prominently in murder trials. A conviction had once been obtained on the basis of shoe polish left on the lethal bruises of a woman who had been kicked to death.

The Chief M. E. excelled at making such findings. And if there was anything to be found in this case, he would surely uncover it. He and his men would go over the bodies inch by inch, leaving nothing to chance. Still, there was that fear . . .

"They'd better come up with something or this case is going to drive me crazy," Becky said on the way up in the elevator. It was new and rose silently with no sense of motion.

"I hate this elevator. Every time I ride in it it scares the hell out of me."

"Imagine how it would be to be trapped in this elevator, Wilson, no way out—"

"Shut up! That's unkind." Wilson was mildly claustrophobic, to add to his list of petty neuroses.

"Sorry, just trying to amuse you."

"You tell me I'm such an s.o.b., but you're really the nasty side of this partnership. That was a rotten thing to do to me."

The doors opened and they stepped into the odor of disinfectant that pervaded the M. E.'s office. The receptionist knew them, and waved them past her desk. Doctor Evans's incredibly cluttered office was open but he wasn't inside. House rules were that you didn't go any farther into the complex without an escort, but as usual there wasn't a soul to be seen or heard. They started toward the operating room when the receptionist yelled Wilson's name.

"Yeah?"

"You got a message," she hollered. "Call Underwood."

"OK!" He stared at Becky. "Underwood wants

me? Why the hell does Underwood want me? I don't remember trying to get you fired recently."

"Maybe you did and forgot."

"Better call, better call." He picked up the phone in Evans's office and dialed the Chief of Detectives. The conversation lasted about a minute and consisted on Wilson's part of a series of yessirs and thankyous. "Just wanted to tell us we're a special detail now, reporting directly to him, and we have the facilities of the department at our disposal. We move to an office at Police Headquarters in Manhattan."

"That's very nice. We get *carte blanche* as long as some of the credit rubs off on him, and the Commissioner gets left in his ivory tower."

Wilson snorted. "Listen, as long as it looks like this case is solvable every parasite from here to the Bulgarian Secret Service is going to try to horn in on the credit. But you just wait. If we don't get it together, we'll be all alone."

"Let's go to the autopsy. I can hardly wait." Her voice was bitter; what Wilson had said could not have been more true.

"Come on, ghoul."

On the way to the operating room Becky wished to hell that Wilson would pull out a bottle of something alcoholic. Unfortunately he rarely drank, and certainly never while he was working—unless events called for it, which they often did about six P.M. But now it was after six.

"I thought you people didn't come back here unless you were invited," Evans growled. He was on his way into the surgery. He stank of chemical soap; his rubber gloves were dripping. "Or don't those rules count where you two are concerned?"

"This is the man who *invites* us on his cases. How sweet."

"I only give you cases that are too easy for me to bother with. Now come on in if you want to, but it won't do a bit of good. And I warn you, they're fragrant."

Becky thought immediately of the families. When she was a child she had been at a funeral where you could smell the corpse—but nowadays they had things for that, didn't they? And anyway, the coffins wouldn't be opened. But still . . . oh, God.

The two bodies lay on surgical tables under merciless lights. There was none of the haphazardness and confusion of the scene out at the auto pound; here everything was neat and orderly except the bodies themselves, which carried their violence and horror with them.

Becky was struck by the sheer *damage*—this attack had been so unbelievably savage. And somehow she found that reassuring; nothing from nature would do this. It had to be the work of human beings, it was too terrible to be anything else.

"The Forensics lab hasn't found a single thing except dog hairs, rat hairs and feathers," Doctor Evans said mildly. He was referring to the results of the examination of the area where the deaths had occurred at the auto pound. "No human detritus that didn't belong to the victims."

"OK," Wilson said, but he took the information like a blow. It was not good news.

Evans turned to Becky. "Look, we're about to start. What do you think it'll take to get Wilson out of here?"

"You can't. There might be something," she replied.

"Something I'd miss?"

"Something we'd see."

"But not him. He won't be able to take it."

"I'll be fine. Just do your job, Doctor."

"There will be no repeat of the Custin mess, Detective Wilson." During the Maude Custin autopsy Wilson had lost his lunch. The reference to his embarrassment hurt his feelings, but he was too proud to acknowledge it before Evans.

"I'll leave if it gets to me," he said, "but not unless it does. We've gotta be here and you know it."

"Just trying to help you, trying to be accommodating."

"Thank you. Why don't you get going?"

"That's what I am doing."

Evans picked up a scalpel and commenced taking a series of tissue samples. An assistant prepared slides of them at a side table, and sent the slides to the lab. The autopsy proceeded swiftly—there was pitifully little to examine. "The main thing we're hunting for is signs of poison, suffocation, anything that would give us a more plausible cause of death," Evans said as he worked. "That good for you two?"

"That's good for us."

"Well, we'll find out all about it from the lab. Look at this." He held up a sharp white tooth. "Embedded in that busted wrist. You know what it means —really what it confirms?"

"The man was alive when his wrist was bitten. Otherwise the tooth wouldn't have been wrenched loose."

"That's right, which confirms that this one was definitely alive when the dogs attacked him."

There was a long silence in the room. Wilson seemed to sink into himself, becoming smaller and more square than he already was. Becky felt a dull powerlessness. As the vague outlines of what they were confronting began to take shape Becky could see all kinds of nasty problems, not the least of which would be simple crowd control. What do people do when they discover a thing like this in their midst? Their placid, workaday lives are suddenly disrupted by a new terror of the most dangerous type—the unknown. And if it can kill two healthy, alert, armed policemen, the run-of-the-mill citizen isn't going to have a prayer.

"I think we'd better get downtown as soon as the lab results are in," Becky said.

"Why bother to wait?"

"Confirming, just so we won't have any loose ends." Convincing Underwood of this wasn't going to be especially easy. She didn't want there to be any stray questions unanswered that might allow him to put off the inevitable decision—admit what killed the cops, seal the area, and kill everything in it that looked faintly like a dog—wild or trained.

The two detectives returned to the M. E.'s office before the autopsies were completed; they didn't spend any more time observing than they had to. Wilson was visibly grateful to leave; Becky was glad to follow.

Wilson seemed unusually quiet, almost chastened. "What do you think Underwood will do?" she asked just to break the silence.

Wilson shrugged. "Two cops got killed by some kind of dogs. It's a pretty flimsy story, you ask me. No matter what's been confirmed, I think we've got to keep digging. Somehow or other we'll uncover a real motive and a real crime."

Becky felt a twinge of concern—didn't Wilson believe the evidence? "But if it was dogs and we don't act pretty fast there could be more deaths. I think we've got to make that assumption. That's certainly where the facts are leading us."

Wilson nodded. If she wasn't sure that it couldn't

be true, she almost would have suspected Wilson of knowing something about the case that she didn't. But they had not been apart since it had happened, not for a minute. Whatever information he had, she also had.

"You know," he said in a low, angry tone, "you damn well never get over smoking. If you weren't armed I'd mug you for your cigarettes right now."

She didn't reply; she was staring past him, toward the door of the office. Evans walked in carrying a clipboard. "Lab says we might have carbon monoxide poisoning as a secondary factor," he said, "but the basic cause of death was the injuries. Primarily the throats in both cases."

"Carbon monoxide? Could those men have been impaired by it?"

"Normally I wouldn't say so. The levels are very low, just residual. You've both probably got higher levels right now just from your drive over here. But it's absolutely the only abnormal thing we found about these men."

"Could it have been higher when they were killed and then dissipated?"

"Not likely. These guys were functioning normally when they were hit. It's just the only other thing."

Wilson seemed greatly relieved; at the moment Becky couldn't understand exactly why this was so.

The Chief Medical Examiner put down his clipboard. "It's as strange as they come," he said, "the strangest case I have worked on in my entire career."

"Why so?" Wilson tried and failed to sound unconcerned.

"Well, they were supposedly killed by dogs, right?"

The detectives nodded like twins; Becky was secretly amused by the similarity of the gesture. She wondered what it was that brought the two of them so close to one another. God knows you couldn't call it love.

"The dogs had to be very unusual. Their mode of attack was extremely clever. It wasn't until DiFalco went for his gun that they attacked."

"So what?"

"So when did you ever hear about a dog smart enough to grab a man's wrist to prevent him from unholstering his gun? Never, is the answer. Dogs don't think like that. They don't know what the hell guns are."

"Maybe and maybe not."

"Oh, come on, they don't know. Point a pistol at a dog's head and not a damn thing will happen. He certainly won't try to defend himself. Whoever heard of dogs working like that?"

"It was a lucky coincidence. The dog went for the movement of the hand, not to prevent it from reaching the gun. I think we can assume that." Wilson picked up the phone. "I'm calling Underwood to tell him we're on the way. His nibs is awaiting us."

"Now don't go running him down, Wilson. Word is he's got the inside track to the big job. Your next Commissioner."

Wilson dialed. "A lot of difference it makes to me. I've been on the promotion list for at least ten years."

Becky was surprised to hear her partner admit this. His own complete inability to handle department politics had assured that he would never move beyond Detective Lieutenant. No matter the level of his achievement; while good work counted in the scramble for top jobs, pull and ass-kissing counted more. And with Wilson not only did he not try to ass-kiss, people were afraid even to *let* him try. You don't let a guy like that get into the delicate politics of the

Police Department. Next thing, he'd unwittingly uncover some scandal and embarrass everybody.

That made him a less than ideal senior partner. The brass would hesitate to promote Becky around Wilson. It just wasn't done unless the senior was completely incompetent—which was far from the case here. So she'd have to sit around as a Detective Sergeant until either she or Wilson rotted, or she was transferred away from him and that was one thing the department would never do. Only Wilson himself in his wisdom would ever consider such a thing. She hated the thought of it right now, too; it could easily mean being moved away from the action, back into the obscurity of a more typical policewoman job.

Wilson muttered into the phone, using no more than a few monosyllables. He had informed the Chief of Detectives that they were coming with just about as much grace as he would inform his building superintendent of a stopped-up toilet.

A wet, shuddering north wind hit them as they left the building; the drizzling cold of the past few days had finally given way to the first real touch of winter. It was seven-thirty and already dark. Thirtieth Street was quiet, with the wind clattering in the skeletons of scrawny trees up and down the block. A few pedestrians hurried past, and out on Fifth Avenue many more figures could be seen amid the flashing lights and the shapes of cars moving slowly downtown. Becky watched the people they passed on their way to her car, looking at the gray, blank faces, thinking about the lives hidden behind those faces, and of how what she and Wilson would soon be telling the Chief of Detectives would affect those lives.

In police work you gradually acquire a distance from nonpolicemen. People on the outside have such a limited concept of what you really do that they might as well know nothing at all. They see only the headlines, the endless propagandizing of the newspapers. Crimes are reported, their solution is not. As a result the people you meet outside of the force see you as incompetent. "You're a cop? Why don't you get the muggers off the street? I never see a cop on the street. I thought that's what we paid you for." Then you might see that same person dead somewhere, the victim of the very crime he said you wouldn't protect him from. It does something to you to realize that you aren't going to protect everybody, you aren't going to make the world a hell of a lot safer by your work. You are there to hold life together, not to bring on the millennium. When you see the incredible suffering and degradation, you begin to realize the truth of that. Sooner or later crooks and victims all merge together into one miserable, bloody mass of whining, twisted bodies and fear-glazed eyes. Murder after murder comes before you, each with its sordid tale of failed lives. . . .

And then you get a thing like this. It doesn't make sense, it scares you. There's a chilly feeling that something *wrong* has happened but you don't quite know what it is. You want like hell to solve the crime because the victims were your people. The twisted bodies were from the inside, from the real world of the department, not from that chaos that swirls around outside.

Usually there is no mystery to a cop's death. He knocks on a door and a junkie blows him away. He hollers freeze at some kid running out of a liquor store and gets a bullet in the face. That's the way cops get killed, suddenly and without mystery. Death in the line of duty—rare, but it happens.

"Here's the car," Wilson said. Becky had walked right past it; she had been too deeply engrossed in her thoughts. But she got in, drove mechanically through the increasingly heavy rain, listening to it drum on the roof, listening to the wind soughing past the closed windows, feeling the pervasive dirty damp of the afternoon.

Headquarters was dark and gray, standing like some black monument in the storm. They pulled into the garage beneath the building, into the sudden flood of fluorescent lights, the squeal of brakes and tires as they maneuvered through the garage and found a parking space in the area marked off for the Homicide Division.

Underwood was not alone in his office. With him was a young man in a polyester suit and round rimless glasses. For an instant Becky was reminded of John Dean, then the face looked up and the impression of boyishness disappeared: the man's eyes were cold, his face thinner than it should be, his lips set in a terse line.

"Good afternoon," Underwood said stiffly, half rising from behind his desk, "this is Assistant District Attorney Kupferman." He then introduced Neff and Wilson. The two detectives pulled up chairs; this was going to be a work session and there was no time to stand on formality.

Becky relaxed into the comfortable leather wing chair Wilson had gotten for her. The Chief's office was all leather and paneling; it looked like an expensive private library without books. Hunting scenes were hung on the wall, a pewter chandelier from the ceiling. The whole impression was one of subdued bad taste—a sort of subtle and completely unintentional self-mockery.

"Let's go," Underwood said. "I told the papers we'd have a statement tonight. Was I right?"

"Yeah," Wilson said. He looked at the assistant

DA. "You're chewing. Got any gum?" The man held out a pack of sugar-free gum. "Thanks. I'm not supposed to smoke."

"I want to know if you've found out anything about those guys that might justify us getting into the act," the assistant DA said.

So that was what he was here for. He was the District Attorney's little watchdog, sent here to sniff out any departmental wrongdoing. Maybe the two dead cops were bent, the thinking would go, maybe that's why they were dead.

"There's nothing like that," Wilson said. "These guys were Auto Squad, not Narcotics. They weren't into anything."

Becky's mind flashed to her husband Dick, to the Narcotics Squad. Just as quickly she pulled her thoughts away, returning them to this conversation. What was it that made her worry so about Dick, especially lately? She couldn't allow herself to think about it now. As firmly as she could, she returned her thoughts to the question at hand.

"You're sure?"

"We haven't investigated that aspect," Becky put in. "We've just now established a cause of death."

This was obviously the part Underwood wanted to hear about. He leaned forward and made a little pulling motion with his hands. "It was the dogs," Wilson said tonelessly.

"Oh, no, you can't tell me that! I can't have that!"

"It's the truth as far as we know. They were killed by dogs."

"Hell no. That's completely unacceptable. I'm not putting that in any press releases. Let the damn Commissioner do it, it's his responsibility."

The way he began to back off would have been funny if it wasn't so sad. He had called them down here hoping to get some glory thrown his way when they solved the crime; but now that it looked like this he wasn't so eager to be associated with it. Let the Commissioner tell the world that two fully armed policemen got themselves killed by a bunch of dogs; Underwood sure as hell wasn't going to do it.

"We didn't believe it ourselves," Becky said, "but Evans is sure. The only thing out of the ordinary was some residual carbon monoxide—"

"Carbon monoxide! That's incapacitating! Then it makes some sense, the guys were out cold. Now that's better, why didn't you start off telling me that?" He glared an instant at Wilson. "That's the crucial piece of change, as far as I'm concerned. Did the M. E. say where they got it?"

"Background atmosphere," Wilson cut in. "It's not important. There are probably higher levels in your blood right now."

"Did anybody check their car, find out if the exhaust system was defective?"

Wilson laughed, a sneering little noise in the back of his throat. Becky wished to God he had never made that sound. "The CO count wasn't high enough."

"It's an angle, man! If I can use that, I don't have to put this case down to The Unexplained. Think about what we're confronting here! Cops were killed by dogs. It's stupid. It's bad for the department, it makes the men look like a bunch of jerkoffs, getting themselves killed by a pack of mutts. You don't tell the papers, yeah, here are a couple of dopes who got themselves done in by a bunch of dogs, didn't even have the sense to defend themselves. I can't make a statement like that."

"Which is why you'll try to get the Commissioner to make the statement. You don't want to be associated with it."

"It's his responsibility, Detective. And I don't think I like your attitude!"

"Thank you."

The Chief's eyes bored into Wilson's impassive face. "What's that supposed to mean?"

"Thank you. Nothing more or less. I've told you all I know about this case. Give me a few more days and a little luck and I'll know more. As far as the cause of death is concerned, it appears to have been the dogs. I don't like it any more than you do, I've got to tell you. But those are the facts. If you want a statement for the press, that's got to be it."

"The hell. The carbon monoxide did it. Had to. And that's damn well what I'm going to say."

"Have you considered the consequences, sir?" Becky said. She had, and a statement like the one Underwood planned to make was a serious mistake, even a dangerous one.

"Like?"

"Well, if the men were conscious—and we all know they probably were—it means that we've got something very dangerous out there. Something the public ought to be made aware of, and the police ought to take steps to eliminate."

"Yeah, but that's no problem because I intend to order that damn dump cleared of wild dogs. I'll send in the Tactical Patrol Force and clean it out. There won't be another problem no matter how those dogs got to DiFalco and Houlihan. Even if the men *were* conscious it doesn't make any difference because by this time tomorrow the dogs are going to be dead. I'm going to say that the officers were suffering from carbon monoxide poisoning and were attacked by the dogs while they were unconscious or semiconscious." He cleared his throat. "All right with you?"

"It's your statement, Chief," Wilson said.

"OK, don't you do or say anything to contradict it, you understand. Just keep your problems to yourself. And as of right now you're off the case."

Becky was astonished. This had never happened to them before; people always put up with Wilson, endured him. Being pulled off this case was a blow to his prestige and to hers. She could have kicked him for his Goddamn bullheadedness.

"It won't last, Underwood," Wilson said quietly. "You can kick us around and you can make any damn statement you want, but in the end you're going to be embarrassed. This thing isn't going to go away."

"The hell it isn't. You wait and see."

"Something damn strange happened out there."

"Nothing the TPF can't deal with." His face was getting blotchy; this was almost too much for his temper. "Nothing we can't deal with! Unlike you! You two can't seem to put this case together! Dogs indeed—that's ludicrous. It isn't even a good excuse, much less a solution. Here I've got this whole town screaming at me for a solution and you give me bullshit!" Suddenly he glared at Becky. "And another thing, sweetheart. I've heard the rumors about your sweet husband. This DA ought to be doing a little investigating into the Neff family instead of trying to dig up some kind of organized crime links to supply motive for the killers of DiFalco and Houlihan. We've got a bent cop's wife right here—or is it a family affair, dear?"

The Assistant DA remained tight-lipped, staring like a statue at the Oriental rug. At the Chief's words the whole room seemed to sway; Becky felt her head tightening, the blood rushing, her heart thundering. What in the name of God was he implying! Was Dick in trouble? She knew that she herself was an honest cop. And Dick had to be too. Had to be. Like Wilson. He had to be as honest as Wilson.

"You think we're incompetent," Wilson said mildly, "why not convene a Board of Inquiry? Present your facts."

"Shut up and get out. Your superior officers will handle this from now on."

"Which means there's going to be a Board?"

"Shut up and get out!"

They left, even Wilson perceiving that the meeting was terminated. "I'm going home," Becky said to her boss as the elevator dropped toward the garage. "Want a lift?"

"Nah. I'm gonna go over to Chinatown, get some supper. I'll see you in the morning."

"See you."

That was that for today. Another charming day in the life of a lady cop.

Traffic was heavy and she had missed the evening news by the time she got home. No matter, the Chief's statement wouldn't make it on the air until eleven o'clock.

When she arrived at their small upper East Side apartment, Becky was disappointed that Dick wasn't there. Mechanically she ran the Phone-Mate. Dick's voice said he'd be in about three A.M. Great. A lonely night just when you need it the most.

At eleven the Chief appeared with his terse statement—carbon monoxide, wild dogs, TPF roundup of dogs, case closed in one day.

The hell it is, she thought, the hell it is.

Chapter 3

Mike O'Donnell hated this part of his daily journey. The streets around here were sullen, dangerous and empty. Openings in the ruined buildings exhaled the stench of damp rot and urine. O'Donnell liked the bustling crowds a few blocks away, but on the money a blind man made you couldn't take cabs through these areas, you had to walk. Over the years the deadly stillness had grown like a cancer, replacing the noisy, kindly clamor that Mike remembered from his childhood. Now it was almost all like this except the block where Mike lived with his daughter and the block near the subway station a twenty-minute walk away.

Those twenty minutes were always bad, always getting worse. Along this route he had encountered addicts, muggers, perverts—every kind of human garbage. And he had survived. He let them shake him down. What could he lose, a few dollars? Only once had he been struck, that by some teenagers, children really. He had appealed to their manhood, shamed them out of their plan to torture him in one of the empty buildings.

Mike was tough and resilient. Sixty sightless years in the Bronx left him no other choice. He and his beloved daughter were on welfare, home relief. She was a good girl with bad taste in husbands. God knows, the kind of men . . . smelling of cologne and hair grease, moving around like cats through the apartment, voices that sneered every word . . . actors, she said. And she was an actress, she said . . . he groped his way along with his cane trying to put trouble out of his mind, not wanting to bring his feelings home, start an argument.

Then he heard a little sound that made the hairs rise along the back of his neck. It didn't quite seem human, yet what else could it be? Not an animal— too much like a voice, too little like a growl.

"Is somebody there?"

The sound came again, right in front of him and down low. He sensed a presence. Somebody *was* there, apparently crouching close to the ground. "Can I help you? Are you hurt?"

Something slid along the pavement. At once the strange sound was taken up from other points—behind him, in the abandoned buildings beside him, in the street. There was a sense of slow, circling movement.

Mike O'Donnell raised his cane, started to swing it back and forth in front of him. The reaction was immediate; Mike O'Donnell's death came so suddenly that all he registered was astonishment.

They worked with practiced efficiency, pulling the body back into the abandoned building while blood was still pumping out of the throat. It was a heavy, old body, but they were determined and there were six of them. They worked against time, against the ever-present danger of being discovered at a vulnerable moment.

Mike O'Donnell hadn't understood how completely this neighborhood had been abandoned in recent years, left by all except junkies and other derelicts, and the ones who were attracted to them for their weakness. And now Mike O'Donnell had joined the unnumbered corpses rotting in the abandoned basements and rubble of the empty neighborhood.

But in his case there was one small difference. He had a home and was missed. Mike's daughter was frantic. She dialed the Lighthouse for the Blind again. No, they hadn't seen Mike, he had never appeared for his assigned duties. Now it was six hours and she wasn't going to waste any more time. Her next call was to the police.

Because missing persons usually turn up on their own or don't turn up at all, and because there are so many of them, the Police Department doesn't react instantly to another such report. At least, not unless it concerns a child or a young woman who had no reason to leave home, or, as in the case of Mike O'Donnell, somebody who wouldn't voluntarily abandon the little security and comfort he had in the world. So Mike O'Donnell's case was special and it got some attention. Not an overwhelming amount, but enough to cause a detective to be assigned to the case. A description of Mike O'Donnell was circulated, given a little more than routine attention. Somebody even questioned the daughter long enough to draw a map of Mike's probable route from his apartment to the subway station. But the case went no farther than that; no body turned up, the police told the daughter to wait, not to give up hope. A week later they told her to give up hope, he wasn't going to be found. Somewhere in the city his body probably lay moldering, effectively and completely hidden by whoever had killed him. Mike O'Donnell's daughter learned in time to accept the idea of his death, to try to replace the awful uncertain void with the comfort of certainty. She did the best she could, but all she really came to understand was that her father had somehow been swallowed by the city.

During these weeks Neff and Wilson worked on other assignments. They heard nothing about the O'Donnell case; they were investigating another murder, locked in the endless, sordid routine of Homicide. Most crimes are no less commonplace than the people who commit them, and Wilson and Neff weren't being assigned to the interesting or dramatic cases these days. It wasn't that they were being muscled aside, but word was out that the Chief of Detectives wasn't exactly in love with them. He knew that they didn't like his handling of the DiFalco/Houlihan murders and he didn't want to be reminded of it, primarily because he didn't like it any more than they did. He was a more literal man than they were and much more concerned with his own potential appointment to the job of Police Commissioner than with following up bizarre theories about what genuinely looked to him like an even more bizarre accident. So the two detectives were kept away from big cases, effectively buried in the sheer size of the New York City Police Department.

The first words Becky Neff heard about Mike O'Donnell came from the Medical Examiner. "I thought you two had retired," he said over the phone. "You got a heavy case?"

"The usual. Not a lot of action." Beside her Wilson raised his eyebrows. The phone on her desk hadn't been ringing too often; an extended conversation like this was of interest.

"I've got a problem up here I'd like you two to take a look at."

"The Chief—"

"So take a coffee break. Just come up here. I think this might be what you've been waiting for."

"What's he got?" Wilson asked as soon as she put down the phone.

"He's got a problem. He thinks it might interest us."

"The Chief—"

"So he said take a coffee break and come up to see him. I think it's a good idea."

They pulled on their coats; outside it was a bright, blustery December afternoon and the cold wind coming around the buildings carried a fierce chill. The cold had been so intense for the past three days, in fact, that there weren't even many cars on the street. The usual afternoon jams were gone, replaced by a smattering of taxis and buses with great plumes of condensing exhaust behind them. The M. E. had been circumspect on the phone, no doubt savoring what little bit of drama might be in this for him.

They didn't speak as the car raced up Third Avenue. In the past few weeks Wilson had become more than usually taciturn; that was fine with Becky, she had problems enough of her own without listening to him complain about his. The last month with Dick had been stormy, full of pain and unexpected realizations. She knew now that Dick was taking money under the table. Strangely enough the money wasn't from narcotics but from gambling. He had tracked a heroin network into an illicit gambling casino about a year ago. Dick's father was in a nursing home, he was sick of the bills, he was sick of the treadmill; he collared the junkies but left the gambling establishment alone—for a few thousand dollars. "It's gambling," he had argued; "what the hell, it shouldn't even be a crime." But since it was, he might as well let it pay the six hundred a month his father was costing. God knows, they might even be able to put enough aside for a decent apartment one of these days.

It hurt her to see this happening to Dick. The truth was, she had sniped at him for it but she hadn't tried to stop him and she hadn't turned him in. Nor would she. But Dick was a corrupt cop, the one thing she had sworn she would never be, the one thing she had sworn she would never allow him to be. Well, he hadn't asked permission.

She had always assumed that she would never give in to the temptations that were so common on the police force—and he had sworn it too. But he had and by not stopping him she had too. Now they bickered, each unwilling to confront the real reason for their anger. They should have had the courage to stop; instead they had let things happen. They had disappointed one another and were bitter about it.

Bitter enough to spend more and more time apart. Often it was days between shared evenings or monosyllabic breakfasts. They used to work their schedules to fit; now they worked them to be apart. Or at least as far as Becky was concerned she just stopped making an effort with her schedule. She drew what she drew, and overtime was just fine. Eventually there would be a confrontation, but not now, not today —today she was heading up to the M. E.'s office to be let in on a new case, maybe something really interesting for the first time in too damn long.

Evans was waiting for them in the reception area. "Don't take off your coats," he said, "we're going to the freezer." That meant the remains were in an advanced state of deterioration. The Medical Examiner's office had a claustrophobic freezer compartment with room enough for three surgical tables and a few people squeezed in tight. Wilson's eyes roved as they went down the disinfectant-scented hall toward the freezer; his claustrophobia had a field day in the thing. More than once he had commented to Becky that the freezer had figured in his nightmares.

"It's rough stuff again," the M. E. said conversationally. "I only call you folks in when I've got some real gore. Hope you don't mind." It could be that Evans lacked taste or it could just possibly be an attempt at banter. Becky didn't bother to laugh; instead she asked a question.

"What are we going to see?"

"Three DOA's, very decomposed." He ushered them into the starkly lit freezer and pulled the door shut behind them. He didn't need to say more; the bodies had clearly been attacked the same way DiFalco and Houlihan were attacked. There was something chilling about seeing the same type of scrape marks on the bones, the same evidence of gnawing. Becky was frightened, too deeply frightened to really understand her feelings. But she knew the moment she saw these corpses that the Chief of Detectives had made exactly the mistake they had feared he was making—this was not an ordinary murder case and it was not a fluke.

"Goddamn," Wilson said.

The Medical Examiner smiled, but this time it was without mirth. "I don't know how to explain these bodies. The condition makes no sense."

"It makes sense," Becky said, "as soon as you assume that they weren't killed by human beings."

"What then?"

"That's what's to be found out. But you're wasting your time with us, Underwood took us off the case."

"Well, he'll put you back on."

"There are a lot of detectives in this department," Wilson put in. "I'm sure he'll find others. And it's likely he'll want more. This is going to be a big embarrassment for him." Wilson shook his head. "A hell of an embarrassment. Let's get out of this icebox. We've seen all we need to see."

Evans opened the door. "You'll get back on," he said, "I'll make sure of that. So start to work. You need a solution."

They didn't bother to ask the M. E. how the bodies had come in; instead they called headquarters and got referred to the right precinct. As soon as he was off the phone to headquarters Wilson called the 41st Precinct in the South Bronx and asked to speak to the Captain. Sure they could come up, but there were already detectives on the case. "Might be a tie-in to another case, one of ours." He put down the phone. "Let's move."

They battled their way across town to the FDR Drive. Despite the fact that the weather had reduced the amount of traffic in the city, getting across town was still difficult. "I read somewhere that it takes longer to cross town in a car today than it used to in a carriage."

"And longer than that when I'm driving, right?"

"Yeah, if you say so."

"Goddamn brass," Becky growled.

"Hey, getting our dander up, my dear."

"Damn right I am. Here we've got two cops buried and forgotten and we knew damn well something wasn't right—damn these politicking bastards. It's a black day when the NYPD won't even mount a proper investigation when officers are killed. Seedman never would have done this."

Wilson sighed, expressing in that single sound all the feelings he could or would not express about the Police Department he so loved to hate. The department had hurt him as well as helped him; in the past few years he had seen its emphasis shift away from solving crimes toward preventing them. Citizens demanded protection in the streets; the once-proud Detectives diminished and foot patrol became the thing. The old-timers were fewer and fewer; Wilson was one, sharp-eyed and careful. And the fact that his young partner was a woman was just another sign of the deterioration of the department. He stared out the window. Becky couldn't see his face but she knew what the expression contained. She knew also that there was no sense in talking to him now; he was beyond communication.

They made their way through the devastated streets of the 41st Precinct, past the vacant brick-strewn lots, the empty buildings, the burned, abandoned ruins, the stripped cars, the dismal, blowing garbage in the streets. And Becky thought, "Somewhere, something is here. It is here." She knew it. And by the way Wilson changed, the stiffening of his posture, the darkening of his face, the little turning-down of the edges of his mouth, she saw that he also had the same feeling.

"Every time I'm up here this place looks worse."

"What street was it again, George?"

"East One Hundred and Forty-fourth Street. Old One Forty-four. Sure is a mess now." Wilson was in the neighborhood of his childhood, looking at the ruins of where he had been a boy. "It was a pretty good place then, not the greatest, but it sure wasn't like this. Jesus."

"Yeah." Becky tried to leave him alone with his thoughts. Considering that the little upstate town where she had grown up was still exactly as it had been, still and seemingly forever, she couldn't imagine what seeing this place must do to Wilson.

"God, I can't believe I'm fifty-four," he said. "I'd swear I was sitting on that stoop last night." He sighed. "We're there," he said, "the old Forty-first." The precinct house was a dismal fortress, an unlikely bastion of reasonable decay in the surrounding ruins. A neighborhood of unabandoned houses clustered around it. The danger and destruction were beyond. In fact, with the strange fecundity of the Bronx, this immediate two blocks showed signs of mild prosperity. There was traffic in the streets, neatly swept sidewalks, curtains in windows, and a well-kept Catholic church on the corner. People were few because of the cold, but Becky could imagine what the area was like when the weather was good—filled with kids on the sidewalks and their parents on the stoops, full of liveliness and noise and the sheer exuberance that can infect city neighborhoods.

The Captain of the 41st Precinct looked up from his desk when Neff and Wilson were shown in. It was clear at once that he still didn't know exactly why they were there. Normally detectives from another borough would have nothing to do with this case— and as far as the Captain was concerned it probably wasn't much of a case. Just another couple of rotting junkie corpses and a poor old man. About the score for the South Bronx these days. Becky knew instinctively to let Wilson handle the Captain. He was the infighter, the resident expert on departmental politics. Look where his political skill had gotten him. The best detective in New York City at dead end. First

Grade, true, but never a division, never a district of his own.

"We got a suggestion from Evans," Wilson said by way of explaining their presence to the Captain.

"Evans pulled rank on the Bronx Medical Examiner and got those cadavers down to Manhattan. We don't know why he did that." There was acid in the man's voice. He didn't like a case being taken from him without a good reason. And it was obvious that so far nobody had given him one.

"He did that because the marks on them were similar to the marks on the DiFalco-Houlihan remains."

The Precinct Captain stared. "That case still open?"

"It is now. We'vo got a new lead."

"Jesus. No wonder you guys are all over us." He stood up from his desk. "We got the scene in good shape," he said. "You want to go over there?"

Wilson nodded. As they followed the Captain out of his office, Becky was exultant. The man had never thought to call downtown to check on Neff and Wilson. If he had he would have found out that they weren't even on the case anymore. But why should he? It would never even occur to him.

The area where the bodies had been found was roped off and plastered with Crime Scene stickers. It was guarded by two patrolmen. "The bodies were found by a gypsy cab driver who stopped to fix a flat and smelled something. He came to us, we were lucky. Usually those guys don't even bother."

The bodies had been found in the basement of an abandoned apartment house. Becky took her flashlight out of her bag and went in under the decaying stoop. Lights had been set up in the dirty room, but the rest of the building was in boarded-up darkness. The flashlight played along the floor, in the unlit corners, up the stairs that led to the first floor. "Door locked?" Wilson asked as Becky shone her light on its blackened surface.

"Haven't been up there," the Captain said. "Remember, we thought this was routine until this morning when the Bronx M. E. told us that Evans had snatched his bodies."

"Ha ha, that was funny," Wilson said tonelessly. The Captain glowered. "Let's go up, partner. We might as well make the search."

They all heard it; a footstep on the stair. They looked to their leader. His hair rose and theirs did too. They functioned with one emotion, one will, one heart. What did the footsteps mean? Obviously, the ones in the basement had decided to come upstairs. And they were familiar. The sound of their tread, their rising smell, their voices were remembered from the dump. As the elders had feared, the killings of young humans had caused an investigation. And these two had been at that investigation. Now they were here, obviously following the pack.

Their scent became more powerful as they drew nearer: an old man and a young woman. No danger, they would be an easy kill.

The leader made a sound that sent the pack into motion.

They were hungry, the children were cold and hungry. Food was needed. Today a new hunt would have begun. Maybe it would be unnecessary, this kill would both remove danger and provide meat. But the strong young woman would have to be separated from the weak old man. How to do that?

Their scents revealed the fact that they were partners, and the way their voices sounded as they talked to one another said that they had worked together a long time. How do you separate such people even for a moment, especially when both recognize danger? The scents became sharp with the smell of fear as the two humans groped through the darkness. It made digestive juices flow and hearts beat faster with lust for the hunt. The leader warned, hold back, hold back. In this situation he sensed hidden dangers. Suddenly he hated the place. He loathed it, despised it. It was thick with humanity. There were strong, young ones outside and these two inside and another old one in the basement. Before there had been many more in the basement. "Our young must not kill their young," he thought fiercely. He found himself moving slowly toward the door of the room they inhabited, moving against his judgment, attracted by the need to kill the two who knew enough of the pack to follow it here. Now the others moved behind him, stealthy, efficient, padding quickly down the darkened hall, down the black stairway toward the wonderful scents, moving too close to humanity and yet only close enough to get what they needed. "Must find a way to split them up," the leader thought. Then he stopped. His whole body seethed with desire to go on, to finish the attack, to feel the death of the prey in his mouth. But he thought carefully, his mind turning over the problem and coming to the solution.

Certain sounds attracted humans. This fact was often used in hunting. A little cry, like one of their children, would bring even the most fearful within range of attack. And the child's cry was most easily heard by the women.

"Sh!"

"What?"

"Listen." It came again, the unmistakable groan of a child. "You hear that?"

"No."

Becky went to the stairwell. She heard it more clearly, coming from above. "Wilson, there's a kid up there." She shone her light into the dimness. "I'm telling you I hear a child."

"So go investigate. I'm not going up there."

The sound came again, full of imperative need.

She found herself standing on the first step, moving upward almost against her own will. Above her the decoy put his heart into the sounds, making them as plaintive and compelling as he could. He imagined himself a helpless little human child lying on the cold floor weeping, and the sound that came out of him was like such a child.

The others moved swiftly to the opposite stairwell and started down. They sensed the positions of the prey. The strong young woman starting up the stairs, the weak old man standing in the dark hallway behind her. "Come up, come up," the decoy pleaded to her in his mind, and made the little sound. It had to be right, to be perfect, just enough to attract her, not enough to let her decide what she wanted to decide—that it was the wind, a creaking board, or something dangerous.

As she reached one landing the hunters reached its twin at the opposite end of the hall. As she rose toward the decoy they descended toward Wilson. As they got closer they became more careful. Hidden strength under the smells of fear and decay. They would have to hit this man with devastating force to get him, hit as hard as they had hit the two young ones at the dump. But their prize would be great; he was heavy and well-fed, unlike the ones they had found among these empty buildings. There was no starvation in him and no sickness to make him dangerous to consume. They loved him, lusted after him, moved closer to him. And they saw his dim shadow, his heavy slow body standing in the dark.

Then standing in a flickering blaze of light.

"What are you doing, George?"

"Lighting a Goddamn cigarette."

Becky came down toward him flashing her light in his face. "You *are* lighting a cigarette. I'll be damned. Where did you get a cigarette?"

"I've been saving it for a special occasion."

"And now is a special occasion?"

He nodded, his face like stone. "I'll be frank with you, Becky, I've got the creeps. I'm scared to death. I won't get out of here without you but I think we ought to leave—now."

"But there's a child—"

"Now! Come on." He grabbed her wrist, pulled her toward the basement door.

"There's something upstairs," he said to the Precinct Captain, who was standing in the middle of the basement as if he had been undecided about whether or not to follow the two detectives upstairs.

"I'm not surprised. The building is probably full of junkies."

"It sounded like a child," Becky said. "I'm sure that's what it was."

"That's possible too," the Captain said mildly. "I'll order up a search party if you think I should. But don't do it with just two people. It'll take ten men with carbines, I think that ought to do it."

Becky acknowledged the wisdom of this plan. No doubt there had been a pack of junkies at the top of the stairs waiting to jump her. Or perhaps there was actually a child. If that was so the ten minutes it would take to assemble the search party would make little difference.

They went outside and got into the Captain's car. As soon as they left, the two patrolmen who had been guarding the scene moved swiftly to their own car and got in to shield themselves from the cold. They turned on their radio so that they would again have advance warning of visits from the precinct and settled back in the warmth.

For this reason they did not hear the howl of rage and frustration that rose from the upper reaches of the tenement. Nor did they see the exodus that took place, a line of gray shadows jumping one by one across the six feet of space that separated this building from the next one.

It didn't take long to assemble the search party. It was now four o'clock and the night men were coming on duty. Three patrol cars returned to the building. With the two men on duty there plus Wilson and Neff there would be exactly ten officers for the search. Of course as soon as the cars drew up to the front of the building you could assume that any junkies in it slipped out the back. But murder had been done here and the precinct so far hadn't mounted a proper search. Pictures had been taken of the victims and a cursory dusting of the area for fingerprints, but that was all. In this part of the city a committed crime was just another statistic. Nobody bothered to find out the circumstances that led to the deaths of a few derelicts. And nobody doubted that the blind man had gotten mugged and then dragged off the street to die. And nobody was right about what happened.

During the search Wilson and Neff were silent. The rooms of the old tenement still bore the marks of the last residents—graffiti on the walls, shreds of curtains in the windows, yellowing wallpaper here and there. Even, in one room, the remains of a carpet. But there was no child, and there were no traces of recent human habitation.

Wilson and Neff made the reluctant patrolmen scoop up some of the fecal matter that was found. They put it in a plastic bag.

"Empty upstairs," a voice called as a group of five came from searching up to the roof. "Nothing suspicious."

What the hell did that mean? These men wouldn't know evidence from cauliflower. "Take us through," Wilson growled. "We've gotta see for ourselves."

The patrolmen went with them, the whole crowd going floor to floor. Becky saw the empty rooms in better light, but her mind could not blot out those plaintive cries. *Something* was up here just a few minutes ago, something that had left without a trace.

They looked carefully in all the rooms but found nothing.

When they got back to the basement Wilson was shaking his head. "I don't get it," he said, "I know you heard something."

"You do?"

"I heard it too, you think I'm deaf?"

Becky was surprised, she hadn't realized that he also had heard the sound. "Why didn't you go up with me then?"

"It wasn't a child."

She looked at him, at the cold fear in his face. "OK," she said, swallowing her intended challenge, "it wasn't a child. What was it?"

He shook his head and pulled out his cigarettes. "Let's get the shit to the lab for analysis. That's all we can do now."

They left the house with the clomping horde of

patrolmen. With their meager evidence tightly enclosed in plastic bags they headed back to Manhattan.

"You think this will reopen the DiFalco case?" Becky asked.

"Probably."

"Good, then we won't be moonlighting on it anymore."

"As I recall we got taken off that case. Or do you recall something else?"

"Well, yeah, but in view of—"

"In view of nothing. We're going to be the scapegoats now. Neff and Wilson get case. Carbon monoxide and wild dogs. Neff and Wilson close case. New evidence comes in. Case reopened. Neff and Wilson scapegoats for closing it in the first place." His throat rumbled in a suppressed cough. "Goddamn Luckies," he said. "Goddamn, you know I could be resigning soon."

"You won't resign."

"No, not voluntarily. But it depends on how hard Underwood wants to stick me with blame for misunderstanding the case."

"But it's only one damn case."

"It's police officers killed in the line of duty. If it gets out that Underwood himself closed the case he'll lose his shot at Commissioner. Therefore you and yours truly are going to be blamed. Might as well relax and enjoy the fun." His shoulders shook with mirthless laughter.

"Maybe there's something more conclusive. If there is it'll help a little." She paused. The silence grew. "Who do you think is doing it?" she asked.

"Not who—what. It's not human."

Now he had said the words, words they had previously been unwilling to face. Not human. Could not be human. "What makes you so sure?" Becky asked, half-knowing the answer.

Wilson looked at her in surprise. "Why, the noise, of course. It wasn't human."

"What's that supposed to mean? It sounded perfectly human to me." Or had it? Becky remembered it now like something that had taken place in a dream, a child's voice or . . . something else. Every few seconds it was as if she woke up and heard it again—horrible, inhuman parody full of snarling menace . . . then child again, soft, wounded, dying.

"Look out!"

She slammed on the brakes. She had been about to glide broadside into the traffic of Third Avenue. "Sorry. Sorry, George, I—"

"Pull over. You're not in good shape."

She obeyed him. Despite the fact that she felt fine, there was no denying what she had almost done. Like the little cries were still taking place, but in a dream. "I feel OK, I don't know what came over me."

"You acted hypnotized," he said.

She heard the noises again, feral, snarling, monstrous. Sweat popped out all over her. She felt cold, her flesh crawling. Her mind turned back to the stair, to the terrible danger that had been waiting for her, the same as the torn, bloodied corpses, the jagged bones and skulls.

With her hands over her mouth she fought not to scream, to give up completely to the terror.

Wilson came across the seat as if he had been waiting for this. He took her in his arms; her body rattled against his thick shoulders; she pressed her face into the warm, scruffy smell of his ancient white shirt, distantly she felt him kissing her hair, her ear, her neck, and felt waves of comfort and surprise overcoming and pushing back the panic. She wanted to pull away from him but she also wanted to do what she did, which was lift her face. He kissed her hard and she accepted it, passively at first, then giving in to the relief of it, and kissed him back.

Then they separated, propelled apart by the fact that they were in a car recognizable to any policeman. Becky put her hands on the steering wheel. She felt sick and sad, as if something had just been lost.

"I've been wanting to get that out of my system," Wilson said gruffly. "I've been—" Then his voice died away. He clutched the dashboard and laid his head on his arm. "Oh, hell, I love you, dammit." She started to talk. "No, don't say it. I know what you'll say. But just let it be known and leave it like that. We go on like we were. Unrequited love won't kill me."

She looked at him, amazed that he could bring up something so . . . extraneous. She had always wondered if he loved her. She loved him in a way. But that wasn't important, it had been accepted a long time ago. And their relationship was established. Certainly it shouldn't intrude now. When he turned his face toward her he registered shock. She knew her mascara must be running with the tears, she knew her face must be twisted in fear. "What happened to me?" she asked. Her voice was not her own, so distorted was it by the rush of emotions. "What was going on back there?"

"Becky, I don't know. But I think we'd better find out."

She laughed. "Oh, that's for sure! I just don't know if I can handle it. We've really got some problems here."

"Yeah. One of them is you. I don't mean that harshly, but I'm going to have to break my cardinal rule at this time. Let's change sides, I'm going to drive."

She hid her amazement. In all the years they had worked together, this was an absolute first. "I must be falling apart," she said as she sank into Wilson's usual seat. "This is really a big deal."

"It's no big deal. You're rattled. But you know you shouldn't be. I mean, you weren't the one in danger. It was me."

"You! I was being lured upstairs."

"To get you away from me."

"Why do you even say that? You're a man, a lot heavier than me, not an obvious target."

"I heard noises on the stairs at the other end of the hall. Breathing noises, like something hungry slavering over its food." The tone of his voice frightened her. She laughed nervously in self defense, the sound pealing out so suddenly that it startled Wilson visibly. He looked at her out of the corner of his eye but kept the car moving.

"I'm sorry. It's just that you're the *last* person I'd think of as one of their victims."

"Why?"

"Well, they eat them, don't they? Isn't that what it's all about? Everybody they've hit has been eaten."

"Old men, junkies, two cops in a hell of a lonely place. The weak and the isolated. I fitted two key criteria in that house—older man, isolated from all except you. And they damn near lured you away upstairs. You ever go hunting?"

"I don't like it. I've never been."

"When I was a kid I hunted with my father. We went after moose up north. We used to track for days sometimes. One summer we tracked for a week. And finally we got on to our moose, a big old bull that moved with a slanty track. A wounded bull. Weak, ready for the slaughter. I'll never forget it. There we were just getting ready to take a shot when wolves stole out of the shadows all around us. They went right past us into the clearing where the moose was grazing. My dad cursed under his breath—those wolves were going to scare our trophy away. But they didn't. That big bull moose looked down at those scrawny wolves and just snorted. They moved in closer and he stopped grazing and stared at them. You'd never believe it. The damn wolves wagged their tails! And the moose let out a great roar and they jumped him. They tore at him, bled him to death. We were fascinated, we were rooted to the spot. But it was like they agreed together that the killing be done. The wolves and the moose agreed. He couldn't make it anymore, they needed meat. So he let them take him. And those timber wolves are scrawny. They're like German shepherds. They look like they'd never be able to bring down a full-grown bull moose. And they wouldn't, unless he agreed to let them try." He was watching her again, barely keeping an eye on traffic. He was no better a driver today than she was.

"What's that supposed to mean?"

"I'm the bull moose in this version of the story. I wasn't scared, but I knew they were coming down those stairs. If they had gotten any closer to me, I think I would have been a goner."

"But you didn't want them to kill you! We're not like animals, we want to survive."

"I don't know what was going on in my mind," he said. By the choked gruffness of his voice she knew that if he hadn't been Wilson he would be sobbing. "All I know is, if they had come any closer I'm not so sure I could have even tried to stop them."

Chapter 4

Becky Neff awoke suddenly out of a restless sleep. She felt that there had been a noise, yet now there was no sound except the wind, and a little snow whispering on the windowpane. The glow from the streetlights far below shone on the ceiling. In the distance a truck clattered its way down Second Avenue.

The hands of the clock showed three forty-five. She had been asleep four hours. She remembered a hint of dream—a flash of blood, a sickly feeling of menace. Perhaps that had awakened her. Dick's steady breathing in the bed beside her was a reassurance. If there had been an unusual noise he would be awake too. Gently she touched him, thinking as she did of how things had been between them such a short time ago, and of how change seeps into even the strongest love. She became sad and afraid. The apartment was cold, the morning heat not yet up. "Dick," she said softly.

There was no response. She hadn't really said it loud enough to wake him; she didn't say it again. Then she leaned over to get her cigarettes from the night table and froze. There was a shadow on the ceiling. She watched it move slowly along, a low lump like something crawling on its belly across the bedroom terrace. Her mind raced to the sliding doors—locked? She had no idea.

Then the shadow was gone and she found she was still lying on her back, not reaching across the bed at all. In the manner of bad nightmares this one had continued even after she seemed to be awake. With the thought her heart stopped pounding. Of course it had been a dream. Nothing could climb sixteen stories to an apartment terrace. And nothing could have followed her. Yet she couldn't quite overcome the feeling that something *was* out there. Something, after all, must have sparked the dream. Something must have waked her up.

The mutilated faces of DiFalco and Houlihan flickered in her mind's eye. She thought of them staring up from the muddy ground. And she thought of Mike O'Donnell, the old blind man dying in his own darkness.

How did the killers look? She had assumed that they would look like wolves, but maybe not. Wolves, she knew, have never been implicated in a human killing. They are generally no more dangerous to man than are dogs. Wolves were interested in moose and deer. Man probably frightened them more than they did him.

A little sound from the terrace made her mind go blank, a shivering coldness pass through her body. It was a growl, very low and indistinct. They *were* here! Somehow they had done the impossible, had followed her here. They must have scented her at the house in the Bronx and followed the trail. They were hunting her down! She felt frozen, as if she could neither speak nor move. This was fear, she knew, so intense that it left her mind floating in a strange, precise world of its own, looking from a distance at her body. Her hand moved across the bed and began shaking her husband's shoulder. She heard her voice saying his name again and again with urgent, whispered intensity.

"What—"

"Don't make a sound. Something's outside."

He slipped his service revolver out of his nighttable drawer. Only then did it occur to her to do the same. Her own gun felt good in her hand. "On the terrace," she said.

Very quietly he got up and went to the door. He moved fast then, pulling back the curtains and stepping outside. The terrace was empty. He turned toward her, his shadow shrugging. "Nothing's here."

"There was something." The conviction grew in her when she said it. A few moments ago she had seen the shadow, heard the growl—and they were certainly real.

"What?"

"I don't know. Some kind of an animal."

"A cat?"

"I don't think so."

He came back to bed, crawling in beside her. "You're really wound up in this case, aren't you, honey?" The gentleness in his voice cut into her, making her feel more lonely than ever. Despite the urge she felt to embrace him, she stayed on her side of the bed.

"It's a strange case, Dick."

"Don't get overinvolved, honey. It's just another case."

That statement caused anger to replace fear. "Don't criticize me, Dick. If you were working on murders like these you'd feel exactly the same way— if you were honest with yourself."

"I wouldn't get worked up."

"I'm not worked up!"

He laughed, a condescending chuckle. The great stone policeman with his tender bride. "You take it easy kid," he said, pulling the quilt up over his head. "Take a Valium if you're upset."

The man was infuriating.

"I'm telling you, George, I know what the hell I saw!"

He stared across the room toward the bleary window. They had been given an office belonging to the Manhattan South Detective Division despite the fact that they were still not officially assigned to it. "It's pretty hard to believe," Wilson said. "Sixteen stories is a long way up." His eyes were pleading when he looked at her—she *had* to be wrong or else they would be dealing with a force of completely unmanageable proportions.

"All I can say is, it happened. And even if you don't believe me it wouldn't hurt to take precautions."

"Maybe and maybe not. We'll know better what we're up against when we talk to the guy we're supposed to see."

"What guy?"

"A guy that Tom Rilker gave some of those paw-print casts to. You remember Tom Rilker?"

"Sure, the kook with the dogs."

"Well, he gave the prints we left behind in his office to another kook who wants us to go interview him. So maybe he'll tell us what you saw."

"Goddamn it, you have the sneakiest way of slipping things in. When do we see this genius?"

"Ten-thirty, up at the Museum of Natural History. He's an animal stuffer or something."

They drove up in silence. The fact that they were even trying this angle testified to their increasing desperation. But at least it meant doing something on the case instead of letting more time slip by. And time seemed to be terribly important.

"At least they aren't throwing other assignments at us these days," Becky said to break the silence. Since this case has been "closed" she and Wilson hadn't exactly been getting more big jobs. Sooner or later they would be transferred somewhere definite instead of remaining in the limbo of reporting directly to the Chief of Detectives. Probably go back to Brooklyn for all the difference it made. At least out there they wouldn't be victimized by high-level departmental politics.

"Underwood knows what we're doing."

"You think so?"

"Of course. Why do you think we're not getting other cases? Underwood's playing it by ear. If we turn up something he can use, OK. If we foul things up, we can always be reprimanded for insubordination." He laughed. "He knows exactly what we're doing."

"Evans told him, I suppose."

Wilson smiled. "Sure. He probably called up and told Underwood he'd better leave us alone if he knew what was good for him. Underwood might not like it since he closed the DiFalco case himself but he's afraid of Evans, so the result is we end up in a vacuum. Damned if we do and et cetera."

"Here's the Goddamn museum."

They went up the wide stone steps past the statue

of Teddy Roosevelt and into the immense dim hall that formed the lobby.

"We're here to see a Doctor Ferguson," Wilson said to the woman sitting behind the information counter. She picked up a telephone and spoke into it for a moment, then smiled up at them.

The workrooms of the museum were a shock. There were stacks of bones, boxes of feathers, beaks, skulls, animals and birds in various states of reconstruction on tables and in cases. The chaos was total, a welter of glue and paint and equipment and bones. A tall young man in a dirty gray smock appeared from behind a box of stuffed owls. "I'm Carl Ferguson," he said in a powerful, cheery voice. "We're preparing the Birds of North America, but that's obviously not why I called you." For an instant Becky saw something chill cross his face, then it was replaced again by the smile. "Let's go into my office, such as it is. I've got something to show you."

It sat on the desk in the office on a piece of plastic. "Ever seen anything like it?"

"What the hell is it?"

"A composite I constructed from the pawprint casts Tim Rilker gave me. Whatever made those prints has paws very much like this one."

"My God. It looks so—"

"Lethal. And that's exactly what it is. An efficient weapon. One of the best I've ever seen in nature, as a matter of fact." He picked it up. "These long, jointed toes can grasp, I think, quite well. And the claw retracts. Very beautifully and very strange." He shook his head. "Only one thing wrong with it."

"Which is?"

"It can't exist. Too perfect a mutation. No defects at all. Plus it's at least three steps ahead of its canine ancestors. Maybe if it was a single mutation it would be acceptable, but there are the prints of five or six different animals in here. There must be a pack of these things." He turned the plaster model in his hand. "The odds against this are billions—trillions—to one."

"But not impossible?"

He held the model out to Wilson, who stared but didn't touch. "We have the evidence right here. And I want to know more about the creatures that made these prints. Rilker couldn't give me a damn bit of information. That's why I called you. I didn't want to get involved, but frankly I'm curious."

Wilson put on a sickly smile. "You're curious," he said. "That's very nice. We're all curious. But we can't help you. You've just told us a lot more than we knew. You're the one who can answer questions."

The scientist looked puzzled and a little sad. He took his glasses off, then dropped into his chair and put the plaster model back on the desk. "I'm sorry to hear that. I had hoped you'd have more information for me. But I don't think you realize how little I know. Where did the prints come from—can you tell me that?"

"The scene of a crime."

"Oh come on, George, don't be so close-mouthed. They came from the scene of the DiFalco-Houlihan murders out in Brooklyn."

"The two policemen?"

"Right. They were found all around the bodies."

"What's being done about this?"

"Exactly nothing," Wilson snapped. "At the moment the case is officially closed."

"But what about these prints? I mean, here's clear evidence that something out of the ordinary is at work. This is no dog or wolf paw, you realize that? Surely somebody must be doing something about it."

Wilson shot Becky a glance and kept staring as if surprised. The feeling that she experienced confused and pleased her—not because of what the look communicated but because of the way his eyes lingered. "Nobody's doing anything about it, Doctor," she said. "That's why we're here. We are the only two police officers in New York on this case and we're about to be reassigned."

"You understand that this claw belongs to a fearsome killer." He said it like it was a revelation.

"We know," Becky replied patiently. In her mind's eye she once again saw the faces of the dead.

Doctor Ferguson seemed to withdraw into himself. His hands hung down at his sides, his head bowed. Becky had seen this kind of reaction to stress before, usually in those who have been unexpectedly close to murderers. "How many have died?" he asked.

"Five so far that we know about," Wilson replied.

"There've probably been more," Ferguson said faintly, "maybe many more, if what I suspect is right."

"Which is?"

He frowned. "I can't say right now. I'm not sure about it. If I'm wrong it could harm my career. We could be dealing with some kind of murderer's hoax. I don't want to get taken in by a hoax."

Wilson sighed. "You got any cigarettes?" he asked. Ferguson produced a pack. Wilson took one, tore off the filter and lit up. He did this all very quickly so that Becky wouldn't have a chance to stop him. "You know, you shouldn't clam up on us. If you don't tell us what you think we aren't going to be able to help you."

The scientist stared at them. "Look, if I get tripped up by a hoax—if I go out on a limb about this thing and it turns out to be a fake—I would lose my reputation. I don't know what would become of me. Or

I guess I do. Teaching at some backwoods college and never quite reaching tenure." He shook his head. "It's not much of a career."

"You're not presenting a paper here. You're talking confidentially to two New York City policemen. There's a difference."

"True enough. Maybe I'm exaggerating."

"So tell us your theory. For God's sake *help us!*" The words came out of Wilson like a bark, causing a sudden pause in the bustle of the workroom beyond the little office. "I'm sorry," he said more softly, "I guess I'm a little upset. Me and my partner here, we're the only ones who even suspect what we're up against. And we've had some bad experiences."

Becky broke in. "These things don't just kill. They hunt. They nearly got us in a house up in the Bronx a few days ago. They hid on an upper floor. One of them tried to lure me with the cries of a baby while the others—"

"Stalked me. They tried to separate us."

"And I think they might have been outside my apartment last night."

The words had come in a rush out of both of them, driven by their rising sense of isolation. Now Ferguson was looking at them with unabashed horror, almost as if they themselves bore some loathsome mark.

"You must be mistaken. They can't be as intelligent as all that."

Becky blinked with surprise—she had never realized that. Not only were they deadly, they were smart!! They had to be damn smart to lure her and Wilson into that stairway, and to seek out her apartment. They had to understand who the enemy was, and know the importance of destroying him before he revealed their presence to the world.

Wilson moved like a man in a dream, his hand gliding up to touch his cheek, the fingers running down the rough line of the throat, down to the seedy brown necktie and back to his lap. As the realization grew also in him his eyes hooded in a deep frown, his mouth opened almost sensually, as if he had fallen asleep and was dreaming of love. "I was beginning to suspect that they were intelligent, too. No matter what you say, Doctor Ferguson, what happened is what happened. You know something—I'll bet they didn't pop out of the ground yesterday either. If they're that smart, they know how to stay well hidden—and they know how important that is, too. That's my thought."

"Well, that's pretty much the theory I didn't want to tell you, too. You've got to get me a cranium or a head, though. Then I can give you an idea of the intelligence. But don't worry about it, I'm sure we're much smarter."

"Doctor, what would a chimp be like if it had the senses of a dog?"

"Lethal—oh God, I see what you mean. If their senses are highly developed enough they don't need our intelligence to best us. I suppose that's right. It's very disturbing, the idea of canine senses and a primate brain."

"And it's more than that."

"What do you mean?"

"Jesus Christ, I thought she just told you she was *hunted!*" His vehemence surprised her. The layers of calm professionalism were stripped away, revealing a Wilson underneath that she had never seen before. Here was a man of intensity and great feeling, protective, angry, full of violence. The cynical surface was gone. What ran beneath was burning with pain.

"Please keep your voice down. I can't have a disturbance in here. So I'll agree that she was hunted. You do something about the problem, you're the police."

"Crap. We don't know what the hell we're confronting."

"And I can't help you unless I've got more information. I'm not going to go spouting out suppositions that could get quoted in the papers. Anyway it's your problem to protect the community, so protect it. My interest is strictly scientific. So bring me a head. If I'm going to give you your answers, I've got to have a head."

Wilson's chin was pulled in, his shoulders were hunched. "Hell, you can count on us! Bring you a head wo can't possibly bring you a head and you know it. Nobody's ever caught one of these things. Even if they've evolved at absolute top speed, how long have they been around?"

"At the very least—and this seems next to impossible—give them ten thousand years."

"Longer than recorded history and you want us to bring you a head! Let's get out of here, Detective Neff, we've got work to do." He got up and left.

"Just one more thing," Becky said as she was leaving, "just one thing I'd like you to think about. If they are following us, they probably know we came to see you." She went out behind Wilson, leaving the scientist staring at the door.

Wilson didn't speak again until they had passed back through the nearly empty museum and were in the car. "That was bullshit you fed that schmuck," he said. "He won't believe us no matter how close to home you try to take it."

"Maybe not. It sure would help us though, to get

a Ph.D. behind us. Think of what would happen if that guy went to Underwood and said these two cops might have a point."

"Don't, Becky. It isn't going to happen that way." They rode on in silence for a few minutes. "Maybe we're spooked," Wilson said. "Maybe it was just our imagination last night."

"Our?"

"I saw something too." He said it as if he didn't want to. "Something watched me from a fire escape when I was on my way to my rooming house. It was a damn strange-looking dog. I only got a glimpse and then it was gone. I've never seen a face like that on a dog—so intense. In fact I've never seen a face like that before except once, when I collared a maniac. He looked at me like that. It was because the bastard was about to pull a hidden shiv on me."

"Why didn't you say something about this earlier?"

"I was wishing it was my imagination. I guess we're in trouble, Becky." This last he said softly, almost in awe of the words. They both knew exactly what the stakes were. Becky felt sick. Wilson, sitting beside her as solid as a statue, had never seemed so frail. She found herself wanting to protect him. She could imagine the thing on the fire escape—she could picture the eager, intent eyes, sense the frustration at the crowds on the sidewalk, imagine the silent anger it felt as Wilson went unmolested on his way, protected by all the unsuspecting witnesses.

"George, I just can't believe it. It's so hard to make it seem real. And if it isn't totally real, I'm not sure that I'll be able to deal with it."

"It's happened before, Becky. There are even legends about it." She waited eagerly for more but he seemed to see no need to continue. Typical of him to lapse into silence after making a leading statement like that.

"So go on. What are you driving at?"

"I was just thinking—you remember what you said to Rilker about werewolves? You might not have been too far wrong."

"That's ridiculous."

"Not really. Say they've existed throughout recorded history. If they really are as smart as we think, people in the past would have believed that they were men turned into wolves."

"Then what happened? Why did the legends die out?"

He braced his knee against the glove compartment and slumped in the seat. "Maybe the reason is that the population of the world grew. Back in the past their hunts were noticed because there were so few people. But as the population got bigger they started concentrating on the dregs, the isolated, the forgotten—people who wouldn't be missed. Typical predators in that respect—they only take the weak."

She glanced at him as she drove. "I think that's a hell of an idea," she said. "I don't think it's very good news for you and me, though."

He laughed. "We're not weak. That probably means they'll be very careful. There also isn't any knowledge about them at all, which must mean that they're very thorough about covering their tracks."

He means that they hunt down people like us, Becky thought as she guided the car through the traffic. It was like being in a bad dream, this feeling of being hunted. Her mind kept going back to the shadow on the ceiling, the shadow on the ceiling ... the patient shadow waiting for that single, perfect instant when it could destroy the woman who knew its secret. The world was whirling around her, around her and Wilson, a world of lights and voices and warmth—except for the darting shape, the shadow leaping in pursuit.

"It's a shame nobody believes us," Wilson said. "I mean, it's a shame the . . . things are wasting their time hunting us down, seeing as how we couldn't reveal them even if we wanted to." He rubbed his face. "Except maybe to Rilker and Evans. Even Ferguson if he'll quit worrying about what they'll say in *Science News*. But we just might be able to convince Rilker and Evans—hell, I don't care *what* they decide is after us, I just want them to know we're in danger and give us a hand!" He turned his head, looking at her with a haggard face. "You know, that Ferguson was a prize jerk. I think he was attracted to you."

He's jealous, she thought, and he doesn't even know it. "I could tell he was a jerk from the first moment I saw him," she said; "he looked like one." There, Wilson will like that. True to her expectations he put his arm out along the seat.

"I like it when you wear that smell."

"I'm not wearing any perfume."

"Must be your deodorant then. It's very nice."

"Thank you." The poor man, his best efforts were so terrible. She felt a twinge of sorrow for him; his loneliness was becoming more and more obvious to her. "You're very sweet to say that," she heard herself say, but the words sounded false.

Apparently they did to him, too, because he didn't say anything more. When they reached Police Headquarters Becky pulled the car to a stop on a crowded nearby street rather than risk the big, empty garage beneath the building.

"We've got to try and get Underwood to assign a special detail," she said when they were back in their office. Wilson nodded. He sat down at their desk and shuffled through the papers heaped on top of it: a day-old *Times* covered with coffee-cup rings, a copy of the *New York* magazine crossword, half a dozen departmental memos.

"Nobody ever calls us," he said.

"So let's call Underwood ourselves. We've got to do something, we can't just let ourselves rot."

"Don't say that! It does bad things to my gut. Why don't *you* call Underwood? Hello, this is the Detective with a capital D. You know the one? Well, please assign me a special protective detail. You see, I'm being chased by these werewolves. That'll get action."

"An invitation from Psychiatric Services and a little confidential note in the old personnel file. I know. But we don't want protection, we want to eliminate the menace!"

"You think we can, Becky?"

"We've got to try."

"So we'll call Evans and Rilker and try to get them on our side. And maybe even the scientist will put his two cents in if Rilker pushes him. Stranger things have happened. Maybe we'll at least get a scratch squad together, enough men to uncover some positive evidence."

Becky didn't feel particularly confident but she got on the phone. Wilson didn't even offer to lend a hand; they both knew that his services were, at best, counterproductive in the area of convincing people to give him help.

Evans listened to the story.

Rilker said he had suspected something like that.

Ferguson was willing to attend the meeting as long as absolutely everything was off the record. Becky considered offering him the loan of a false beard and dark glasses but let it go.

"Three hits," Wilson said, "they can't resist you."

"Now, now, don't get jealous. All that's left is for you to get an appointment with Underwood."

Despite his lack of skill with people, there was no way that Wilson could avoid being the one to call Underwood. He was senior man on the team, and their mere connection with the Chief of Detectives was a major disruption of the chain of command. Officially Neff and Wilson weren't assigned at the moment to any particular division. The Chief was keeping them in cold storage until he was sure the DiFalco case held no further surprises. Obviously he wasn't completely convinced that his quick closing of the case had been wise. With Neff and Wilson apparently still assigned to it he could keep them from uncovering embarrassing new evidence and also cover himself if that happened some other way, because he could always say that the department had kept a special team active on the case the whole time. He didn't want the case reopened, but if it was he was prepared.

For him it was a very economical solution to a problem. For Neff and Wilson it was agony—they didn't know where they stood and neither did anybody else. This meant that they could get nothing done. The resources of Manhattan South were not theirs to use—except for a dingy office. And the Brooklyn Division considered them off its roster. So they had only each other, and whatever help they could get outside the department.

It wasn't going to be enough, that had become very clear.

Underwood was polite, when Wilson finally got through. He set a meeting for three o'clock and didn't even ask what it was about. And why should he—he knew that there could be only two topics of conversation. Either they wanted to reopen the DiFalco case or they wanted to be reassigned. And he had one simple answer for both questions. It was no.

"We've got a couple of hours, we might as well go up to Chinatown for lunch."

Wilson glanced out the window. "Looks like plenty of people in the streets. I guess we can go."

They took a cab. Despite the crowds it seemed the safest thing to do. Pell Street, the center of Chinatown, was cheerfully crowded. They left the cab, Becky feeling a little more at ease, Wilson nervously studying the fire escapes and alleyways. Becky chose a restaurant that was neither familiar from her courting days with Dick nor one of the dingy chop suey parlors Wilson would have selected. He liked to eat lunch for under two dollars. And when he was treating he would go even cheaper unless his victim was very alert.

Becky was very alert. During lunch they spoke little because he was pouting at the cost. Or at least that was what she assumed until he finally did speak. "I wonder what it'll feel like."

"What in the world makes you say something like that!"

"Nothing. Just thinking is all." She saw that he was ashen. In his left hand he held his napkin pressed against the middle of his chest as if he was stopping a wound. "I can't get that damn claw out of my mind." Now his lips drew back across his teeth, sweat popped out on his cheeks and forehead. "I just keep thinking of it snagging my shirt, grabbing at me. God knows you couldn't do a thing once something like that was in you."

"Now wait a minute. Just listen to me. You're getting scared. I don't blame you, George, but you can't afford it. You cannot afford to get scared! We can't let that happen to us. They'll move right in if it does. I've got a feeling the only thing that's kept them from doing it before is the fact that we haven't been scared."

He smiled his familiar sickly smile.

"Don't do that, I expect you to take me seriously. Listen to me—without you I haven't got any hope at all." Her own words surprised her. How deeply did she mean that? As deep as her very life came the instant answer. "We'll get through this."

"How?"

It was an innocent enough question, but under the circumstances it exposed a weakness she wished wasn't there.

"However the hell we can. Now shut up and let me finish my lunch in peace."

They ate mechanically. To Becky the food tasted like metal. She wanted desperately to turn around, to see whether the doorway behind her led to the kitchen or to the basement. For Wilson's sake, though, she did not. There was no sense compounding his fear with her own.

"Maybe that claw is what we need. When the Chief sees it maybe he'll figure things more our way."

"I didn't even remember to ask Ferguson to bring the damn thing."

"But he will. He's very proud of that claw."

"I don't blame him. He can carry it instead of a shiv."

Wilson chuckled and sipped the last of his tea, his fears seemingly forgotten. But the napkin was still clasped convulsively against his chest.

As soon as they got back to headquarters they went to Underwood's office. It was actually a suite of offices, and in the outer office was the kind of policewoman Becky most disliked, the typist in uniform.

"You're Becky Neff," the woman said as soon as the two of them came in; "the Chief of Detectives said you'd be coming up. I'm so pleased to meet you."

"Pleased to meet you too, Lieutenant," Becky muttered. "This is my partner, Detective Wilson." Wilson stood uncertainly staring past them. There was nothing on the wall he was staring at except a hunting scene. "Wilson—you're being introduced."

"Oh! Yeah, hiya. You got any cigarettes?"

"I don't smoke, the Chief doesn't like it."

"Yeah. What's he doing? We're supposed to see him at three."

"It's only two forty-five. He's still in his other meeting."

"Still at lunch, you mean. Why don't you let me sleep on that couch he's got in his office. I gotta sleep off about three pounds of chicken chow mein."

The lieutenant glanced at Becky, but continued without a pause: "No, he's really in there. He's got some people from the Museum of Natural History and Doctor Evans—"

They went in.

"Sorry we're late," Wilson growled. "We got slowed down by your house genius."

"Well, you're not late. Still fifteen minutes to go. But since these men were all here, I thought we'd get started. Everybody knows everybody?"

"We know them," Wilson said. "Anybody in here smoke?"

"I don't have any ashtrays," Underwood said firmly. Wilson pulled up a chair, crossed his legs, and sighed.

There was a silence. The silence got longer. Becky looked from face to face. Rigid, expressionless, Evans a little embarrassed. She felt herself slump into the chair. This silence could only mean that they didn't believe. These men thought of the two detectives as being a little off their rockers. Two famous detectives driven a little crazy. Worse things have happened, more unlikely things.

"Apparently you gentlemen don't know what it is to be hunted," Wilson said. Becky was amazed— when he was up against the wall he revealed hidden resources. "And since you don't know, you can't imagine the state me and Neff are in. We are being hunted, you know. Sure. By things that have claws like this." With a swift motion he picked it up. "Can you imagine how it would feel to get one of these in the chest? Rip your heart right out. Hell, you might look at the sunset out there and think it's beautiful. And it was for us too, until last night. Now we don't look at a sunset that way anymore. We look at it the way deer and moose do—with fear. How do you think that feels, eh? Any of you know?"

"Detective Wilson, you're overwrought—"

"Shut up, Underwood. I'm maybe making my last speech and I want to be heard." He waved the claw as he spoke, and measured his words with uncharacteristic care. "We are being hunted down by whatever has these claws. They *exist*, don't forget that! They have for thousands of years. We have seen them, gentlemen, and they are very ugly. They are also very fast, and very smart. People used to call them werewolves. Now they don't call them anything because they've gotten so damn good at covering their tracks that there are no legends left. But they're here. They damn well are here."

The two who had to be killed were hard to find. They had been scented clearly as they walked through the house where the pack had been feeding. Their car had been seen as it left, and seen again a few days later, this time far down Manhattan toward the sea. Patience had been needed. The man was watched as he went through the streets, and his house was finally discovered. The woman also was followed, and her scent traced into a building with many stories. It was watched until they knew that the bedroom behind one of the balconies must certainly hold her.

They were not rightful prey, but they had to be taken. If their knowledge of this pack spread, all the race would suffer. First, the many packs in this city would be hurt, then others nearby, and finally all everywhere. Better that man not know of the packs. If the numberless hordes of men knew of the many packs that thrived on them, they would surely resist. Essential that man not know.

Whenever man came close this was done. It had always been thus, and that was the first law of caution. For many years they had roamed free in the world and they had prospered. There was so much humanity that packs were growing through the world, in every one of the human cities. When they were occasionally glimpsed by man the pack passed as a group of stray dogs. Normally they hunted at night. By day they slept in lairs so carefully concealed—in basements, abandoned buildings, wherever they could find a spot—that man never realized they were there. Dogs also posed no problem. To them the scent of the packs was a familiar part of city life and they ignored it.

Now these two humans had to die else they go among all the human cities and warn them of the presence of death in their midst.

So they had followed the scent of the two humans, they had followed this scent through the streets, tracked it until it entered a great gray building in lower Manhattan. When it came out again and separated they split up, following both parts.

The man's lair was easy to find. It was close to the ground, in a house with weak outer doors and an easily accessible basement. But the man's own room was locked and barred, with gates on the windows. The whole place stank of fear. This man lived in a fortress. Even the chimney leading to his fireplace had been blocked up long ago. It was pitiful to see one so sick and full of fear, sitting his nights away in a chair with all the lights in his room on. Such a one needed death, and the pack longed to take him not only because he was potentially dangerous but because he was in the condition of prey. He needed death, this one, and they all hoped to give it to him.

And they had found a way to move against him.

The woman lived far up in her building. Not all of the pack were adept climbers, but some were and one of them climbed. He moved from balcony to balcony, grasping with his forepaws, hauling himself up, doing it again and again. Below him the rest of the pack stood in the black alley longing with their hearts to howl their joy at his heroism, at his true love for all of his kind. But they kept their voices still. It was unnecessary anyway—even as he climbed he would scent the respect and gladness of those far below him.

And he climbed toward the smell of the human woman. She was here, closer and closer. He climbed, he longed to reach her, to feel her blood pouring down his throat, to taste the meat of her, to feel as her body died and the threat to the race ended. The pack was glad he could climb, and he was glad to climb for them!

When he got to her balcony he moved as softly as he could. But not softly enough. One of his toenails clicked against the glass door as he tested the lock. To him the sound was bell-clear. Had the humans inside heard it? Had she heard it?

Her scent changed from the thickness of sleep to the sharpness of fear. The accursed creature *had* heard him! Slowly he inched across the balcony. She knew he was out here. Now the sound of her breath changed. She was growing so terribly afraid that he longed to help her into death even though she was not weak enough to be prey. But this was so dangerous. If they opened that curtain, he would be seen. You cannot be seen by those who will live! To avoid that he was prepared to throw himself off the balcony. Or was he? Die, for that? His own heart began to pound. She made a little cry—she had seen his shadow on the ceiling. His instincts screamed at him —growl, lunge, kill—but all that came out was a tiny noise.

A noise which she heard.

Now it was too late! They were getting up. He glanced at the light fixture in the ceiling of the balcony. The turning of a switch inside would reveal him! Desperately he climbed up to the next floor, and not a moment too soon. He heard the sliding door scrape, a footfall on her balcony. Her male companion looked about, moving through the dense body-heat and smell of himself and, in the marvelous blindness of humans, not even noticing. These poor creatures were blind in all except the visual sense. Nose-blind, ear-blind, touch-blind. They were the best prey in the world.

When the man went back inside and all once again fell into darkness he returned to the alley. His heart was full of sorrow. When he faced the pack—he had failed, she still lived.

But they found a way to move against her also, and now they were ready.

Chapter 5

Carl Ferguson had gone back to his office. His lamp provided the last glimmer of light in the empty workrooms of the museum basement. Beyond his open door the evening shadows spread slowly across the workbenches, turning the half-finished specimens into indistinct, angular shapes.

Under his light Ferguson held the model he had constructed of the paw.

The paw. He turned it in his hands, looking at its supple efficiency for the hundredth time. He placed it on the desk, then picked it up again and ran its claws along his cheek. It would do its job well, this paw. The long toes with their extra joints. The broad, sensitive pads. The needle-sharp claws. Almost... what a human being might have if people had claws. It had the same functional beauty as a hand, a lethal one.

Suddenly he frowned. Wasn't that a noise? He jumped up and started toward his door—then saw that some moving air was ruffling a box of feathers.

"I'm getting crazy," he said aloud. His voice had a flat echo in the empty space beyond his office.

Ferguson glanced at his watch. Seven P.M. It was dark, the winter sun had set. He was tired, exhausted from the harrowing meeting downtown and from his own hectic schedule. The new exhibit was going to be a great achievement, one that would be sure to get him tenure at the museum. A beautiful concept— the birds of North America. Not just static cases but a whole room of meticulous reconstructions, soaring, wonderful creatures . . . he looked at some of them, their great wings spread in the darkness, barely visible, in the process of being feathered quill by careful quill.

But where did this—thing—belong among the creatures of North America? What the hell was it, dammit!

The detectives had babbled about werewolves . . . superstitious fools. But they certainly had uncovered a problem. Surely the city police could capture one of the things, bring it in, let him evaluate it more thoroughly. Judging from this paw it was on the large side, maybe bigger than a wolf. Possibly a hundred and eighty pounds. Even alone such a creature could be extremely dangerous, highly so in a pack. Unlikely it was a mutant wolf, they were too radically adapted to their traditional prey. Coyotes—too much of a size variance. Whatever had a paw like this had split off from the canine mainstream a long time ago, and had reached a very, very high level of evolution.

Which brought up the question of why there were no bones, no specimens, nothing.

It was uncanny and chilling to think that a whole

subspecies of canine carnivore existed without even a hint of it in science.

He jumped again—this time he heard a scraping sound. Now he took it seriously. "Luis," he said, hoping it was the night man coming down to check on the light, "it's me, Carl Ferguson." The scraping continued, insistent, patient . . . something trying to worry one of the basement windows open.

He looked at the paw. Yes, it could do that.

He turned out his lamp, closed his eyes to hasten their getting used to the dark. He stood up from his desk swaying, his skin crawling.

The scraping stopped, was followed by a slight creak. A puff of icy air made the box of feathers in the hallway rustle again. There was a sliding sound and a thump as something came in the window, then another.

Then there was silence. Carl Ferguson stood with his plaster paw in his hand, his throat and mouth agonizingly dry.

"Somebody's over there."

A light flashed in the scientist's eyes.

"Hello, Doctor," said a gruff voice. "Sorry we startled you."

"What the hell—"

"Wait a minute, wait a minute, don't go off half-cocked. We're cops, this is an investigation."

"What in hell do you mean coming in here like this? You—you scared me! I thought—"

"It was them?" Wilson flipped a bank of switches flooding the basement with a stark neon glow. "I don't blame you for being afraid, Doctor. This place is spooky."

Becky Neff pulled the window closed. "The truth is, Doctor, we were looking for you. We figured we'd find you here, that's why we came."

"Why didn't you come in the damn front door? My heart's still pounding, for God's sake! I don't think I've ever been that scared."

"Think how we feel, Doctor. We feel that way all the time. At least I do. I don't know about Detective Wilson."

Wilson pulled his chin into his chest and said nothing.

"Well, you could have come in the right way. I don't think that's asking too much." He was angry and aggrieved. They had no right to do this to him! Typical cops, completely indifferent to the law. They didn't even have a right to be here! "I think you should leave."

"No, Doctor. We came here to talk to you." She said it sweetly, but the way she and Wilson advanced toward him made him take an involuntary step back. When he did Wilson sighed, long, ragged and sad—and Ferguson saw for an instant how tired the man was, how tired and afraid.

"Come into my office, then. But I fail to see what you're expecting to get out of me."

They pulled up chairs in the tiny office. Ferguson noticed that Wilson lingered at the door, Neff sat so that she was looking out. Together they had most of the workroom in view. "Those are easy windows," Wilson murmured, "very easy windows."

"The museum has guards."

"Yeah, we figured that out."

"All right, what is it you want—but don't think I'm going to let this matter drop. I want you to know I'm calling the Police Complaint Department in the morning."

"The Police Department doesn't have a complaint department."

"Well, I'm calling somebody. Cops don't run

around breaking and entering without citizen complaint. You people get away with enough as it is."

Wilson remained silent. Becky took over. "We wouldn't be here if we weren't desperate," she said softly. "And we realize that you've told us all the facts you know, that's not what we want. We want your theories, Doctor, your speculations."

"Anything might help us stay alive, Doctor," Wilson added. "We are going to have a hard time doing that as things stand now."

"Why?"

Becky closed her eyes, ignored the question. "Imagine, Doctor," she said, "what these creatures might want, what they might need—if they are as we say they are."

"You mean intelligent, predatory, all that."

"That's right."

"It's barely a hypothesis."

"Try it."

"Detective Neff, I cannot try it. It's worse than a hypothesis, it's rank speculation."

"Please, Doctor."

"But what if I'm wrong—what if I confuse you more than you've already confused yourselves? Can't you see the risk that's involved? I can't work on unfounded imagination, I'm a scientist! The truth is I *want* to help you. I really do! But I can't. I know that this damn paw is something special but I don't know how to apply that knowledge! Can't you understand?"

Becky watched him, her eyes filled with the desperation that she felt. Wilson covered their backs, listening to every word but watching the long row of black windows at the far end of the workroom. From the sound of Ferguson's voice, she knew that he was telling the truth. No longer was he holding back to protect his reputation. Now, in the dead of night when the three of them were alone and the customary bustle of his little kingdom around him was missing, he had forgotten worries of reputation and was forced to face the real truth—that the two cops needed help that he could not give.

Or could he? Often the trouble with scientists is that they do not realize how little others really know. "Anything you can say might be of help to us, Doctor," Becky said with what she hoped was gentle calmness. "Why not tell us about something you do understand."

"Like what?"

"Well, like the sense of smell. How effective is it and what can we do to cover our trails?"

"It varies greatly. A bloodhound might be seven or eight times more effective than a terrier—"

"Assume the bloodhound," Wilson said from the doorway. "Assume the best, the most sensitive."

"It's a very extraordinary organ, a bloodhound's nose. What it is, basically, is a concentration of nerve endings that fill the whole muzzle, not just the tip, although the tip is the most sensitive. For a bloodhound, you've got about a hundred million separate cells in the olfactory mucosa. For a terrier, twenty-five million." He looked to Becky as if to ask if this sort of thing was any help.

"If we understood their capabilities we might be able to throw them off our tracks," Becky said. She wished that the man would explain how the hell the sense of smell worked—if she understood it she would think of something, or Wilson would.

Wilson. His instinct had told them that they would find Ferguson sitting in here worrying about his plaster paw. Wilson had very good instincts. Now added to them was the overriding feeling of desperation, the certain knowledge that something was following them *now*. From the way he was beginning to twist the edge of the blotter on his desk Ferguson was having the same thought. If so, he didn't acknowledge it directly. "You want me to tell you how to throw the . . . animals off your tracks?"

Becky nodded. "Give me a cigarette," Wilson growled. "I don't think I'm gonna like what the doctor's gonna say."

"Well, I'm afraid you won't. A lot of people have tried to figure out how to shake a tracking hound. Not much will do it except rain and a lot of wind."

"How about snow? It's snowing now."

"A bloodhound in Switzerland once followed a track that had been under snow for forty-seven days. Heavy snow. A massive blizzard, in fact. Snow isn't going to stop a bloodhound."

"Doctor," Becky said, "maybe we ought to approach this from another angle. Why can't anything stop a hound from tracking?"

"Aside from rain and wind? Well, it's because of their sensitivity and the long-lasting nature of odors."

"How sensitive are they?"

"Let me see if I can quantify it for you. The nose of a bloodhound is perhaps one hundred million times more sensitive than that of a man."

"That means nothing to me."

"I'm not surprised, Lieutenant Wilson. It's a very difficult number to grasp. Look at it this way." He went outside and returned with a tiny pinch of oily-looking powder between his fingers. "This is about one milligram of brown paint pigment. Now visualize a hundred million cubic centimeters of air—about as much air as covers Manhattan. A good bloodhound could detect this amount of pigment in that amount of air."

Becky felt as if she had been hit. They were that sensitive! She had never realized just what an animal's sense of smell meant before now. She fought to stay calm, her eyes darting toward the windows that revealed only the reflection of the workroom itself. Wilson got his cigarette lit and drew on it, exhaling with a long sigh. "What if you neutralized the odor, if you covered it with ammonia, say?"

"Makes absolutely no difference. The dog won't like it but it will still be able to distinguish the odor. People have tried everything to break track, but very little works. One thing—floating down a river, completely submerged, with the wind going in the same direction as the water. If you can make it half a mile without putting your head out of water you might break track. I say might because a single breath coming up through the water could be enough for a dog if the wind wasn't too strong."

"Breath?"

"We don't know the exact mechanism of a dog's scent, but we believe that they track by body oils and exhaled breath. They may also go by the odor of clothing."

"There's nothing you can do to yourself to nullify your odor?"

"Sure. Take a bath. You'll be safe for a while as long as you don't put on your clothes."

Wilson raised his eyebrows. "How long?"

"A good three or four minutes. Until your skin oils start replacing themselves."

"Wonderful! That's very helpful." There was a ragged edge in Wilson's voice that Becky didn't like.

"There must be something, something you haven't mentioned that would help us. If we can't get rid of our odor, what about neutralizing their sense of smell?"

"Good question. You can cause osmoanaesthesia with something like cocaine, although I've never heard of a dog that would inhale it willingly. Also, you could use a phenamine. You'd get a temporary paralysis of the olfactory sense with that, too, and administration would be a little easier. That stuff you could disguise in meat. It doesn't have to be inhaled, just eaten."

"Here doggie, have a little snacker!"

"Shut up, George. We might learn something if you'd just keep your trap shut!"

"Oh, Little Miss Muffet becomes Dragon Lady. So solly, missy!" He bowed, his hands folded across his belly, his eyes in a mocking squint. Then he froze. His hand dropped to the Colt he was carrying under his jacket.

"What?" Becky was on her feet, her own pistol in her hand.

"Good heavens, put those things—"

"Shut up, Sonny! I saw something at that window, Becky." The mocking tone was gone, the voice was grave and a little sad. "Something pressing against it, gray fur. Like something had banged against the glass and gone off into the night."

"We would have heard it."

"Maybe. How thick is the glass in those windows?"

"I have no idea. It's just glass."

Becky remembered back to their entry. "It's thick," she said, "about a quarter inch."

Wilson suddenly holstered his gun. "Saw it again. It's a bush blowing against the glass. Sorry for the false alarm."

"Keep your shirt on, Detective," Becky said. "I can't handle many more of those."

"Sorry. Lucky I was wrong."

Left unsaid was the fact that they had now been here a long time, longer than must be safe. The plan was to keep to the car, keep moving. That way at least they'd be harder to follow. In fact now that she thought of it, Becky didn't know how they could be tracked at all if they were in a car. She asked the question.

"The tires. Each set of tires has a distinctive odor. Tracking dogs can follow bicycles, cars, even carriages with iron wheels. In fact it's easier in some cases than following people on foot. There's more odor laid down."

"But in the city—hundreds of thousands of cars —it seems almost impossible."

Ferguson shook his head. "It's difficult but not out of the question. And if you two are right about being followed all the way from the Bronx our specimens are quite capable of doing it."

"So let's sum up. We can't get rid of our odors. We can't neutralize their noses without getting a hell of a lot closer than we want to be. Is there any other bad news?"

"Is he always this acerbic, Miss Neff?"

"It's Mrs. And the answer is 'yes.'"

Ferguson held his eyes on her a moment, as if to ask something more. She stared right back at him. In an instant he looked away, faintly confused by the challenge. Becky did not like men to strip her with their eyes, and when they did she stripped right back. Some it turned on, some it frightened, some it angered. She really didn't care how they reacted, although from the way Ferguson both crossed his legs and brushed his hand along his cheek it looked as if he had been turned on and frightened at the same time. He was scared of a lot of things, this scientist. His face was powerful, only the eyes giving away the inner man. Yet there was also something else about him—a sort of buried competence that Becky felt was a positive factor in his makeup. He must be very professional and very smart. Too bad, it probably meant he was giving them the best information they were going to get.

"I wonder what it's like," Wilson said, "to have a sense of smell like that."

Ferguson brightened. "I've been extremely interested in that, Lieutenant. I think I can give you something of an idea. Canine intelligence is of intense interest to me. We've studied dogs here at the museum."

"And cats."

Becky winced. The Museum of Natural History had been embroiled in a violent controversy about some experiments using live cats, which Wilson naturally brought up.

"That's irrelevant," Ferguson said quickly, "another department. I'm in exhibits. My work on dogs ended in 1974 when the Federal money ran out. But up to then we were making great strides. I worked very closely with Tom Rilker." He raised his eyebrows. "Rilker's a hell of a dog man. We were trying to breed increased sensitivity to certain odors. Drugs, weapons—bred right in, no training needed."

"Did you succeed?"

He smiled. "A secret. Classified information, compliments of Uncle Sam. Sadly enough, I cannot even publish a paper on it."

"You were telling us about canine intelligence."

"Right. Well, I think dogs know a lot more about the human world than we do about theirs. The reason is that their sensory input is so different. Smell, sound—those are their primary senses. Sight is a distant third. For example, if you put on a friend's clothes your dog won't recognize you until you speak. Then he'll be confused. The same way if you take a bath and walk out naked without talking your dog won't know who, or necessarily what, you are. He'll see a shape moving, smell the water. He might attack. Then when he hears your voice he'll be very relieved. Dogs can't stand the unknown, the unfamiliar. They have a tremendous amount of information pouring in through their noses and ears. Under certain circumstances it's more than they can handle. For example, a bloodhound will get completely exhausted on a track long before he would if he was just running free. It's psychic exhaustion. Generally the more intelligent the dog, the more all this data coming through the nose means. To a wolf, for example, it all means much more than to a dog."

"A wolf?"

"Sure. They're much more intelligent and more sensitive than dogs. A good bloodhound might have a nose a hundred million times more sensitive than a human nose. A wolf would be two hundred million times more sensitive. And wolves are correspondingly more intelligent, to handle the data. But even so there's a tremendous richness of data, more than their minds can possibly assimilate."

Wilson moved from his spot by the door and picked up the plaster paw model. "Is this closer to a wolf or a dog?"

"A wolf, I'd say. Actually it does look more like the paw of a giant wolf—except for those extended toes. The toes are really wonderful. A marvelous evolution. They are beyond canine, as I understand the genus. That's why I keep asking you for a head. I just can't do more with this thing unless I get more of the body. It's too new, too extraordinary. Right now whatever made those pawprints is outside of science. That's why I'm asking for more."

"We can't give you more, Doctor," Becky said, it seemed for the hundredth time. "You know the trouble we're in. We'd be lucky even to get a picture."

"We wouldn't, and live," Wilson put in. "These things are too vicious for that."

He signalled Becky with his eyes. He wanted to get moving. Since night had fallen Wilson had kept on the move. Officially they were on an eight-to-four, but neither of them was recognizing duty hours right now. They had been cut loose from their division, their squad, their block and put on this thing alone. Nobody was marking their names on a blotter. Nobody was counting their presence or giving them calls.

They were on the case because the Chief felt there was a remote chance that something unusual was indeed happening. Not enough to really do anything about, just enough to keep the wheels turning very, very slowly. Which meant a single team, alone, digging as best they could. And being available as scapegoats—if needed.

"We ought to go," Becky said to Ferguson. "We figure our best bet is to keep on the move."

"You're probably right."

Wilson stared at him. "Sorry about the way we came in. No other way to reach you, the museum was closed."

Ferguson smiled. "What if I hadn't been here?"

"No chance. You're really running after this. It's got under your skin. I knew you'd be here."

Ferguson walked with them through the dim corridors, to a side door where a single guard nodded under a small light. "I'm leaving with you," he said. "I haven't had a bite to eat since lunch and I don't think I can accomplish anything just sitting and staring at that paw."

Their feet crunched in the snow as they crossed the quiet grounds of the museum. Becky could see their car on Seventy-seventh Street where they had left it, now covered with a dusting of snow. They had perhaps twenty yards to walk up a disused driveway before they reached the safety of the car. Nothing seemed to be moving among the shadows of the trees that surrounded the museum, and there were no tracks visible in the new snow. The wind was blowing softly, adding the crackle of bare limbs to the hiss of the falling snow. The clouds hung low, reflecting the light of the city and covering everything with a green glow stronger than moonlight. Even so, the trip to the car seemed long. By the position of his hand Becky knew Wilson felt the same way: he was touching the butt of the pistol he kept holstered under his jacket.

As they reached the car Ferguson turned, saying he was going to take the Number 10 bus up Central Park West to his apartment. They let him go.

"I wonder if we should have done that," Becky said as she started the car.

"What?"

"Let him go off on his own. We have no way of knowing how much danger he's in. If they were watching us, they saw us with him. What would that mean to them? Kill him too, maybe? I think he's in more danger than he knows."

"Get moving. Put on the damn radio. Let's listen to the traffic."

"You handle the radio, man, you're not doing anything else."

He flipped it on and settled with his knee against

the dash. "It's too cold for junkies on the streets, it'll be a quiet night."

They listened to a rookie call and immediately cancel a signal 13 at Seventy-second and Amsterdam. But you can't cancel an assist officer call just like that. Guys would move in on him anyway and then rib him about it later. "What made him jump, you suppose?" Wilson asked. He didn't really expect an answer and Becky didn't talk. Who the hell cared about some rookie and his erroneous 13. Becky headed the car east across Central Park on the Seventy-ninth Street transverse. She was heading toward a Chinese restaurant in her home neighborhood the other side of the park. She wasn't particularly hungry, but they had to eat. And what they would do after that, how they would pass the night she had no idea. And what about the days and nights to come, what about the future?

"What the hell are they going to do about us?"

"Do, Becky? Not a damn thing. They're just gonna leave us hanging on this here string. Hey, where're you going—you live over here, don't you?"

"Don't get your hopes up, I'm not taking you to my place. We're going to stop for a little supper. We need to eat, remember."

"Yeah. Anyway, the brass isn't going to do a damn thing about us. They're too busy pushing paper and worrying—who has this division, who has that precinct, who's moving up, who's getting flopped. That's their whole career, that and figuring who has the biggest hook, who *is* the biggest hook for that matter. You know that's what they do. That's about it in Commissioner country."

"Bitter boy. I think maybe Underwood actually thinks we belong on the case. He respects us."

"Who belongs on a closed case? Oh Jesus, Becky, this is a Szechuan restaurant—I can't eat here."

She double-parked the car and pulled out the key. "You can eat here. Just ask them to hold the hot sauce on your chow mein."

"I can't even get Goddamn chow mein in a place like this," he sulked.

She got out of the car and he followed reluctantly. They entered the dimly lit restaurant knocking snow off their clothes. "Getting heavier?" the coatcheck girl asked.

"Heavier," Wilson said. "Becky, this place is going to cost a fortune. It's got a hatcheck girl. I never eat in places with hatcheck girls." He followed her into the restaurant still complaining, but he subsided into subvocal grumbling when he received the menu. She could see the gears turning over as he calculated whether he could eat for less than two dollars.

"I'll order for both of us since I've been here before," she said, taking his menu. "I'll get you out for five bucks."

"Five!"

"Maybe six. I hope you're not too hungry though, because it'll only be one dish."

"What?"

The waiter came. She ordered prawns in garlic sauce for Wilson and Chicken Tang for herself. At least she would enjoy what could easily be her last meal. But she stopped that line of thought—you think that way, it happens. She also ordered a drink, and Wilson got beer. "A buck for a Bud," he muttered. "Goddamn Chinks."

"Come on, relax. You'll enjoy the food. Let's talk about it."

"What Ferguson said?"

"What he said. What ideas did it give you?"

"We could set up living quarters in Evans's meat locker."

"It gave me a better idea than that. It's something I think we've got to do if we're going to survive. Obviously it's only a matter of time before our friends see their chance and move in. Sooner or later the two of us are going to join DiFalco and Houlihan. *Then* the department will wade into this thing all the way. But it won't make a damn bit of difference to us."

"Insufficient evidence, that's what's got the wheels gummed up. We have provided theories, hearsay, suppositions and a funny-looking piece of plaster of Paris made by Doctor Whozis."

"So why not provide photographs. Pictures. It's not a cadaver but it sure would improve our case."

"How do you photograph what you never see? If there's light enough for a picture there's too much light. These things won't get close to us in light. Although we *could* use infrared equipment. Special Services could probably give us the loan of a scope. But it's bulky stuff—hard to handle."

"I've got a better idea. Narcotics has been experimenting with computerized image intensification equipment, stuff developed during the Vietnam war. We can get a really super picture even in total darkness with it. Dick's unit's been using it experimentally."

"What's involved, a support truck or something?"

"Not at all. The whole thing looks like an oversize pair of binoculars. Camera's built in. You just look through the thing and what you can see you can photograph."

"What you can see? There's the hole in the idea. We have to be close enough to see them."

"Not so close. You've got a five-hundred-millimeter lens."

"My God, that's the damnedest thing I ever heard of. We could be a quarter of a mile away."

"Like staked out on the roof of my building watching the alley, watching for them to come back."

"Yeah, we could do that. We could get our pictures and pull out before they even started climbing the terraces."

"There's only one small hitch. Dick's got to be convinced to help us. He's got to give us the equipment, and it's classified."

Wilson frowned. It meant a departmental infraction, something he didn't need. He had too many enemies to be able to afford getting things like that in his file. "Goddamn, the PD'd classify mechanical pencils if they had time. I don't like to get into that kind of stuff, it's not going to help me."

"Dick owes you a favor, George."

"Why?"

"You know perfectly well why." She said it lightly but felt the anger nevertheless. Her staying in Detectives had depended on finding a place in a block of four men, and to do that you had to get one of those men as a partner. Wilson had taken her on and she had not been shunted off into administration like many lady cops. And Wilson had taken her on because Dick Neff had asked him to.

"He may think it was a favor, but it wasn't."

"Jesus. You're going to seed, Wilson. You actually complimented my police work just then."

He laughed, his face breaking for a few moments into a mass of merry wrinkles, then as abruptly returning to its usual glower. "You got some good points," he said, "but I guess you're right. Taking you on was a favor to Dick when I did it. Maybe he'll let me collect."

Becky excused herself and called ahead to the

apartment. She wanted to be sure Dick was there;
she didn't want to end up alone with Wilson in the
apartment. It wouldn't look good, especially if Dick
came home.

He was there, his voice sounding thick. She
wanted to ask him what was wrong but she held back.
When she told him she was bringing Wilson over
his only comment was a noncommittal grunt.

They ate their food in silence, Wilson digging
into his with glazed indifference. If you fed him silage,
he'd probably eat it exactly the same way.

Becky was excited about the idea of getting photographs of the animals; excited and worried. The
whole situation contained menace, every part of it.
There was something about the way these creatures
killed—the extreme violence of it—that made it impossible to put the problem out of your mind even
for a short time. You just kept turning it over and
over . . . and Becky had a recurring picture of what
they must look like with their long toes that ended in
delicate pads and were tipped by claws, with their
razor-sharp teeth, and their heavy bodies. But what
were their faces like? Human beings had such complex faces, not at all like the more-or-less frozen expressions of animals; would these creatures also have
such faces, full of emotion and understanding? And
if so, what would those faces tell their victims?

"Look we just come right out and ask Dick—
right? Just ask him without fooling around?"

"You mean no diplomatic subtleties?"

"Not my strong point."

"So we just ask. Everybody's heard rumors about
the optical gear Special Services is using. Just logical
that a Narcotics wire man could get his hands on it,
isn't it? We don't have to tell him we know the stuff is
classified. Maybe he'll never even bring the matter

up, just give us the damn thing and not think any more about it. That's what I'm hoping anyway."

But that wasn't what happened. As soon as she opened the door to their apartment, Becky felt something was wrong. She left Wilson in the hall while she went to Dick in the living room. "Why'd you pick tonight to bring that old fart up here?" were his first words.

"I had to, honey. It can't wait."

"I got burned."

There it was, as simple as that. To undercover cops like Dick getting burned meant being recognized as police officers by their suspects. "Bad?"

"Real bad. Some sonofabitch really put it on me. I might as well graduate to the Goddamn movies."

"Dick, that's terrible! How—"

"Never mind how, honey. Just say it was two years of work blown to hell. And I think I've got a shoofly on my ass, too."

She leaned down and kissed his hair. He was slumped into the couch, staring at the TV. "You're clean, aren't you?" But her heart was sinking, she knew something was wrong. And the inspectors from the Internal Affairs Division knew it too or they wouldn't have put a man on him—shoofly was what cops called other cops who investigated them.

"You know damn well I'm not clean." He said it with such infinite tiredness that she was surprised. And he looked older, more hollow, than she had ever seen him before. "Look, let's get drunk or something later, celebrate my early retirement, but bring Wilson in now, let him do his thing."

"It's not much, won't take a second." She called Wilson, who moved forward from the foyer where he had been standing.

They shook hands. Dick offered him a beer. They

settled into the living room, the TV cut down but not off. Becky closed the curtains.

"What's up?" Dick said.

"We need your help," Wilson replied. "I gotta get some pictures, I need your night-vision camera."

"What night-vision camera?"

"The one you can get from Special. The five-hundred-mil lens, the image-intensification circuit. You know what camera."

"Why not order it up yourself?" He looked at Becky, a question in his eyes.

"We haven't got authorization, honey," she said. "We need it for the creatures."

"Oh, Christ almighty, that bullshit again! Can't you get off that? What are you two, nuts or something? I can't get that Goddamn camera, not while I've got shooflies hanging from my Goddamn ears. Come on, lay off it. Why don't you two earn your damn salaries instead of monkeyin' around with that shit."

"We need your help, Neff." Wilson sat hunched in his chair, his eyes glistening like dots beneath the heavy folds of his brows. "I helped you."

"Oh, Christ." He smiled, turned his head away. "Oh, Christ, the favor. The great big favor. Let me tell you, Wilson, I don't give a rat's ass about your big favor. That's not a factor."

"That camera could solve this case for us, honey, get the damn thing out of our hair. We only need it for a night or so."

"You need more than the camera, you need me to work the damn thing. It's balky as hell, you gotta know how to use it."

"You can teach us."

He shook his head. "Took me weeks to learn. You don't get it just right you don't get any picture."

She stared at him. "Dick, please. Just one night is all we ask."

He frowned at her, as if asking "Is this for real?" She nodded gravely. "A night, then," he said, "maybe it'll be a few laughs."

So he agreed, just like that. She wished she felt more than grateful, but she didn't. His anger and tiredness made her wish to hell that she would not have to spend the rest of this night with him.

She showed Wilson to the door. "See you at headquarters," she said as he pulled on his coat. "Eight o'clock?"

"Eight's fine."

"Where are you going now, George?"

"Not home. You're crazy to stay here, as a matter of fact."

"I don't know where else I'd go."

"That's your business." He stepped out into the hallway and was gone. She started to wonder if she would ever see him alive again, then stopped herself. Not allowed. She turned, took a deep breath, and prepared to face the rest of the night with her husband.

Chapter 6

They were hungry, they wanted food. Normally they preferred the darker, desolate sections of the city, but their need to follow their enemies had brought them into its very eye. Here the smell of man lay over everything like a dense fog, and there was not much cover.

But even the brightest places have shadows. They moved in single file behind the wall that separates Central Park from the street. They did not need to look over the wall to know that few of the benches that lined the other side were occupied—they could smell that fact perfectly well. But they also smelled something else, the rich scent of a human being perhaps a quarter of a mile farther on. On one of the benches a man was sleeping, a man whose pores were exuding the smell of alcohol. To them the reek meant food, easily gotten.

As they moved closer they could hear his breathing. It was long and troubled, full of age. They stopped behind him. There was no need to discuss what they would do; each one knew his role.

Three jumped up on the wall, standing there perfectly still, balanced on the sharply angled stone. He was on the bench below them. The one nearest the victim's head inclined her ears back. She would get the throat. The other two would move in only if there was a struggle.

She held her breath a moment to clear her head. Then she examined her victim with her eyes. The flesh was not visible—it was under thick folds of cloth. She would have to jump, plunge her muzzle into the cloth and rip out the throat all at once. If there were more than a few convulsions on the part of the food she would disappoint the pack. She opened her nose, letting the rich smells of the world back in. She listened up and down the street. Only automobile traffic, nobody on foot for at least fifty yards. She cocked her ears toward a man leaning in a chair inside the brightly lit foyer of a building across the street. He was listening to a radio. She watched his head turn. He was glancing into the lobby.

Now. She was down, she was pushing her nose past cloth, slick hot flesh, feeling the vibration of subvocal response in the man, feeling his muscles stiffening as his body reacted to her standing on it, then opening her mouth against the flesh, feeling her teeth scrape back and down, pressing her tongue against the deliciously salty skin and *ripping* with all the strength in her jaws and neck and chest, and jumping back to the wall with the bloody throat in her mouth. The body on the bench barely rustled as its dying blood poured out.

And the man in the doorway returned his glance to the street. Nothing had moved, as far as he was concerned. Ever watchful, she scented him and lis-

tened to him. His breathing was steady, his smell
bland. Good, he had noticed nothing.

Now her job was over, she dropped back behind
the wall and ate her trophy. It was rich and sweet
with blood. Around her the pack was very happy as
it worked. Three of them lifted the body over the
wall and let it drop with a thud. The two others,
skilled in just this art, stripped the clothing away.
They would carry the material to the other side of the
park, shred it and hide it in shrubs before they returned to their meal.

As soon as the corpse was stripped it was pulled
open. The organs were sniffed carefully. One lung,
the stomach, the colon were put aside because of rot.

Then the pack ate in rank order.

The mother took the brain. The father took a
thigh and buttock. The first-mated pair ate the clean
organs. When they returned from their duty the second-mated pair took the rest. And then they pulled
apart the remains and took them piece by piece and
dropped them in the nearby lake. The bones would
sink and would not be found at least until spring, if
then. The clothing they had shredded and scattered
half a mile away. And now they kicked as much new
snow as they could over the blood of their feast. When
this was done they went to a place they had seen
earlier, a great meadow full of the beautiful new
snow that had been falling.

They ran and danced in the snow, feeling the
pleasure of their bodies, the joy of racing headlong
across the wide expanse, and because they knew that
no human was in earshot they had a joyous howl full
of the pulsing rhythm they liked best after a hunt.
The sound rose through the park, echoing off the
buildings that surrounded it. Inside those buildings a
few wakeful people stirred, made restive by the cold

and ancient terror that the sound communicated to man.

Then they went to a tunnel they had slept in these past four nights and settled down. By long-learned habit they slept in the small hours of the morning when men mostly did not stir. During daylight, man's strongest time, they remained awake and alert and rarely broke cover unless they had to. In the evening they hunted.

This traditional order of life went back forever.

Before sleeping the second-mated pair made love, both to entertain the others and to prepare for spring. And afterward the father and mother licked them, and then the pack slept.

But they did not sleep long, not until the hour before dawn as was their custom. This night they still had something to accomplish, and instead of sleeping through the wee hours they left their hiding place and moved out into the silent streets.

Becky listened to the phone on the other end of the line ring once, twice, three times. Finally Wilson picked up. He had gone home after all. "Yeah?"

"You OK?" she asked.

"Yes, Mama."

"Now now, don't get sarcastic. Just bedchecking."

He hung up. The thought of slamming down the phone crossed her mind but what good would it do? She returned the receiver to its cradle and went back into the living room. Dick had not heard her and she paused behind him. Sitting slumped in his chair he seemed smaller than life—diminished. She would have to do everything she could to help him defeat the investigation. She had to; by simply being his wife she was implicated. "You knew he was getting extra money," they would say. "Where did you think it was coming from?" And there could only be one answer to that question.

It wasn't that she minded helping him, either. He had been a good husband for a long time and she supposed that what was happening between them was very sad. The trouble was she didn't care. The intimacy that had once united them had died through inattention. Where once she had been full of love there was now just stone boredom. There wasn't even a sense of loss. Or maybe—just maybe—there was a sense of loss, for a love that had never been real.

She had to ask herself, if a love can die like this, was it ever real? She remembered the long happiness of the past, the happiness that had seemed so eternal. When they had gone sleighriding up in the Catskills five Christmases ago, the love they shared had *been* real. And in the hard times before she was a cop, that love had been very real indeed. It wasn't just that Dick was a good lover, it was that he was a partner and friend of a deep and special kind. "You're beautiful," he would say, "you're wonderful." And it had meant more than the physical. Maybe the waning of his enthusiasm was inevitable as she reached middle age. But his enthusiasm wasn't the problem, it was hers. Try as she might she could not love Dick Neff anymore.

Wilson waited five minutes to be certain she wouldn't call back. The phone didn't ring again. His rudeness had evidently made her mad enough to ignore him for the rest of the night.

Fine. He went into his bedroom and unlocked a chest he kept in his closet. Inside were a number of highly illegal weapons—a sawed-off shotgun, a WWII vintage BAR in working order, and an Ingram M-11 Automatic Pistol. He pulled the automatic pistol from its case and got a box of shells. Carefully he worked the pistol's action, then hefted it in his hand. Its balance was a pleasure to feel. It was unquestionably the finest automatic handgun ever designed, lightweight, sound-suppressed, with a 20-round-a-second punch. It was not designed to frighten, slow down, or confuse, but purely and simply to kill. One bullet would blow a man's head apart. The best automatic weapon ever made. The fastest. The most murderous. He opened the ammo box and snapped a clip of the special .380 subsonic velocity bullets into the gun. Now it was heavier but the balance hadn't changed. Only three and a half pounds of weapon, it could be hefted nicely. And aimed. The sights were precise. For a handgun, its range was almost incredible. You could shoot a man at a hundred and fifty yards with this weapon. A burst of three or four bullets would get him even if he was on the run.

He laid the pistol on his bed and put on an overcoat he rarely wore. When it was on he dropped the M-11 into a pocket which had been especially tailored to fit the nine-inch pistol. Wilson had had the coat modified when he had acquired the pistol. The pocket carried the M-11 almost invisibly. Despite the size and weight of the pistol only a careful observer would note that he was carrying a piece at all. His hand felt the weapon in his pocket, his thumb triggering the lever that moved the mechanism from safe to fire. A single press of the trigger could now deliver from one bullet to a full clip in a matter of seconds. Good enough. Now he got out his winter hat, old, wrinkled, perfect for both protecting the head and hiding the face. Next the shoes—black sneakers, surprisingly warm with two pair of socks, surprisingly agile even in the snow. They had been winterized with a polyurethane coating, and the soles scored to provide traction. The sneakers gave him the advantages of quiet and quick movement, most useful on an icy winter night. The last item was a pair of gloves. These were made of the finest Moroccan leather, softer and thinner than kid. Through them he could feel the M-11 perfectly, almost as if the gloves weren't there at all.

As a final precaution he took out the pistol and removed fingerprints. Not even a gold shield policeman goes around printing up a weapon like the Ingram. There isn't anything in the rule book about policemen carrying machine pistols, but that's only because there doesn't need to be. You need a special permit to own one, and permission to move it from one premises to another. As far as carrying one around in the street fully loaded, that is illegal for policeman and civilian alike.

He replaced the M-11 in its pocket and stood for a short time in the middle of the room. Mentally he checked himself out. He was ready to move. Too bad his plan to de-scent himself had been wishful thinking. Now the M-11 was really his only advantage. That and the fact that hunters aren't used to being hunted. Or at least he hoped they weren't. His logic seemed strong—how suspecting would a human hunter be if the deer suddenly turned on him, or a lion if it was attacked by a gazelle?

While he saw the danger of what he was doing he nevertheless felt that he had to act to give Becky some kind of a chance of survival. She deserved to live, she was young and strong; as for him he could take a few chances. And it was a hell of a long chance he was taking. The thought of being killed—by things —made clammy sweat break out.

But he knew that he and Becky had to have help

if either of them was going to live much longer. And to get the kind of support they needed, they had to have a specimen. Irrefutable, undeniable evidence that would force Underwood to act, to assign this problem the kind of manpower it demanded.

Wilson was going to get that evidence if he could. And if he got killed trying—oh God, he wanted to live! No matter how old, how beat-up, he still wanted to live! But he was going after a carcass anyway. Had to.

He left his apartment after making sure all the lights were on. He triple-locked his door and moved quickly to the rear of the dim hallway, where a fire escape was barred by an accordion gate. He unhooked it and pulled it back, then raised the window and stepped into the winter night. He took some putty out of his pocket—carried for just this purpose—and pressed it into the locking mechanism so that when he closed the gate again the latch fell into place but could be raised if you jiggled it just right. If you yanked at it or shook it hard the putty would give way and the lock would secure itself. Then he closed the window and moved his bulky body down the ice-covered fire escape to the street.

The snow was becoming heavier. Not good, impeded his vision but not their sense of smell. Perhaps the muffling effect would reduce the acuity of their hearing a little.

He put his hand in his pocket, closing his finger around the trigger of the M-11. It was a mean weapon, designed for anti-guerrilla work, the kind of police work where you killed it if it moved. Right now it felt good. It was the right pistol for this hunt—the bullets would knock a man ten feet. A hundred-pound animal should go considerably farther.

He set out to find his quarry. He reasoned that the creatures would be more likely to hit Becky first because she was younger and presumably stronger, therefore more dangerous to them. Wilson, slow, old, sick, would be second in line. His theory was borne out by the fact that they had gone to such great lengths to get to Becky and had left him pretty much alone. Of course they had come in the basement window, Wilson was well aware of that. He had left it ajar as an invitation. His dusting of the basement of the rooming house last night had revealed two sets of pawprints as distinctively different as human fingerprints. They had gone up the basement stairs to the door. There were marks on the lock where they had tried to spring it with their claws.

But they had reserved their best effort for Becky, of that he felt reasonably sure. If he was wrong, if they were around him now . . . with luck he would take a few with him.

He walked through the deserted late-night streets with his hand in his pocket clutching the M-11. Despite the gun, he kept close to the curb, away from any trashcans and shadowy entranceways, out from under overhanging fire escapes. And every few steps he stopped and looked behind him. Only once did he see another human form, a man bundled against the snow and hurrying in the opposite direction.

When he reached the lights of Eighth Avenue he felt much better. He was safer out here under the bright sodium-arc lamps, with the passing cars and the more frequent pedestrians. Somehow he felt more anonymous taking the bus, so he waited at the bus stop instead of hailing a cab. Ten minutes passed before a bus came. He got on and rode it far uptown, to Eighty-sixth and Central Park West. Now all he had to do was cross the park and he would be in Becky's neighborhood. Upper East Side cardboard box neighborhood . . . well, if that's what she liked . . .

He thought better of crossing the park on foot—in fact he never really considered it at all. To the danger of the creatures he would add the dangers of the park, very foolhardy indeed.

After what seemed an hour a crosstown bus appeared, moving slowly in the deepening snow. Wilson got on, glad for the heated interior. He let himself relax in the bus, but he never took his hand out of his pocket.

When he got off he spotted Becky's building at once. He counted the balconies. Good, she had left her lights on, an intelligent precaution. She would probably be furious at him for coming out alone like this, but it had to be done. If you're going to take crazy risks, you take them alone.

He moved toward the alley where the creatures must have congregated. The snow had, of course, covered up all trace of them. They would be coming back here sooner or later, of that much he felt sure. But if their sense of smell was as good as Ferguson had implied they would know he was here long before they were even in sight. So what, let them move in on him. He hefted the M-11 a little in his pocket, then settled down behind a garbage bin to wait.

One o'clock. The wind moaned out of the north. Two o'clock. The snow blew in great waves past the streetlights. Three o'clock. Wilson flexed his toes, rubbed his nose hard, listened to his heartbeat. He began to fight sleep about three-fifteen. Taking his cheek between thumb and forefinger he pinched hard. The pain startled him into wakefulness.

Then it was quiet. The snow had stopped. Involuntarily he gasped—he *had* fallen asleep. What time—four-twenty. Damn, over an hour out. And across the street, through the alley, standing in the light, were six of the ugliest, most horrifying things he had ever seen. He didn't move a muscle, just his eyes.

These things were big, big as timber wolves. Their coats were dusky brown, their heads perched on necks much longer than that of a wolf. They had large pointed ears, all cocked directly at this alley. He could practically *feel* them listening to him. Somewhere his mind began to scream, Fire the Goddamn pistol, fire the pistol! But he couldn't move, he couldn't take his eyes off those faces. The eyes were light gray, under jutting brows. And they were looking where the ears were pointing. The faces were . . . almost serene in their deadliness. And they had lips, strange sensitive lips. The faces were not even a little human but they were clearly intelligent. They were worse than the faces of tigers, more totally ruthless, more intractable.

Fire the pistol!

Slowly the pistol started coming out of his pocket. It seemed to take an hour for it to be raised, but at last the long barrel swung up and . . . without a sound they were gone.

Not a trace, not even the rustle of a foot in the snow. They had *moved!* Goddamn, he hadn't counted on speed like that. Then he was running too—as fast as he could out of the alley and into the middle of the snowy street, running frantically, feeling like an old, old man as he wheezed along, running toward a lighted window, an all-night deli, and then through the door.

"Jesus, don't scare me like that, man!"

"Sorry-sorry. I—I'm cold. You got coffee?"

"Yeah, comin' up. You runnin' your ass off out there. You in trouble, man?"

"Just trying to keep warm is all. Trying to keep warm."

The counterman held out the coffee—and held on to it. "You got fifty cents, daddy? That's fifty cents in advance."

"Oh, yeah, sure." Wilson paid him, took the hot coffee cup in his hands, moved it to his face, and sipped.

Great God *I'm alive!* I got that Goddamn gun out f-a-s-t! One second later and they would have had me, the s.o.b.'s! It was exhilarating—it might have felt slow but he had drawn that gun Goddamn fast. Fast enough to save himself from them and they were fast beyond imagining.

He sipped again, noticing how his hand trembled. That had to stop. Long ago he had learned how to overcome the special fear that came with the close proximity of death. Now he went through the routine, a system that had been taught to him by his first partner, back in the forties when he was a rookie cop. There was a man—shot dead by his oldest son in '52.

Now wait a minute, Wilson thought, you're digressing. You're shocked. Come on now, policeman, snap out of it! Relax shoulders, let them fall. Let your gut hang out. Slack your lips. Breathe deeply . . . one . . . two . . . and think about nothing, just let it roll over you.

Now when he sipped the coffee he tasted it, and for the first time noticed that it was black and unsweetened.

"Hey, I said light, this coffee's black."

"You need it black, man. You don't need no light coffee. You drink that, then I'll give you a light."

"Thank you, Doctor, but I'm not drunk."

The counterman laughed softly, then looked straight at Wilson. "I wouldn't say you were. You scared. You the scaredest motherfucker I've seen in a good long while. Maybe that coffee'll help you get it back together, man."

"Well, it is back together, man. And I want a light coffee. I can't drink this stuff."

"Sure, you got money I'll fix you a carbonated coffee if you want it. I don't give a damn. But don't say you can't drink what you got."

"Why the hell not! What are you, some kind of a nut? I said I wanted light. I can't drink this junk."

"Look in the cup, man."

It was empty. He hadn't even been aware of swallowing it! He shut up, returned to his thoughts, to how incredibly fast they had been. It was almost as if they had vanished; but he had glimpsed flashes of running bodies. Then it occurred to him that if they were that fast they would have gotten past his defenses before he had even realized they were there.

Why hadn't they? For some unknown reason this particular gold shield had been allowed to live. The M-11 still felt good in his pocket but it had been no protection at all. None at all. It certainly hadn't been the speed of his draw that had scared them away. Something, then . . . almost but not quite like a memory. He almost knew why they had run, then—he didn't. "Shit."

"You ready to go, mister?"

"No."

"Well, you notice we ain't got no chairs in here. This is a deli, not no coffee shop. You got to buy and go in a place like this, that's the rules."

"So what if I don't go?"

"Nothin'. Just I feel like you got trouble all

around you. You gonna bring it in here with you."

Wilson debated whether to go back outside or to flash his shield. What the hell, outside probably wasn't the healthiest place for him to be right now. Whatever had stopped them before might not again. So he flashed. "Police," he said tonelessly, "I'm stayin' put."

"Sure enough."

"There a back room, some place I can bunk out? I'm tired, I've just been in a bad spot."

"I'd have to agree, judging from the way you look. We got a storeroom. It's good, there's plenty of place to lie, and it's pretty warm. I get a little back there now and then myself." He showed Wilson into a low-ceilinged room, obviously a shed attached to the rear of the old brownstone building that housed the deli. There was one window, barred, and a triple-locked door. Very good, very cozy, very safe until the morning brought crowds back to the street and he could safely go out. As he settled back he reviewed his strange, terrifying failure. Obviously they were way, way ahead of him—fast, smart, in complete control of the situation. There was only one reason that he wasn't dead right now—they wanted him alive a little longer.

When he closed his eyes he saw them, their steady, eager eyes, the cruel beauty of their faces . . . and he remembered the moose and the wolves. What did the spent old moose feel for the ravening timber wolf—was it love, or fear so great that it mimicked love?

When they realized who was concealed in the alley they were full of glee. He had come to protect the female, just as the father had said he would. The father knew man very well and could detect nuances of scent that the younger ones could scarcely imagine. And Father had detected the fact that the

man who had seen them loved his female coworker.
Father had said, we can move against them both at
the same time because the male will try to protect the
female. And Father had selected the place and time:
where the female was most defenseless, when she was
most vulnerable.

And they went and there he was. Asleep! The
second-mated pair prepared for the attack, moving
into position across the street. They were just about to
move when the man raised his head and looked at
them. The pack froze and smelled it all at the same
time: sweat from the hand that held the gun.

It was a hard decision, instantly made by Mother
—we leave; we do not risk moving so far against the
gun, we get him another time.

Now the pack ran, rushing through the streets to
the ruined building where they would spend the day.
Each heart beat with the same agonizing knowledge:
they live, they live, they live. And they know about
us. Even as the sun rises they must be telling others,
spreading the fear that the old legends speak about,
the fear that would make life among men hard and
dangerous for future generations.

The second-mated pair was especially anguished:
in the spring they would litter, and they did not want
to bring forth children if man knew of the hunter.

Not that they feared anything from single individuals, or even groups. But endless numbers of men
could overwhelm them or at least force them into
furtive, tormented lives unworthy of free beings. As
they moved warily through the deserted streets one
thought consumed them all: kill the dangerous ones,
kill them fast. And it was this that they talked about
when they reached their sanctuary, a long, intense
conversation that left them all shuddering with a
furious urge for blood, all except Father, who said,

we have won. Soon he will give himself to us as men did of old, for the death wish is coming upon him.

Wilson opened his eyes. The light coming in the window was yellow-gray. A steady tapping against the windowpane indicated that it was snowing again.

"Who the hell are you?"

A man was standing over him, a fat man in gray slacks and a white shirt. He was bald, his face pinched with the long habit of unsatisfied greed.

"I'm a cop. Wilson's the name."

"Oh Christ almighty—why'd you let this damn bum in here, Eddie? Throw the fucker out, he'll get weevils in the Goddamn bread."

"He got a gold shield, man. I'm not gonna say no to a gold shield."

"You can buy a Goddamn gold shield on Forty-second Street. Get the jerk out."

"Don't worry, sweetheart, I was just leaving. Thanks, Eddie, from the NYPD."

Wilson left to a snort of scornful laughter from the white guy, a disgusted stare from the black. Sleeping over in storerooms was pretty unorthodox behavior for a cop. What the hell, he didn't give a damn.

It was still pretty damn lonely on the street. Lonely and snowy too. This was practically a blizzard, must be five or six inches by now. He started to walk back by Becky's building, then stopped himself. It hit him like a haymaker—they had come when they did because they knew he would be there. They were *hunters*, for Chrissake, they knew damn well where he'd be. Oh, they were beautiful! They had him figured from way back. It was probably exactly what one of them would have done—protect the one he loved.

What the hell, the bitch was beautiful. Fair cop

too—but so beautiful. Becky had creamy skin, Irish coloring. Wilson was partial to that kind of coloring. And she had those soft, yet piercing eyes. He thought of looking into those eyes. "Becky, I love you," he would say, and she would open her mouth slightly, inviting the first long kiss . . .

But not now. Now it was cold and he was hungry. He trudged toward the Lexington Avenue subway to ride down to headquarters. His watch said six-thirty. The Merit Bar was open by now, and they served up a fair breakfast. Then he felt the M-11. You didn't go into Police Headquarters with a loaded M-11, you just did not do that. He'd have to stop by his rooming house first and exchange it for his regulation piece.

The subway wasn't much warmer than the street, but at least it was well-lighted and there were a few people around. Not many at this hour, but enough to keep the things away from him. They were after him and Becky because they had been seen—certainly they wouldn't attack except when their targets were alone. But you can be alone enough for just a few seconds. That he had to remember.

He got off and returned to his rooming house, entering this time by the front door. At the top of the stairs he carefully removed the putty he had left in the fire escape lock and returned to his room. He dropped off the overcoat containing the M-11 and put on the one containing the .38. That was all. The way he kept his place locked, he wasn't worried that a burglar would rip off the pistol, or anything else in his apartment for that matter.

He double-locked his door, tested it, and left the building as quickly and quietly as he had come. And as he did it he laughed at himself. There was no need to be so quiet, it was just that it was second nature to him now. Unless he was acting the part of an un-

concerned civilian he was always wary, always
stealthy. He walked the short distance from his place
to headquarters the same way, like a thief or someone
tracking a thief.

He went through the quiet, brightly lit corridors
of Police Headquarters until he got to the little office
occupied by him and Neff. When he opened the door,
his eyes widened with surprise.

There sat Evans.

"Hiya, Doc. Do I owe you money?"

Evans wasn't interested in bantering with Wilson.
"We got another one," he said simply.

"What's the story?"

Evans looked at him. "Call Neff. Tell her to meet
us at the scene."

"Anything new?" Wilson asked as he dialed the
phone.

"Plenty."

"Why didn't you call Neff yourself?"

"You're the senior man on the case. I tried you
first. When you didn't answer I came over. I figured
you were on your way in."

"Emergency, Doctor. You could have called Neff
when you didn't find me."

"I have no emergencies. My line of business only
concerns emergencies after they're over."

Somewhere out there the phone was ringing. Dick
was subvocalizing a few choice curses each time the
bell burst the silence. Ring and curse, ring and curse.
"It could be for you," Becky said.

"Nah. I'm burned, remember. It ain't for me."

"Then it's for me."

"So answer the fucker. One of us has gotta do it."

She picked up the receiver. Wilson didn't waste

hellos. "Oh, Christ. OK, see you there." She hung up. "Gotta go. Homicide in the park."

"Since when are you assigned uptown?"

"Evans called us in. He says it looks like our friends got hungry again."

"The big bad wolves." He raised himself up on his elbow. "What about our picture-taking expedition, will it be on?"

"I hope. I'll call you."

"OK, honey."

She was dressing as quickly as possible, but the gentleness in his voice made her stop. They looked at one another. The delirious, unexpected intensity of the night before was written in Dick's face. She saw clearly: he was grateful. It touched her, made her think that maybe there was still something left after all.

"I " The words seemed to die in her throat. They were so unfamiliar, so long unsaid.

Dick had come to her wordlessly, in the dark, just as she was falling asleep. He had embraced her, his body hot and trembling, and had awakened in her a painful rush of feeling. Maybe she *did* care—so much that she just couldn't face it. Maybe that was the true source of the wall that was being built between them. And realizing that she had responded to his intensity with passion of her own and had enjoyed the violent insistence of his body, finally crying out with the pleasure.

"What, Becky?"

"I don't know. Just wanted to say good-bye." But not I love you, not that again, not yet. And she felt like a heel for holding back, a selfish heel.

"Don't make it sound so final."' He chuckled. "The worst I'll get is early retirement. If the shooflies are

real good they might give you a five-day. Don't let it
bug you, darling. And by the way, there's something
else I want to say to you before you go." He rolled
over on his back, throwing off the covers, exposing
his naked body and erect penis with delightful lack
of modesty. "You still remain one of the great Ameri-
can lays, darling."

And she was beside him, bending over him, kissing his smiling face. "Dick, you silly fool, look at you.
You never get enough."

"I'm a morning man."

"And a night man and an afternoon man. I wish
I didn't have to go! I'll call you when I get the
chance." She drew herself away from him, full of a
confusion of emotions. Why couldn't she make up her
mind about this: did she still love Dick Neff or didn't
she? And what about Wilson, what did her feelings for
him mean?

She rode the elevator down to the garage level
and got in her car. As soon as she started driving her
mind closed around the case. The night with Dick
receded, as did the welter of emotions she had been
feeling. Like a murky, ugly fog the case rose and re-
captured her. Wilson hadn't said much over the phone,
not much. But he had sounded uncharacteristically
upset. Evans had been with him at Police Headquarters. She glanced at her watch: seven A.M. An early
hour for Doctor Evans. She stepped on the accelerator,
racing across Seventy-ninth Street in the snow, heading for the point of rendezvous, Central Park West
and Seventy-second.

The streets were empty as she maneuvered the
car around the corner at Seventy-ninth and CPW.
She was now in the 20th Precinct. Ahead she could
see the flashing lights, the dismal little crowd of
emergency vehicles that always marked a crime scene.

She pulled up behind a parked radio car. "I'm Neff," she said to the lieutenant on the scene.

"We got a funny one," he intoned. "Anticrime boys found this bench covered with frozen blood about an hour ago. We took it to pathology and sure enough it's human. O-negative, to be exact. But we got no corpse, nothin'."

"How do you know it was a murder?"

"There's evidence enough. First off, too much blood, whoever lost it had to die. Second, we can see where the body was pulled across the wall." Her eyes went to the indentations in the snow that lay along the wall. More snow had fallen since the murder, but not enough to completely obliterate the signs. "By the way, Detective Neff, if I may be so blunt, why are you here?"

"Well, I'm on special assignment with my partner, Detective Wilson. We're investigating a certain M.O. When the M. E. finds a case that seems to fit he gives us a call."

"You take your orders from the M. E.?"

"We were instructed by the Commissioner." She hadn't wanted to pull rank, but she sensed that he was needling her. He smiled a little sheepishly and strolled away. "Lieutenant," Neff called, "is this blood all you have? No body, no clothing, nothing?"

"Hold on, Becky," a voice said behind her. It was Evans, followed closely by Wilson. The two men came up and the three of them huddled together under the curious eyes of the men of the 20th and Central Park precincts. "There's more," Evans said, "there's some hair."

"He's examined some hairs that were stuck in the blood."

"Right. This is my interpreter, Detective Wilson. I found hairs—"

"That match the hairs found at the DiFalco scene."

Evans frowned. "Come on, Wilson, lay off. The hairs match the ones we've found at every scene."

"They're pretty voracious if they only left blood," Becky said.

"They didn't. Don't you see what happened? They hid the remains. They've learned that we're on their tail and they're trying to slow us down. They're very bright."

"That's for certain," Wilson said. Becky noticed how haggard he looked, his face waxen, his jaw unshaven. Had he slept at all? It didn't look like it. He cleared his throat. "Are they searching for the corpse?" he asked the Lieutenant, who was standing nearby.

"Yeah. There's some sign of something being dragged, but the snow covered most of the evidence up. We're just not sure what happened."

Becky motioned to Wilson and Evans. They followed her into her car. "It's warmer here," she said, "and the Loo won't overhear us."

Evans was the first to speak. "Obviously they were hiding behind the wall when somebody sat on the bench. Judging from the blood it happened five or six hours ago. They must have jumped over the wall, killed fast and dragged the corpse away."

"Not in one piece," Wilson said. "There'd be more marks. I think they tore it up and carried it."

"Jesus. But what about the clothes?"

"That's what we ought to be able to find. The bones, too, for that matter, there aren't too many places they could have hidden them."

"How about the pond?"

"You mean because it's frozen over? I doubt if they'd think of busting the ice in the pond, that's *too* smart."

"We need to find clothes, some kind of identification."

"Yeah. Where the hell to look, though? This friggin' snow . . ."

"I have the hairs. I don't need anything more to convince me. They came here last night and they killed this person. I'm certain of that. It was them. Their hairs are unique, as unique as a fingerprint."

"So they kill a lot. That's to be expected for a carnivorous animal."

Becky corrected her partner. "Carnivorous humanoid."

Wilson laughed. "From what I've seen they could hardly be described as humanoid."

"And what have you seen?"

"Them."

Becky and the M. E. stared at him. "You've seen them?" Evans finally managed to ask.

"That's right. Last night."

"What the hell are you saying?" Becky asked.

"I saw six of them outside of your apartment last night. I was hunting them, trying to get Ferguson his specimen." He sighed. "They're fast, though. I missed 'em by a mile. Lucky I'm still alive."

Becky was stunned. She looked at her partner's tired face, at his watery, aging eyes. He had been out there guarding her! The crazy, sweet old romantic jerk. At this moment she felt like she was seeing a hidden, secret Wilson, seeing him for the very first time. She could have kissed him.

Chapter 7

Carl Ferguson was horrified and excited at the same time by what he was reading. He seemed to drift away, to a quiet and safe place. But he came back. Around him the prosaic realities of the Main Reading Room of the New York Public Library reasserted themselves. Across from him a painfully pretty schoolgirl cracked her gum. Beside him an old man breathed long and slow, paging through an equally old book. All around him there was a subdued clatter, the scuttle of pen on paper, the coughs, the whispers, the drone of clerks calling numbers from the front of the room.

Because you could not enter the stacks and because you could neither enter nor leave this room with a book, its collection had not been stolen and was still among the best in the world. And it was because of the book that he had finally obtained from this superb collection that Carl Ferguson felt such an extremity of fear. What he read, what he saw before him was almost too fantastic and too horrible to believe. And yet the words were there.

"In Normany," Ferguson read for the third time, "tradition tells of certain fantastic beings known as lupins or lubins. They pass the night chattering together and twattling in an unknown tongue. They take their stand by the walls of country cemeteries and howl dismally at the moon. Timorous and fearful of man they will flee away scared at a footstep or distant voice. In some districts, however, they are fierce and of the werewolf race, since they are said to scratch up graves with their hands and gnaw poor dead bones."

An ancient story, repeated by Montague Summers in his classic *The Werewolf*. Summers assumed that the werewolf tales were folklore, hearsay conjured up to frighten the gullible. But Summers was totally, incredibly wrong. The old legends and tales were true. Only one small element was incorrect—in the past it was assumed that their intelligence and cunning meant that werewolves were men who had assumed the shape of animals. But they weren't. They were not that at all, but rather a completely separate species of intelligent creature. And they had been sharing planet Earth with us all these long eons and we never understood it. What marvellous beings they must be—a virtual alien intelligence right here at home. It was a frightening discovery, but to Ferguson also one of awesome wonder.

Here were legends, stories, tales going back thousands of years, repeating again and again the mythology of the werewolf. And then suddenly, in the latter part of the nineteenth century, silence.

The legends died.

The stories were no longer told.

But why? To Ferguson's mind the answer was simple: the werewolves, tormented for generations by humanity's vigilance and fear, had found a way to hide from man. Their cover was now perfect. They lived among us, fed off our living flesh, but were unknown to all except those who didn't live to tell the tale. They were a race of living ghosts, unseen but very much a part of the world. They understood human society well enough to take only the abandoned, the weak, the isolated. And toward the end of the nineteenth century the human population all over the world had started to explode, poverty and filth had spread. Huge masses of people were ignored and abandoned by the societies in which they lived. And they were fodder for these werewolves, who range through the shadows devouring the beggars, the wanderers, those without name or home.

And no doubt the population of werewolves had exploded right along with the human population. Ferguson pictured hundreds, thousands of them scavenging the great cities of the earth for their human prey, rarely being glimpsed, using their sensitive ears and noses to keep well distant of all but the weak and helpless, taking advantage of man's increasing multitudes and increasing poverty. Their faculties combined with their intelligence must make them fearsome indeed—but what an opportunity they also represented to science—to him—as another intelligence capable of study, even perhaps communication.

But there was something else about Summers' book, something even more disquieting, and that was the continual references to men and werewolves in communication with one another. "Two gentlemen who were crossing a forest glade after dark suddenly came upon an open space where an old woodsman was standing, a man well-known to them, who was making passes in the air, weaving strange signs and signals. The two friends concealed themselves behind a tree, whence they saw thirteen wolves come trotting along. The leader was a huge grey wolf who went up to the old man fawning upon him and being caressed. Presently the forester uttered a sing-song chant and plunged into the woods followed by the wolves."

Just a story, but tremendously interesting in the context of the information that the two detectives had brought him. Obviously the references to signs and a "sing-song" chant referred to human attempts to mimic the language of the werewolves, to communicate. Why did men once run with the werewolves?

Summers said that vampires were often connected to werewolves. Vampires—the eaters of blood. In other words, cannibals. To a less knowledgeable person such an idea might have seemed fantastic, but Ferguson knew enough about old Europe to understand the probable truth behind the legend. Men did indeed run with werewolves, and those men were called vampires because they fed off human flesh like the wolves themselves. Cannibalism must have been common in the Europe of the Dark Ages, when grinding poverty was the fate of all except a tiny minority. When men were the weakest and most numerous creatures around it must have tempted the hungry . . . to go out and find the werewolves, somehow build up a rapport, and then hunt with them, living like a scavenger off the pickings.

So much for the image of the vampire as a count with a castle and a silk dinner jacket. The truth was more like Summers' description—a filthy old forester scrabbling along with a pack of werewolves to glean the leavings of their monstrous feasts.

Man the scavenger, in the same role among werewolves that dogs play among men! And the human prey, unsuspecting now, but in those days it knew. People approached the night with terror crackling in their hearts. And when darkness fell only the desperate and the mad remained out of doors.

What, then, was the role of the human scavenger, the vampire, that ran with the werewolves? Why did they tolerate him? Simple enough, to coax people out of their houses, to lure them into the shadows where they would be ripped apart. It was ugly but it also meant that there had been communication of a sort between man and werewolf in the past, and could be again. And how immeasurably richer communication between this extraordinary species and modern science might be. There could be no comparison between the promise of the future and the sordid mistakes of the distant past.

It had gotten much easier for the werewolves in recent centuries. No longer were the human vampires needed. Nowadays the werewolves could do it on their own. Just take up residence in any big city, live in abandoned buildings among the city's million byways, and prey on the human strays.

Man and wolf. It had been an age-old animosity. The image of the wolf baying at the moon on a winter's night still calls primitive terrors to the heart of man.

And with good reason, except that the innocent timber wolf with his loud howling and once conspicuous presence was not the enemy. Lurking back there in the shadows, perhaps along the path to the well, was the real enemy, unnoticed, patient, lethal beyond imagining. The wolf-being with its long finger-like paws, the werewolf, the other intelligent species that shared this planet.

We killed off the innocent timber wolf and never

even discovered the real danger. While the timber wolf bayed to the oblivious moon the real enemy crept up the basement steps and used one of those clever paws to throw the bolt on the door.

Ferguson ran his fingers through his hair, his mind trying to accept the fearful truth he had uncovered. That damn detective—Wilson was his name —had an absolutely uncanny intuition about this whole matter. It was Detective Wilson who had first said the word werewolf, the word that had gotten Ferguson really thinking about that strange paw. And Wilson had claimed that the werewolves were hunting him and the woman down. With good reason! Once their secret was out the life of the werewolf would be made immeasurably harder, like it was in the old days in Europe when humanity bolted its doors and locked its windows, or in the Americas where the Indian used his knowledge of the forest to play a deadly game of hide and seek, a game commemorated to this day in the traditional dances of many tribes. The werewolf undoubtedly followed man to this continent across the Bering land bridge eons ago. But always and everywhere he kept himself as well hidden as he could. And it made good sense. You wouldn't find beggars sleeping on sidewalks if the werewolf was common knowledge. A wave of terror would sweep the city and the world unlike anything known since the Middle Ages. Unspeakable things would be done in the name of human safety. Man would declare all-out war on his adversary.

And at last he would have a fair fight on his hands. With all our technology, we have never faced an alien intelligence before, have never faced a species with its own built-in technology far superior to our own. Ferguson could not imagine what the mind behind the nose and ears of the werewolf must be like.

The sheer quantity of information pouring in must literally be millions of times greater than that reaching a man through his eyes. The mind that gave meaning to all that information must be a miracle indeed. Maybe even greater than the mind of man. And man must, this time, react responsibly. If there was intelligence there it could be reasoned with, and eventually the two enemy species could learn to live together in peace. If Carl Ferguson had any part in this at all it was as the missionary of reason and understanding. Man could either declare war on this species or try to come to an understanding. Carl Ferguson raised his head, closed his eyes and hoped with every fiber of his being that reason would for once prevail.

He was surprised to notice somebody was standing beside him.

"You've got to take this call slip to the rare books department. We don't have this book in the reading room. All of our stuff is post-1825 and this book was written in 1597." The call clerk dropped the card on the table in front of Ferguson and went away. Ferguson got up and headed for the rare books collection, card clutched in his hand.

He moved through the empty, echoing halls of the great library, finally arriving at the rare books collection. A middle-aged woman sat at a desk working on a catalogue under a green-shaded lamp. The only sound in the room was the faint clatter of the steam pipes and the snow-muted mutter of the city beyond the windows.

"I'm Carl Ferguson of the Museum of Natural History. I'd like to take a look at this book." He handed her the card.

"Do we have this?"

"It's catalogued."

She got up and disappeared behind a wire-covered doorway. Ferguson waited standing expectantly for a few moments, then found a chair. There was no sound from the direction the woman had gone. He was alone in the room. The place smelled of books. And he was impatient for her to return. It was urgent that she produce the book he needed. It was by Beauvoys de Chauvincourt, a man considered an authority on werewolves in his day, and more interestingly, a familiar of them. The manner of his death was what had excited Ferguson—it indicated that the man may indeed have known the creatures firsthand. Beauvoys de Chauvincourt had gone out one night in search of his friends the werewolves and had simply disappeared. The dark suspicions of the time notwithstanding, Ferguson felt that he almost certainly had met his end observing the ancestors of the very creatures whose work the two cops had uncovered.

"Do you know books, Mr. Ferguson?"

"It's Doctor. Y-yes, I do. I can handle antique books."

"That's exactly what shouldn't be done with them." She eyed him. "I'll turn for you," she said firmly. "Let's go over there." She placed the book before him at a table and turned on one of the green-shaded lights.

"*Discours de la Lycanthropie, ou de la transformation des hommes en loups,*" read the title page.

"Turn."

She opened the book, turning the stiff pages to the frontispiece. And Ferguson felt sweat trickling down his temples. What he was seeing was so extraordinary that it was almost too much to bear without crying out. For there on the frontispiece of the ancient book was engraved a most amazing picture.

In this ancient engraving a sparse plain was

shown lit by a full moon. And walking through the plain was a man surrounded by things that looked somewhat like wolves but were not wolves. The man appeared at ease, strolling along playing a bagpipe that was slung over his shoulder. And the werewolves walked with him. The artist had rendered his subjects faithfully, Ferguson guessed. The heads with their high, wide brain cases and large eyes, the delicate and sinister paws, the voracious, knowing faces—it all fit the image Ferguson had created in his own mind of what the creatures must look like. And the man with them—incredible. In those days there must certainly have been communication between humans —some humans—and werewolves. De Chauvincourt himself must have . . . known them. And in the end they destroyed him.

"Turn."

Ferguson cursed his French. Here were lists of names—no, they were invocations of demons. Nothing to be learned here. "Turn."

More invocations.

"Keep turning."

The pages rolled past until something caught Ferguson's eye. "The Language They Assume."

Here followed a description of a complex language composed of tail movements, ear movements, growls, changes in facial expression, movements of the tongue and even clicks of the nails. It was as if human language had consisted not only of words but also of myriad gestures to augment those words.

And Ferguson knew something he hadn't known before. The creatures had vocal cords inadequate to the needs of true verbal language. How fast their brain must have evolved! Perhaps it took only fifty or a hundred thousand years and there they were, strange intelligent beings roaming the world in pursuit of man, engaged in the age-long hunt that occupied them to this day.

"Turn."

Here the book had another engraving—hand movements. "Can I get a Xerox of this page?"

"We can't copy this book."

He had brought paper and pencil and made rough sketches of the positions shown noting the meaning of each: stop, run, kill, attack, flee.

Stop—the tips of the fingers drawn down to the edge of the palm.

Run—the hands held straight out before the face.

Kill—the fists clenched, held against the throat.

Attack—the hands clutching the stomach like claws.

Flee—the palms against the forehead.

But these were human signals. Obviously the werewolves did not use such gestures among themselves because they were four-legged. There must have been a mutual language composed of signals like these between the werewolves and—

"Les vampires." The book said it. And there was the source of another legend, the vampires again. This must be the language they used to communicate with the werewolves. The vampires, those who followed the wolves and scavenged the remains. And the wolves needed them to induce people to come out of their locked houses.

What a different world it had been then! Werewolves and vampires stalking the night, the vampires luring people from their homes to be devoured. No wonder the Middle Ages were such a dark and cruel time. The terrors of the night were not imaginary at all, but stark realities faced from birth by everybody. Only as the sheer numbers of mankind had increased had the threat seemed to disappear. Man grew so numerous that the work of the werewolves was no longer noticed. In the days of de Chauvincourt the human helpers must already have been unnecessary in most places . . . and so as soon as the vampire weakened with age the werewolves turned on him. The librarian turned the page.

Ferguson jumped up. He tried to stop himself, but took an involuntary step backward and knocked over the chair.

"Sir!"

"I-I'm sorry!" He grabbed the chair, righted it. Now he felt like a fool. But the engraving that covered both of the pages facing was so terrible that he almost could not look at it.

He was seeing the werewolf close up, face to face. This would be a reliable rendition of the features. Even in this three-hundred-and-eighty-year-old engraving he could see the savagery, the sheer voraciousness of the creature. The eyes stared out at him like something from a nightmare.

And they *were* from a nightmare. His mind was racing now as he remembered, an incident that had occurred when he was no more than six or seven. They were in the Catskills, spending the summer near New Paltz in upstate New York. He was asleep in his ground-floor bedroom. Something awakened him. Moonlight was streaming in the open window. And a monstrous animal was leaning in, poking its muzzle toward him, the face clear in the moonlight.

He had screamed and the thing had disappeared in a flash. Nightmare, they said. And here it was staring at him again, the face of the werewolf.

The librarian closed the book. "That will be enough," she said. "I think you're upset."

"Those engravings—"

"They are horrible but I don't think it quite calls for—hysterics."

This amazed Ferguson. How dare she accuse him like that. "What would you say, madam, if those were engravings of real animals?"

"These are werewolves, Mr. Ferguson."

"*Doctor*. And I assure you that those animals are very real. You can imagine my shock when I saw them engraved in a book of that age, when the discovery was supposed to have taken place only a few weeks ago."

He left her to sort that one out. Too bad, too, she was a nice-looking woman, he wouldn't have minded getting to know her. But not now. He went down to the basement cloakroom and picked up his coat. Outside it had stopped snowing and the pedestrian traffic had transformed the sidewalk into gray slush. He turned the collar of his coat up against the surging wind and walked toward Sixth Avenue. He was going to see Tom Rilker, to get his help in determining a logical forage in the city for these creatures. There must be some area where lots of homeless people congregated. Not the Bowery, it was surrounded by heavily populated areas. Rilker would have some ideas.

Then he stopped. "My God," he thought, "those two cops have a point, what if the damn things are hunting me too?" Had they seen him with the cops last night? No way to tell. But if they *had* made the connection then he could be in mortal danger right now, even here in the middle of Forty-second Street.

He jammed his hands into his pockets and walked more quickly on. And he remembered the face of the nightmare in the moonlit window.

Dick Neff padded naked into the kitchen to fix himself another drink. He glanced at the kitchen clock—nearly noon. A shaft of sunlight shone in the kitchen window, as sharp and silver as a blade. First the snow had stopped and then the clouds had blown away. Now the wind moaned around the corner of the building and a bright dust of snow glittered through the sunlight. The glare hurt Dick's eyes, and he fumbled as he fixed his third Bloody Mary.

His mind was working, turning in a haze of anguish that would not go away. Becky, shooflies, burns, sorrow. He took a long pull on the drink and went into the living room. Goddamn, he couldn't believe what had *almost* happened to him, how close he had come to death. Burned and didn't even know it. He had been moving with Andy Jakes for six months, really working in with him. Hell, the guy was the biggest dealer in the Northeast. The Goddamn biggest fuckin' dealer. And Andy Jakes had been playing with Mr. Narcotics Cop. Jesus Christ! If he had collared Andy Jakes the shooflies would have laid off out of respect. Let it ride. But now he was just another victim of that brilliant crook's mind.

He had been about to enter Jakes's apartment, just heading toward the elevator when his teammates had gotten to him. Hold it, Dick, we got trouble. Bobby says the bug's pickin' up a lot of movement in there. Jakes's supposed to be alone?

—Yeah, he's alone. He's got the stuff in there. Ten kilos, let me go.

—Not alone. Don't go in. There's people in there, lots of people movin' around, not talkin'.

—Not talkin'? Shit, that must mean—

—They suspect a bug. And they suspect you. They're waiting for you, Dick.

—Oh, shit shit shit.

And he had stopped. He had not gone in. Follow your instincts, boy. Don't go in there. Another man might have shrugged it off and gone in. But not Dick.

And then they were off trying to get a warrant to bust the place when another call had come from the wire man. They were leaving. Christ! They *had* left. Surveillance followed them to Teterboro Airport, to a flight plan filed for Guadeloupe, Honduras, Brazil. Shit.

And they got the warrant and entered the apartment. So it's empty, of course, completely empty except for the Goddamn note. A note on nice engraved stationery, just as nice as you please. "Sorry, Richard," says the note. "I know how much of an embarrassment this will be to you. You be careful now. Cordially, Andy."

The guys got a whoop out of that note. "Hey *Richard*, Andy's some cool sonofabitch! Hey, beautiful, what a shit-heel."

The other guys were almost happy that Dick hadn't made his collar. Robin Hood. Sam Bass. The beautiful crook. Although there was also the other thing. Every gold shield in the division lusted after Andy Jakes and now it was open season on him again. Now other guys could take a crack, now Neff had blown it.

"Dick, you know what was waiting for you in there," Captain Fogarty had said. Good old Fogarty, always looking on the bright side. "A Goddamn arsenal. Wires says six or seven people were in there creepin' around as silent as cats. Waiting for you, Dick. Blown you away. I doubt if we'd ever laid eyes on you again, old buddy."

Maybe that would have been better. Because another captain, Captain Lesser of the Internal Affairs

Division, was closing in on Dick Neff. Another job blown. Somehow or other IAD had gotten wind of Dick's little deal with Mort Harper. What the hell was it anyway, a nice clean gambling establishment. The best clientele, even the fuckin' DA was there once. The fuckin' DA playing blackjack and lovin' it. Mort was protected! But he had put the finger on Neff, had built up his City Hall connections to the point that he didn't need Neff's silence anymore. "Hey, Mr. DA, y'know I got this monkey on my back, a little shit shakin' me down—"

"What the hell, this is a decent place." Movie stars. Politicians. Stockbrokers. Marble bar. Crushed-velvet carpets. Honest tables.

"Takin' out a grand a month, Mr. DA."

"Oh stop singin', Morty, I'll take care of it."

Oh, Morty was beautiful too. Smarter than Dick Neff. Everybody was smarter than Dick Neff. Even the shoofly Captain with his funny questions. "How many bank accounts you got? Your wife? Fine, could we see your income tax returns? Just routine. Somebody turned up a little dirt, Dick. Nothing really. Just routine. I got to go through the motions is all."

Go through the motions like hell! Dick Neff was due for a Board. Early retirement—hell, he'd be lucky to stay out of Attica! "You have a right to remain silent. You have a right to an attorney."

Silent, damn right. An attorney, damn right. He swallowed the last of the Bloody Mary and went to the sliding doors, looked out on the bright snow that covered the balcony.

And what he saw there made him gape. Pawprints as nice and clear as you please. He stared at them confused and disbelieving. Pawprints? And on the glass door a smear of another print. He squatted down and examined it. It could just be . . . a smeared pawprint . . . where something had tried the door. These prints must have been laid in the early morning after the snow had stopped. Shit, Becky wasn't imagining things after all. These damn prints were real. No way to deny it, and they didn't belong here.

He felt suddenly exposed in his nakedness and returned to the bedroom to dress. He shook his head, physically trying to shake out the welter of thoughts that clamored for attention. Dressing automatically, he fought for clarity. Those two crazies were right then? That scabrous old shitkicker Wilson wasn't senile after all. It seemed impossible, a trivial detail suddenly expanded to fill his whole consciousness with its importance. If she was in danger! If she was in danger and he didn't help her he would kill himself. That was the size of it, he would take out his Goddamn .38 and put the barrel in his mouth and pull the Goddamn trigger. Let the department face that one.

He put on a conservative suit and brushed down his hair until he looked reasonably presentable. He had to get that Starlight camera out of Yablonski in the Photo Unit. He had to look the part. Would the good news about Dick Neff have traveled as far as Yablonski? Probably not. Just routine, gimme the camera. Orders? Shit, c'mon man, I got to use this thing tonight. Easy. Peaches.

He left the apartment, then returned. As soon as he had gotten into the hall he had felt the absence of his pistol. Like he wasn't wearing underpants or something. The gun. He dropped off his overcoat and his jacket and pulled the holster containing the .32 out of his bureau drawer. The larger .38 he left behind. This pistol fitted neatly into a holster nestled in the small of his back, easy to get to, hard to spot. You weren't too comfortable when you sat down in a hard chair but other than that the small of the back was a beautiful hiding place for a weapon.

Now he glanced at the pawprints again. They were ugly, frightening. He tested the door and then pulled the curtains closed. This time he left and did not return. Outside the wind hit him with the force of a powerful shove. It bit right through his coat and made his muscles grow taut with cold. He wanted another drink, better make a pit stop on the way down. What the hell, make it now. Across the street was O'Faolian's where he usually made a stop on his way to the apartment. He went there now.

"Hiya, Frenchie," he said as he slipped up to the bar, "gimme a Bloody." The bartender made it and set it in front of him. Instead of going about his business, though, he hovered there fooling with glasses.

"You want something?" Dick asked. Frenchie was not a friendly guy, not the type to make small talk.

"Nah. A guy's been in is all. A guy wantin' to know about you."

"So?"

"So I don't say nothin'."

"Good. What else is new?"

"You don't wanna know what he's askin' about?" Frenchie looked surprised, a little disappointed.

"I can pretty well guess," Dick said expansively. "He wanted to know if I had ever been seen in here with a little kike five-two, greasy black hair, wire-rimmed glasses, name of Mort Harper. And you said no."

"Hell I didn't say nothin'. Not yes or no." He looked pleadingly at Neff. "The guy, he flashed on me, see. What could I do? You don't get 'em flashin' unless it's serious business."

Dick chuckled. "Thanks, Frenchie," he said. He put a five on the bar and left. Damn decent of the little jerk to tell him that Captain Lesser had been in here confirming that this was where Dick met Mort Harper to take the pass. How long had it been going on? Dick couldn't remember exactly. God, though, it must be years. All that money right up to the Stranger Nursing Home. Right up there to keep the old man in cigars.

The old man. A pang of sentiment went through him, thinking of the old senile man who had once been so powerful, so determined. Drove a bus for the Red and Tan Line. Retirement pay plus Social Security: $177.90 a lousy month. Senile decay, Parkinson's disease, helplessness had turned to violence, periodic seizures, a thousand-dollar-a-month problem. You don't give your old man over to the tender care of the State, not when you've seen the inside of those places firsthand. "Gonna make you go naked for a day, you old fart, you don't stop that shakin'. Stop it, you gettin' on my *nerves*. OK, fuck you, gimme that gown!" That's the kind of thing that went on. A bunch of monsters making life hell for the old and helpless. "Come on, guinea, light my cigarette! Fuckin' old shit." Dick had seen what it was like in those State hospitals, a playground for sadistic perverts masquerading as attendants. No place for his old man.

All of a sudden he was shaking uncontrollably, standing there in the doorway of the bar. He grabbed at the door handle to steady himself, then reeled back into the bar. He dropped to a table. "Shit, Frenchie," he said, "get some food in me. I feel like shit."

Frenchie produced a hamburger and some stale fries and as soon as he bit into the food Dick found that he was ravenously hungry. He wolfed down the burger, ordered another. Now he leaned back, relaxed into the mild fog that the drinks had produced, that and the ease of the food.

What the fuck had he been doing? Oh yeah, going to get that damn camera for Becky, his kid bride. Kid, hell, she was only a year younger than him and he was no kid. She was still a damn good lay, though, especially the way she came. Like a Goddamn female freight train. She made you feel like you were worth something. None of the others ever really did that. They were all pretending, wanting to fuck a cop for reasons that had nothing to do with love. Pros that needed a friend, most of them. What the hell, they threw it at you. Becky didn't know and never would if Dick had anything to say about it. What they had together was something special, something no pro was going to take away from them.

Well, what the hell, what she didn't know wasn't going to hurt her.

"Frenchie! Bring me another Bloody."

Frenchie came over. "Nosir," he said, "can't do that."

"Why the fuck not! What is this, a Salvation Army Shelter?"

"You're on duty. I'm not gettin' you drunk in here. Shit, you came in here half looped. Now you go on about your business. I don't want no cops gettin' drunk in here. It's a bad rap with the department and you know it. Go somewhere else."

"I'm not on duty. I'm graveyard this week."

"You're carryin' a piece, Lieutenant Neff. I can't serve you any more booze."

"Jesus Christ, Mr. Hot Shit—OK, I'll take my trade elsewhere. But don't say I didn't warn you, Frenchie. You look out for your ass, hear. Just look out real careful, you never know what's gonna come up your back."

Frenchie walked away shaking his head.

Dick left, wanting at once to say something to appease Frenchie, wishing he hadn't been so nasty, yet still feeling in himself the urge to be even nastier, to strike out at somebody. He hailed a cab to go to headquarters.

Yablonski's office was a clutter of photographic equipment, report forms, pictures tacked to walls, half-empty coffee cups. "Hey, Dick," the little man said when he looked up. "What brings you down here?"

"Your beautiful face. I need some night photography equipment."

"Yeah? You got infrared uptown. If you need a photographer forget it until next week, my guys are—"

"Hooked up. No, we don't need a photographer."

"You guys take up time. I can't spare men to spend days and days sitting in cars doing what any moron—"

"Like me can do."

"Yeah. So why don't you just use your own infrared equipment and let me the fuck alone."

"Because I don't need infrared. I need high power and long range. You know infrared's no good over fifty yards."

"No, I didn't know that. Hell, Dick, it's my business, don't take that tone with me."

Neff closed his eyes. What made this little fart so Goddamn difficult to deal with? He always talked in arguments. "I need the Starlight camera."

"Like hell."

"For one night."

"I repeat: like hell. That camera doesn't leave this Bureau without a trained operator, meaning me. And I'm not takin' it out without a signed letter from somebody I can't turn down."

"Come on now, don't get crazy. I only need it for

one night. Think if you don't give it to me and I lose an important collar as a result. Think how that'll look."

"It won't look like nothin'. Officially you don't even know that camera exists."

"Oh, cut the crap. We got an eyes only on it in 1975. That thing's been goin' in and out of Narcotics ever since."

"Well, I didn't know that." Yablonski glowered, pugnacious, aware that Dick was somehow edging him into a corner.

"How's the wife?"

"What's she got to do with it? She the suspect?"

"Just trying to be friendly. Look, I'll level with you. I got a big collar coming up but we need evidence. We got to have pictures."

"Big deal. Use fast film. There's plenty of light in the streets."

Dick sighed, pretended to give up on something. "I guess I gotta tell you more than you need to know. We got a big pass comin' up. We just can't risk missin' it. We gotta have that camera."

Yablonski glared at him. He did not like to let his precious Starlight camera out of his personal control. On the other hand he had no intention of spending the night on some dangerous narcotics stakeout. He stood up, brought out his keys and went to a bank of lockers that covered one wall of the office.

"I'm gonna be a sucker," he said, "let you take this thing out and get it smashed. You know how much this thing cost the City of New York?"

"Nothin'."

"About a hundred grand. Hardly nothing."

"It's CIA surplus circa Vietnam. You know damn well we got it for nothing."

"Well, I'm not sure we'd get another if we lost or busted this one." He removed a metal case from the locker and placed it gently on his desk. "You used this before?"

"You know I have."

"Well I'm gonna go through the drill anyway!" He opened the case and pulled out a boxy object made of gray, burnished metal. It was about the size and shape of a two-pound can of coffee with binocular eyepieces on one end and a large, gleaming fisheye of a lens on the other. The body of the thing was entirely featureless, except for a barely visible indentation obviously intended for a thumb.

"You open the control panel like this," Yablonski said, pressing on the indentation. A three-inch square of surface metal slid back to reveal a panel containing two black knobs and a small slit. "You slide in the film." He pushed a small black rectangle into the opening. "That gives you two hundred shots. That's the bottom number in the readout you'll see in the lower right quadrant of the frame when you look through the camera. Above that's the ambient light reading. You set the top knob so that it reads the same value. Here—" He held the camera out. Dick took it, put it up to his eyes. The image was blurred but the three numbers were clear. "Read off from the bottom up."

"The bottom number says two hundred. The middle one sixty-six, the top point-oh-six."

"Meaning you've got two hundred shots left, the ambient light level is sixty-six and you are pointing the camera at an object point-oh-six meters away. Now gimme." He took it back. "You set the top knob at sixty-six and the bottom one at point-oh-six. Now look."

"What the hell is it?"

"The top corner of the locker, dummy. It's magnified so much you can't tell what you're seeing that close. Point the camera out the window." Dick swung the camera around. The top two readings flickered and changed as he moved it, then the limbs of a tree down near street level leaped into view. He could see where ice adhered to the twigs and where the sun had made it drop away. Yablonski guided his hand to the thumb indentation. "Pull back on it." There was a click. The little door had closed on the side of the camera and a red light had gone on above the three green numbers of the readout. "You get a light?"

"Right."

"Ready to shoot. Push forward."

The camera made five shots in quick succession. The film indicator now read 195.

"It always shoots in increments of five. Now press inward on the indentation." The scene pulled back and revealed the sidewalk below. "You go down to fifty millimeters. Fifty to five hundred, that's the lens. If you push forward and down at the same time the camera will take a series of shots while the lens is moving. No problem. Just remember to always close the control housing before you try to shoot." Dick took the camera from his eyes. Yablonski was pointing at the control housing. "That activates the camera. And if you change position always check focus. In operation it doesn't matter too much, but remember that the camera is at its sharpest focus when the object you are shooting is exactly as far away as that little indicator in there says. You want it to change, you've got to adjust it with the knob."

"That's all? I remembered everything."

"Well, aren't we wonderful. Just don't bring it back to me in a shoebox, for Chrissake. And get the fucker back here before noon tomorrow or I'll be on your ass."

"Oh, yes sir, Mr. Commissioner, just like you say."

"Come on, Dick, take it easy. How much film you want?"

"Another couple of boxes. That stuff's really compact. You sure there are two hundred shots?"

"Of course. You think the camera would lie?"

Dick put the machine back in its case and hefted it. He left Yablonski staring after him.

As soon as he was gone, Yablonski was on the phone. "Captain Lesser," he said crisply, "you told me you wanted a call if Dick Neff came around here for anything. Well, he did. He checked out the Starlight camera."

Chapter 8

The search teams kept coming back empty-handed. It looked as if the park wasn't going to yield any worthwhile clues. A bench covered with a slick of red ice—human blood. Some tattered remnants that might have been the victim's clothes. That was all. No body, no ID, no witnesses. And so far, no report of a missing person. The cops were waiting for orders to move them out. The precinct wasn't going to spend much more time on this, it was just another one of those mysteries that the city tossed up. Obviously somebody had died here, but in the absence of anything except blood there wasn't much that could be done to find the killer.

"Maybe it'll tell us something," the Medical Examiner said as a patrolman handed him a clear plastic bag full of tattered cloth.

Becky Neff said nothing. More vague evidence.

Even Wilson's experience last night was nothing but
hearsay. Hell, maybe he got panicked by some dogs.
The trouble was, you weren't going to get headquarters to take a chance on the theory. The man
who sanctioned an investigation of werewolves in this
city was headed for early retirement if that investigation didn't prove itself.

"Do you believe me?" Wilson said into the silence
in the car.

"Yeah," Becky replied, surprised at the question.

"Not you, dummy. The genius. I want to know
if he believes me."

"If it wasn't delirium tremens, I'd say you saw
what you saw."

"Thanks." Since relating his story Wilson had
fallen into a silence. Becky didn't know whether he
was thinking something out or simply sinking into
depression. If possible he seemed to be getting more
morose.

When Wilson turned to stare again out of the car
window, Evans raised his eyebrows. "Listen," he said
to Wilson's back, "if it makes any difference I really do
believe you. I just wish to God I could do more for
you than that."

"Every little bit helps," Becky said acidly.

"I'm sure. It must be hell."

"Yeah," Wilson said, "it's that."

Suddenly there was a flurry of activity. A couple
of park cops jumped on scooters; guys from the 20th
Precinct piled into squad cars. Becky flipped on the
radio to catch the activity. "—thirteen, repeat, thirteen to Bethesda Fountain."

"Jesus—" Becky started the car and followed the
others into the park. They slurried in the new snow,
heading for the emergency. A signal-13 was the most

serious call a policeman could put out: it meant that
an officer was in distress. It would cause immediate
response from all nearby units—and often some from
farther away. It was the call that cops hated most to
hear and wanted most to answer.

The area around Bethesda Fountain was once
elegant. Once, during summer, there was an open-air
restaurant where you could drink wine and watch the
fountain. Then the sixties had come, and drugs, and
Bethesda Fountain had become an open-air drug
bazaar. The restaurant had closed. The fountain had
become choked with filth. Graffiti had appeared. Murders had taken place. Now the once-bustling spot was
the same in summer as in winter: empty, abandoned,
destroyed. And crumpled on the esplanade overlook-
ing the fountain was a blue uniform, its occupant bent
over almost with his forehead touching the snow. The
scooter cops were the first to get to him. "Shot," one
of them shouted. An ambulance could already be
heard screaming over from Roosevelt Hospital.

Becky pulled the Pontiac up behind the scooters
and the three of them jumped out. "I'm a doctor,"
Evans shouted pointlessly. There wasn't a person in
the NYPD who didn't know that the Medical Examiner was a doctor. Evans reached the wounded man,
followed closely by Becky. He was a middle-aged
cop, one of the guys who had been out beating the
bushes for evidence, one of the searchers. "Fuckin'
dog," he said almost laughing, "fuckin' dog bit a hole
in my side." The voice was anguished and confused.
"Fuckin' *dog*!"

"Holy shit," Evans said.

"Is it bad, Doc?" the man said through gathering
tears.

Evans looked away. "I'm not movin' you till the

stretcher gets here, buddy. You aren't losing any blood out of it, however bad it is."

"Oh, fuck, it hurts!" he shouted. Then his eyes rolled and his head slumped to his chest.

"Get some pressure on it, he's passed out," Evans said. Two of the man's friends applied a pressure bandage to the gash in his overcoat. "Where's that friggin' meatwagon!" Evans rasped. "This man's not gonna make it if they don't hurry."

Just then it pulled up and the medics piled out with their equipment. They cut the coat away and for the first time the wound was visible.

It was devastating. You could see the blue-black bulge of the man's intestine pulsing in the blood. Becky started to sob, stifling it as it came. *They* had done this! Just now, just minutes ago. They were right around here! She put a trembling hand on the M. E.'s shoulder.

"Leave me alone." He was examining the wound. "Move him out," he murmured to the orderlies. He looked up at Becky. "He ain't gonna live," he said simply.

They got the man on the stretcher and took him to the ambulance, heading for the emergency room as fast as they could go. There was an M.D. on the wagon so Evans returned to Becky's car.

The other cops were still standing in a little clump, staring at the blood-smeared thrash marks in the snow. For a moment nobody spoke. What could you say? A man had just had his intestines laid open— and he claimed it had been done by a dog. The Precinct Captain came up puffing hard. For some reason he hadn't made it into a car. "What the fuck— what the fuck happened?"

"Baker got hit."

"What by? Hit and run?"

"Something took about nine inches of hide off his gut. Laid him open."

"What the fuck—"

"You said that, sir. He says it was a dog."

Becky felt Wilson's hand grasp her shoulder. A sharp pang of fear ran through her. "Listen, kid," he said in an unnaturally calm tone, "stroll real easy-like over to those two scooters." He breathed it into her ear. "You can ride a scooter?"

"I suppose."

"Good, because you gotta. Just go real easy."

"What about our car?"

"Stay the hell away from our car! And when you get on that scooter, *move.*"

She didn't ask questions even though she didn't quite understand why he wanted to do this. You get to trust a good partner, and Becky trusted Wilson more than enough to just do what he said without asking why. He'd do the same for her. Hell, he had often enough.

As she walked she noticed that he was meandering in the same direction, getting closer and closer to the scooters without making it particularly obvious.

"Now, Becky!"

They leaped, the scooters coughed to life, they skidded onto the snowy pavement, Becky swayed, righted herself and headed straight down the Mall, which stretched to Park East Drive and the safety of the streets. She heard a shout behind, an incredulous shout from one of the scooter cops who saw the two detectives suddenly hijack his transportation. Then something else was there, a gray shape moving like the wind, a furious pulsing mass of hair and muscle. And she knew what had happened. "Oh God God God," she said softly as she rode. She turned the gas all the way up and the scooter darted through the snow, bouncing and shaking, threatening from instant to instant to go into a skid. Thirty. Forty. Fifty. Was the thing dropping back? She risked a glance. God, it was right there. Its teeth were bared, and its *face*, something unbelievable, twisted with hate and fury and effort—animal, man, *something*. She choked out a sob and just held on. The thing's breathing was clearly audible for a moment, then it fell back, fell back making little sharp noises, sounds of pure anger! It was gone and the scooters bounded off the Mall, crashed through ripping naked shrubs, shot into the roadway and tore down toward the park entrance at Fifth Avenue. Ahead the Plaza Hotel and the General Motors Building. General Sherman with his permanent toupee of pigeon droppings. Horse-drawn carriages waiting in rows, the breath of the horses steaming. Then stopping, bringing the scooters to a halt at the bustling entrance to the hotel. "We're at the Plaza," Wilson was growling into the scooter's radio, "come get us."

A squad car appeared. "What's the problem, Lieutenant?" the driver said. "You just got reported for stealing two scooters."

"Fuck that. We were under orders. We thought we saw a suspect."

"Yeah. So get in. We'll drive you up to the Twentieth."

They left the scooters for the men from the park precinct who were approaching in another car. Wilson and Neff were silent as they rode toward the precinct, Wilson because he had nothing to say, Becky because she couldn't have talked if she had wanted to. It felt funny to her to be alive right now, like she had just broken through a wall into a time she was never intended to see. "I was supposed to die back there," she thought. She looked at her partner. He had figured it out just in time—a trap. God, what a clever trap! And they had slipped out just as it had been sprung.

"You know what happened," Wilson asked.

"Yeah."

He nodded, silent for a few minutes. The squad car wheeled up Central Park West. Wilson touched the door lock; the windows were closed. "They're very smart," he said.

"We knew that."

"But that was a very neat trap. Wounding that guy . . . knowing that we would respond . . . setting an ambush. All very smart."

"How did you figure it out? I've gotta confess I was completely taken in."

"You oughta start thinking defensively. They wounded that guy, didn't kill him. That's what tipped me off. Why wound, when killing is easier? It had to be the same reason a hunter wounds. To lure. When I figured that out, I decided we ought to go for the scooters. Frankly I'm surprised we made it."

The squad car pulled up to the precinct house. After a long look up and down the street the two detectives got out and hurried up the steps. The desk sergeant looked up. "Captain's waiting for you," he said.

"Must be antsy as hell," Wilson muttered as they walked into the Captain's office.

He was a trim, neatly turned out man with steel-gray hair and a deeply wrinkled face. But his movements, his posture, belonged to a younger man. He had just taken off his overcoat and sat down at his desk. Now he looked up, raising his eyebrows. "I'm Captain Walker," he said. "What the hell's going on?"

"We saw a suspect—"

"Can that bullshit. Everybody saw those dogs come out from under your car and chase you half-way to Grand Army Plaza. What the hell was that all about?"

"Dogs?" Wilson was no actor. The fact that he was hiding something was perfectly clear to Becky. But maybe she underestimated him.

"Yes, dogs. I saw them. We all did. And Baker said it was dogs that laid him open."

Wilson shook his head. "Beats the hell out of me."

"Look, I don't know quite what's going on here—I mean you two are some kind of special team, that's OK by me—but I got a guy hurt bad down at Roosevelt and he says a dog did it. I saw you two light out like you were runnin' from death itself. And you were chased by two dogs. Now I'd like to know what the fuck's goin' on." His phone rang. A few muttered words, a curse, then he hung up. "And so would the New York *Post*. They got a photographer and a reporter waiting out front to see me right now. What do I tell them?"

Becky stepped in. Wilson had tucked his chin into his neck, squared his shoulders, and was about to blow it. "Tell them what's probably true. Your man was wounded in an unknown manner. I mean if somebody's colon is lying on the sidewalk they might get a little delirious. He passed out right after his statement, didn't he? And as for dogs chasing us, it might have happened, but it was a complete coincidence."

The man stared at them. "You're bullshitting. I don't know why but I'm not gonna push it. Just get one thing straight: I don't owe you two a Goddamn thing. Now take off. Go wherever you go."

"What about the reporter?" Becky asked. That was important. You couldn't leak this to the press, not unless the problem could be solved.

"So I'll tell the reporters what Baker said. And I'll tell them that he was delirious. Is that sufficient?"

"What do you mean, sufficient? How should we know?"

"You're the people keeping this thing under wraps, aren't you? You're the ones who go around and make sure no shaggy dog stories get into the paper, aren't you?"

Wilson closed his eyes and shook his head. "Let's get out of here," he said. "We got better things to do."

They left the precinct and hailed a cab. Obviously there was no point in asking the precinct for transportation back to Bethesda Fountain where their car was waiting. As they approached the car Wilson craned his neck out of the cab window to make sure nothing was under it. But he needn't have bothered. The car wasn't going anywhere.

The doors were open. The interior of the car was ripped to shreds. And it was full of bloody pulp. "Jesus," the cabdriver blurted, "this your car?"

"Yeah. It was."

"We gotta get a cop." He gunned the motor. "Who's in there? What a fuckin' mess!"

"We *are* the police." Becky held her shield against the bulletproof glass separating the passenger seat from the driver's compartment. The driver nodded and headed for the Central Park precinct house on Seventy-ninth Street. A few moments later they pulled to a stop in front. Neff, Wilson and the driver got out and approached the desk sergeant through the worn double-doors of the building. "Yeah," he said looking up. "You two. I hear you're a couple of mean motherfuckers on a scooter."

"Get your guys back over to the Fountain," Wilson rasped. "The Chief Medical Examiner just got himself killed."

Becky felt the blood drain out of her face. Of course, that must be who was in the car. It had to be. Poor Evans, he was a hell of a good man! "Goddamn it," Becky said.

"We were stupid," Wilson said softly. "We should have warned him in advance." He laughed, a bitter little noise. "They missed out on the main event. So they went for the consolation prize. Let's get Underwood on the phone."

Wilson took on Underwood. Becky watched him, annoyed that her usual role was being usurped. "Look," Wilson said into the phone, "you got problems. You got a cop on critical at Roosevelt with his guts laid open. Says dogs did it. You got that? Dogs. Plus you got a reporter from the *Post* on it, and more to follow. So listen, dummy. You got one Chief Medical Examiner just murdered out by Bethesda Fountain. And you're gonna find it was done by claws and teeth. And if you want this one wrapped up real good—"

"Oh my God, what about Ferguson!"

"—just sit on your can and wait for it." He slammed down the phone. "You're right! Let's go!" They headed for the motor pool.

"Get a car," Becky snapped at the dispatcher.

"Well, you gotta—"

"Matter of life and death, Sergeant. What number?"

"Let's see—two-two-nine. Green Chevy, you'll see it against the wall out near the gas pumps."

They headed for the car. To the south the sorrowful moan of sirens sounded their dirge for Evans. "Lot of fucking good they'll do," Wilson said quietly. "That guy was just goo."

"You're sure?"

"What?"

"It was him."

"Just drive the car, Becky."

God, he was a condescending bastard. Even if it

was self-evident to Wilson, she could still hope. Evans was a great man, a civic institution in New York City for forty years. Probably the best practitioner of forensic medicine in the world. Plus he was a good friend. His loss left a damn big hole. And the manner of his death was going to stop the presses even over at the *Times*.

"This story's gonna get out."

"You don't say. By the way, Ferguson'll be at the museum."

"Look, I don't give a damn how bad things are, it's no excuse to pretend I'm some kind of a dummy. I know where the hell he is."

"Yeah, well—"

"Well nothing, just keep your jerkoff opinions about lady cops to yourself and do your Goddamn job."

"Oh, come on, Becky, I didn't mean that."

"You did, but I don't mind. I guess I'm just nervous."

"That's funny. Can't imagine why."

They got to the museum, stopped the car right in front of the main entrance and ran in as quickly as possible. It was necessary to go through the drill of getting downstairs to see Ferguson. When they were finally on it the elevator seemed to take hours to reach the sub-basement.

The room was full of people working on the birds. There was a smell of glue and paint, and an air of quiet intensity. Ferguson's office door was closed. Becky opened it and stuck her head in.

"You! I've been trying to call you all over town!"

They went in, closing the door behind them. Wilson leaned against it. "I wish this cubicle had a ceiling," Becky said, "it'd be more secure."

"Secure?"

"We'd better fill you in. I'm afraid you're in great danger, Doctor. Evans—the Medical Examiner—he's just been mauled to death."

Ferguson reacted as if he had been hit. His hands moved trembling to his face. Then he slowly lowered them, staring into them. "I've found out a lot about the werewolves this morning," he said almost inaudibly. "I've been down to the public library." He looked up, his face impassively concealing the determination he had formed to try to communicate with the creatures. "It's all there, just like I thought it would be. The evidence that this species is intelligent is pretty strong. Canis Lupus Sapiens. The Wolfen. That's what I want to call them."

Wilson didn't say anything; Becky didn't want to. She stared at the scientist. Wolfen indeed. They were killers. Ferguson's expression betrayed his innocent excitement at his discovery. It was obvious that he still didn't understand the extremity of his danger. She felt sorry for him—sorry in a detached, professional way like she felt sorry for the people left behind after murders. Residue, Wilson called them, the red-eyed wives and numbed husbands who were usually found slobbering over their victim's body. Most murder is a family affair. But far worse were the cases where you had to call some frantic soul who had been waiting hours for a loved one to come home—somebody who wasn't on the way anymore. "Hello, Mr. X, we're detectives. May we come in? Very sorry to tell you, Mrs. X was found murdered at blah blah," the rest of it said into a fog of grief beyond communication.

"Join the hunted," Wilson said, "and welcome. Maybe we'll form a co-op."

The humor was strained but it seemed to get a positive reaction from Ferguson. "You know," he said, "the damn thing of it is, these creatures are so *murder-*

ous. That's what makes them unusual. Canines are a notably friendly race. Take the timber wolf—all the legends, the Jack London stories, that's mostly crap. I mean, you threaten a wolf and you know what'll happen? That wolf will turn over on its back like a dog. They aren't dangerous." He laughed. "It's ironic. Science just figured that out about the wolf in the past few years. Here we were so sure that the great canine predator was just a myth—and now this. But I think we have an extraordinary chance here—there must be some point of communication between us and them."

"To a deer, Doctor Ferguson, the wolf is incredibly dangerous. No wolf is going to turn turtle if it's threatened by a deer. The wolf isn't dangerous to man because he doesn't count us among his prey. But look at the deer—to them the wolf is a scourge from hell."

Ferguson nodded slowly. "So these . . . things are to us as wolves are to deer. I agree. They are also an intelligent species and as such represent an extraordinary opportunity."

Wilson laughed out loud. The sound sent a chill down Becky's spine. It was not the laugh of a normal human being but that of somebody deeply frightened, bordering on hysteria. She wondered how much longer she would have his help. And his mind! He had saved them in the park by bare seconds. How many more times would he do it? Or could he? Would the traps just keep getting more and more subtle until finally the hunted were down? As far as Ferguson and his ideas about communication, she dismissed them. He hadn't seen what these creatures did to people.

"Let's plan out our next moves," she said. "We've got to be very damn careful if what just happened is any example of what's on the way." Ferguson asked for the details of Evans' death. Wilson related the story, very factually, very coldly, how the werewolves had wounded a patrolman out searching for evidence, how this had lured them into an ambush, the escape on scooters just at the moment Wilson pieced the thing together, the subsequent discovery of the M. E.'s body in the car.

"So they missed you and took him instead."

Wilson was silent for a long moment. "Yeah," he said at last, "I wish to hell I had realized—but I didn't. I just never thought of him being in danger."

"Why not?"

"In retrospect I suppose it's obvious. But I didn't think of it then. That's the damn truth." He breathed a ragged sigh. "The old s.o.b. was a good man. He was a hell of a pro."

Coming from Wilson that was a soaring epitaph indeed. "Let's plan our moves," Becky said again.

"Plan what! We haven't got anything to plan!"

"Oh come on, Wilson, take it easy. We might as well try. I thought we were going to try to take pictures tonight. Let's plan that."

"How about planning how to survive until tonight? Wouldn't that be a better thing to plan, since it looks kind of hard to do?"

She shook her head and said nothing. He was a petulant bastard. Up to now she had relied on him, had always assumed that he would pull them through. And he had. This morning was an example. But he was cracking now, getting closer and closer to the edge. Wilson had always been afraid of life, now he was afraid of death when it came close. And how did Becky herself feel? As if she didn't intend to die. She was afraid and not sure that any of them would survive—least of all herself—but she wasn't about to give in. Wilson had taken charge of this case so far and he had done fine. But he was getting tired. It looked like her turn now.

"Wilson, I said we were going to plan our moves. Now listen. First, we've got to let Underwood know the score. We've got evidence that's going to be God-damn hard to ignore. I mean, Evans getting murdered is international news. They've got to say something about it. And you can be damn sure the TV stations and the papers are on the scene. How are they going to take it? Medical Examiner mutilated beyond recognition. It's going to require a damn good explanation."

"Don't breathe a word of this to the papers," Ferguson said, suddenly understanding the significance of Becky's statements. "You'll cause all kinds of trouble—panic, fear, it'll be hell. And the Wolfen will be threatened in just the way we don't want—grossly, by idiots with shotguns. Some might get hurt at first but they'll adapt quickly, and when they do they'll be that much harder to find. Our chance will be lost—maybe for generations to come."

"How hard to find are they now?" Wilson asked bitterly.

"Well, obviously hard. I wasn't saying that they were easy to deal with at all. But you might not realize it, Detective Wilson—if these creatures get it into their heads to completely disappear, they can do it."

"You mean become invisible?" Wilson's voice was rising. He seemed about to lunge at the scientist.

"For all practical purposes. Right now they're being very careless. Witness the fact that you've seen them. That's a sign of carelessness on their part. And there's a reason. They know that it's a risk to allow themselves to be seen by you, but it's very limited because they also know that you will in all likelihood not live to describe them to others."

"Maybe and maybe not."

"They're predators, Detective, and they have the arrogance of predators. Don't expect them to fear man. Do we fear hogs and sheep? Do we respect them?"

"We damn well aren't sheep, Doctor! We're people, we have brains and souls!"

"Sheep have brains. As for souls, I have no way of measuring that. But we know every possible move a sheep might make. There is no way a sheep can fool a man. I suspect that the analogy holds true here too."

"Wonderful. Then what am I doing alive? Wouldn't they have killed me last night in the alley of Becky's building? Wouldn't that make sense? But they didn't. They weren't fast enough. I got my gun out before they made their move."

Becky broke in. "I hope they *are* arrogant, frankly. It's our only chance."

Ferguson raised his eyebrows and smiled. "Yes," he said, "unless they're playing a little game with you."

"A game," Wilson said, "what do you mean a game?"

"Well, they're intelligent, they're hunters, creatures of action. Most of their hunting must be pretty damn easy. You're different, though, you're a challenge. They might be spreading it out for fun."

Wilson looked as if he would like to throttle the scientist. "Fine," he said, "if they're playing games with us let 'em play. Maybe we'll get the fuck out of the trap in the meantime." He spat. "Who the hell knows?"

They ran, desperate for cover. Humanity was pouring into the park, policemen by the hundreds swarming down every path, passing over in helicopters, roaring along in cars and on scooters. The sharp scent of human flesh exposed to cold air mingled with the suffocating sweetness of exhaust fumes. And they came from every direction. All around the park the sirens shrieked, the tone causing sharp agony in the ears of the fleeing pack. Voices called back and forth over radios; men shouted to one another. And then there was a new smell, thick and putrid—a parody of their own scent. It was dogs. The pack stopped, cocked ears: three dogs by the sound of their claws clattering on ice; eager to be unleashed by the exciting rasp of their breathing. Three dogs, heavy, strong, excited. And they had the scent, the pack could practically feel them yearning on their tethers, choking themselves with eagerness to give chase.

Very well, let them come and die. Dogs could no more hunt the pack than chimpanzees could hunt men. Defense against these animals was based on established procedures because the pattern of the animals' attack never varied. The only trouble was that it meant more time wasted in this accursed park— more time for the swarm of policemen to get closer, more time for their luck to run out.

And the pack was divided now: on one side were the two old ones and the second-mated pair. On the other was the third-mated pair. This pair, the youngest, had run after the two humans who had escaped just an instant too soon, and given up the chase a few moments early. Another breath, another footstep and the quarry would have been down. The beautifully laid plan was wasted—or almost wasted; the old man in the car had been all they could kill. Very well. Certainly he had known of the pack. They had heard him in the car, his booming old voice muttering human words with the others . . . words like wolf . . . wolf . . . wolf . . .

Human language, so complex and rapidly spoken, was hard to follow, but they all knew certain words that had been handed down from generation to generation. Among these was "wolf." Traveling between cities the pack sometimes encountered these gentle things of the forest. They had soft, beautiful faces and sweet eyes, and the blank expressions of animals. Yet one almost wanted to speak to them, to wave the tail or knock the paw, but they had not the brains to answer. They would trot along behind a pack for days, their empty smiling heads wagging from side to side— and cower away when the pack took a man for food. After that the wolves would slink out of sight, fascinated and terrified by the ways of the pack. But wolves were wild and never accompanied the packs into the cities. Among men only the packs were safe— and so safe! Such a huge quantity of food in the cities, all of it blankly oblivious, as easy to hunt as a tree would be.

The wolf looked not unlike the werewolf. And in the car they had been saying the word over and over —wolf . . . wolf. So the little old man was contaminated by the other two, the two who knew. He died instantly. They had crept up to the car the moment the other cars had left in search of the two on the scooters. They had crept closer and closer, and one of them had opened the door. The man's hands fluttered up before his face and his bowels let loose. That was all that happened. Then they were on him, pulling and tearing, ripping full of rage, spitting the bloody bits out, angry that the two important ones had been missed, angry that this one also dared to confront them with his evil knowledge. They had cracked open the head and plunged their claws into the brains, plunged and torn to utterly and completely destroy the filthy knowledge.

And in their anger they had also shredded the interior of the car, ripping at the seats for sheer hate, feeling the red pulse of their frustration well up inside them as they tasted the very salt of the two that were to be killed. They tore the interior of the car apart, and would have done more to it if they had known how. Somehow the humans made these things move, and they made other similar things fly in the air. Humans flew in these. And then one of them caused this thing to make a noise. They abandoned it at once, afraid that it would begin to move with the pack still inside. Man was of two faces: naked and weak, clothed and powerful. The same man who had no defense on his own might be completely invulnerable in a car with a gun.

The pack had speed and hearing and eyesight and most of all smell to protect itself. Man had metal and weapons. They envied man his big flat paddles that could do so much more than their hands. The things looked clumsy but they were flexible. It was with his paddles or hands that man fashioned these mysterious objects that rolled and flew, and the guns that shot. And it was because of them that man had been able to inhabit the cities. No pack knew how these cities came about, but man inhabited them, keeping for himself the warmth they produced in winter, and the dryness that was not affected even by the most violent rain. While the sky poured water or snow man sat comfortably in the cities. How these things grew and why man possessed them nobody could say.

Just as well—it kept the herds of men closely gathered so that hunting was easy.

But hunting could also be fun, if, for example, you left the city and went into the forest during the season of dead leaves. Then you would find men armed with guns, men stalking deer and moose, men who could be dangerous if you let them. It was a good game—you made a little extra noise and let the man become aware of you. Then you hunted him, letting him see just enough so that he would try hard to escape. And they tried so hard! They swam into rivers, climbed trees, covered themselves with leaves. They tried all manner of stratagem, doubling back, leaping ravines, swinging through forests in the tree-tops. And all the time their scent followed them like a blaring noise. But the pack made conditions for itself during these hunts. If the man got to a certain point, he couldn't be chased again for a hundred heartbeats. If he got to another point, two hundred. So the better he was, the harder they made it for themselves. Finally, with the very good ones there was a last desperate chase before he reached his car, a chase that ended with him rolling up useless windows, fumbling with keys, and dying there, being eaten while the blood still pulsed through his exhausted heart.

But not many of them were fun to hunt. For the most part it was the same routine as it would be with these eager, stupid dogs. Certainly the humans were closing in, but it was very hard to believe that a man not encased in metal was a threat. Killing the three dogs would waste a little time, but in the end the pack would escape from these human beings. Only if the whole city was aware would humanity become dangerous. Everybody knew that this was possible, that the two enemies could contaminate all the men of this city with the dirty knowledge. Then the pack would be endangered, then the pack would flee. But it wasn't necessary just yet.

The dogs were released. Their voices pealed, communicating the crazed, heedless excitement that was characteristic of the creature. Their breath began to pulse, their feet to pad faster and faster as they ran madly toward the pack.

They had chosen their stand carefully. A tree overhung the path, which was itself choked by heavy underbrush. The only way to the pack was up a slope, through this brush. The second female went down to the base of the low hill. She sat on her haunches, waiting to trot into the trap as soon as the dogs saw her. They were stupid animals, and you had to make it very clear what they were supposed to do if you expected them to do it.

They swarmed up the path howling, saw the female, who growled and leaped to make sure, then ran into the underbrush. The dogs were hot behind her when the rest of the pack dropped out of the trees onto them. Their bodies writhed, the howls of excitement changed to shrieks of agony, and then nothing. The carcasses were hurled deep into the brush and the pack moved quickly on.

They went in the direction where the smell of man was the least, coming out onto a snowy roadway and moving to the stone wall that surrounded the park. A short trot down the wall was where they had made their kill the night before. Already it was afternoon and their minds were turning to food. But they would not kill anywhere near their last hunt—that might awaken man's understanding. Best to spread the kills far apart, as far as possible.

As one the pack stopped. They raised their muzzles and inhaled deeply. Across the street was a large building with a statue in front of it. And in the air was the faintest whiff of . . . the two.

Had they passed by here recently or were they just possibly inside that building? It was hard to tell by the quality of the odor, it was too faint. Just the slightest trace, not enough to tell even whether the body was hot or cold, indoors or out.

They crossed the snowy street and went into the grounds around the building. Yes, that scent was now a little stronger. Caution! These creatures were not dumb and they knew that they were being hunted. Better be very slow and careful. They trotted around the building, three in one direction and three in the other, easily leaping the small balustrades that surrounded the place. In this way they identified by scent which doors were in use and which were not. Without even needing to converse they came together again, then spread out to watch the doors that might be used. They hid themselves wherever they could, crouching along fences, curling up in the small clumps of bushes, lying behind stone retainers. And the scent hung here, that distinctive sweet smell that went with the woman, the denser smell of the man. And there was another familiar odor, lighter and more salty: one they had smelled near the two before.

Each human's distinctive odor separated him from all the others, and the pack separated these three from the great mass of odors around them. And they settled down to wait. Waiting was easy for them. It added the excitement of anticipation.

Sam Garner pulled his car to a stop in front of the Museum of Natural History. He got out, relying on his press ID in the window to ward off the tow-away patrol. He paused before the imposing building, looking up at the statue of Teddy Roosevelt. The Great White Hunter with a guilt complex. Sweet guy. Sam trotted up the stairs. Two detectives were in there whom he wanted to see. He didn't know exactly why he wanted to do this. He didn't especially like detectives, and it hadn't been easy to track these two down. But here he was and here they were, and he wanted very much to find out how they would react when he gave them a certain piece of information.

He had it planned. He would say, "You understand that Medical Examiner Evans was mauled to death in the park this morning." They would say yes to that. Then he would say, "The incident occurred in your car." He was very interested in watching their reaction to that. Somewhere along through here there was some kind of a story, maybe big. And these two just might have some idea what it was.

Chapter 9

Carl Ferguson's phone rang. He picked it up, then handed it to Wilson. "For you. Underwood."

Wilson took the phone. "Jesus, Herb, how'd you know I was here?"

"Lucky guess. Actually I've made about six calls. This was a last resort."

"That's accurate. What's on your mind?"

"Evans. What killed him?"

"You know perfectly well, Herbie-boy."

"Wolves?"

"Werewolves. Same as killed the other six."

"Six?"

"Sure. The bloody bench we found this morning was all that remained of number six. O-negative blood. No ID as yet beyond that."

"Look, I gotta tell you there's a hell of a lot of press out pounding the pavements on this one. We're crawlin' with 'em down here, plus the park's full of 'em. Reporters from every damn where—Evans was a famous man. So far nobody's made the connection between his death and the other murders. I mean, obviously there're similarities. So don't, if you know what I mean."

"Oh, I won't. I haven't got enough proof so it might not embarrass you as much as it should. There's a cake, but I ain't got icing."

"Like what?"

"Like evidence that will convince even you. When I've got that, I'll go to the papers, but not before. That much you can count on."

"Goddamn you, George. If it weren't for Old One Forty-seven I'd sign your fuckin' walking papers."

"Well, Herbie, now what can you expect? You were a dumb kid and you're a dumb grown-up. You should have given in a long time ago, when you first knew I was right."

"Which was?"

"The first time you heard my story. It's dead right and you know it. You're just too damn stubborn to admit it, or too dumb. Probably both."

This was followed by a silence at the other end of the line that lengthened until Wilson thought that Underwood had hung up on him. Finally he spoke. "Detective Wilson," he said, "have you ever considered, if your story is true, what kind of public reaction it will cause?"

"Panic, mayhem, blood in the streets. Plus heads will roll. The heads of the people who didn't do anything about it when they could."

"My head. You'd sacrifice this city for *that*? Can you imagine the economic loss, the destruction? Thousands of people would pour the hell out of the city. Mass exodus. Looting. This is a great city, Detective Wilson, but I think that would break it."

Wilson closed his eyes, bowed his head and put
s fists to his temples. He looked like a man shielding
mself from an explosion.

"Goddamn, I wish to hell we were out of this!"
e had shouted it so loud that the faint hubbub be-
ond the tiny office came to a halt.

"Please," Ferguson said, "you could cause me
roblems."

"Sorry, Doctor, *excuse* me."

"Well, you have to admit—"

"Yeah, yeah, save it. Becky, I'm sorry."

"Yeah. I'm sorry too." His eyes pleaded up at her,
and she met them with what she hoped was a look of
reassurance.

"Don't think about death. You thought about
death. Think about our camera. Tonight we'll get
our pictures and then things'll start to move. All the
evidence, plus the pictures—nobody will be able to
deny it."

"And we'll get some protection?"

"Damn right. Whatever the hell happens, it'll be
something. Better than this, God knows."

For the first time Becky allowed herself to imagine
t. What form would protection take? A cold stab of
ealization went through her—about the only thing
hat would help would be virtual imprisonment. At
st it would mean a good night's sleep, but then it
uld get stifling, finally unendurable, and she would
o it up—and every moment outside would hold
ger, every shadow the potential to kill. It was hard
urn her mind away from this train of thought. And
death flashed into her own imagination—how
it feel to be ripped to pieces: will there be des-
e agony or will some mechanism of the brain pro-
elief?

he couldn't think about that either. Think about

"Yeah. And you along with it. People will come
back when they realize that the werewolves aren't
just a local attraction. But you won't come back,
Herbie. You'll be completely retired."

Underwood's voice was bitter. "I must say, I
hope to hell you're wrong. Right now I can't think of
anything that'll give me more pleasure than kicking
your ass off the force. Now *that* would be a hell of a
good feeling." This time Wilson was sure that he had
hung up because of the bang the phone made.

"Good God," Becky said, "what in hell ever possessed you to talk to him like that!"

"He's a jerk. He was always a fuckin' jerk. Hell,
he was a jerk when he was runnin' around in a dirty
bathing suit half the summer. A fuckin' two-bit jerk."

"That doesn't give you the right   I mean, I
know you grew up together and all that . . . but my
God, you'll destroy both of us!"

"What in the world are you two talking about?"

They turned, surprised at the strange voice. A
small man in a cheap raincoat stood there smiling
more than he should. "Name's Garner. New York *Post*.
You folks Detectives Neff and Wilson?"

"Come back later. We don't want any right now."

"Oh, come on, Wilson, let him—"

"We don't want any now!"

"Just one question—how come Doctor Evans was
murdered in your car? You have any comment on
that?" His eyes watched them. Of course he didn't
expect a straight answer. It was how they looked that
counted. One way, he would know there was a story.
Another way, he would know zip.

"Get the hell out of here!! Whassamatter, you
deaf! Move!"

He scurried away, down the hall and up the
stairs, smiling from ear to ear. He loved it! There was

going to be a damn *good* story! As soon as he got back to his car he called in for a photographer. A couple of pictures of them as they left the museum wouldn't hurt. Nice pictures, come in handy later.

"Sometimes I think maybe we should tell them something," Ferguson asked when the reporter was gone. "I think it'll help us if we got more people involved."

"You tell them."

"Oh, I couldn't possibly. I haven't got enough—"

"Evidence. Neither have we, and that's why we can't tell them either. We've got to wait until we get that clincher. Once we have it, we can blow the story from here to Moscow for all I care, but I'm certainly not going to break it early. Can you imagine—detective alleges werewolf killed M. E.? Underwood would dearly love that."

His own voice made Wilson suddenly very tired. The long night ahead was bearing down remorselessly; he felt a knot growing in his stomach. Already the light in the room had changed. This time of year the days were quick, the nights long. And tonight moonrise would be late. Despite the lights of the city there would be shadows everywhere in just a few hours. The world around him seemed to be frowning, looming down at him, revealing within its softness a savagery he had never suspected. You think that the world is one thing, it turns out to be another. What appeared to be a flower is actually a gaping wound. The fact that time was passing ate at him, drove him closer and closer to—the truth, and the truth was they were going to die. Soon he would feel it, he knew it. He would feel what Evans had felt, the sensation of those *things* pulling him apart with their teeth. And Becky too, that beautiful skin torn open—he could hardly tolerate the thought.

He had always had a knack for pro he had a premonition. He was standing in of Becky's bedroom when one of them jur the curtains and buried its head in his stom sheer pain killed, he saw its tail wagging.

Then something hit him.

"Come on! Good Christ, kid, what the into you?" Becky? Becky was shaking him.

"Now, now calm down—here, sit him a stress reaction, that's all. Call his name, dor get away."

"Wilson!"

"Wha—"

"Call a doctor, you jerk! What the h matter, he acts like he's made of rubber!"

"Stress did it, extreme stress. Keep callir he's coming back."

"Wilson, you motherfucker, wake up!" sponse he pulled her down to the chair and clumsily embraced her, held her against him. A choked noise started in his chest. She felt his stubbly bea-d rub against her cheek, felt his dry lips come into with her neck, felt his body trembling, sm sour, rumpled jacket. After a moment she d pushing at his shoulders, and was immed leased.

"God, I feel awful."

Ferguson gave him some water in cup, which he spilled at once. "Hell, I—"

"Take it easy. Something happened

"It was a stress reaction," Ferguso uncommon. People in crashing planes ings, trapped people, experience it. isn't terminal, the condition passe trying to smile but his face was to seem very real. "I've read about it, it before," he added lamely.

the next moment, not the future. Think about the camera. Men in battle must do it that way, keeping their minds fixed on the next shell hole, shutting out the deadly whisper of bullets, the groans of the unlucky, until they themselves . . .

She turned her mind from it again and said in a tired voice, "Dick probably has the camera by now. It's nearly three. What say we get over there and plan the stakeout? It's gonna be a long night."

Ferguson smiled a little. "Frankly, I think it'll be exciting. Obviously there's danger. But my God, look at the magnitude of the discovery! All of history mankind has been living in a dream, and suddenly we're about to discover reality. It's an extraordinary moment."

Both the detectives stared at him in amazement. Their lives and habits of thought emphasized the danger of the quest, not its beauty. Ferguson's words made them realize that there was beauty there too. The presence of the werewolf, once proven, would completely change the life of man. Of course there would be panic and terror—but there would also be the new challenge. Man the hunted—and his hunter, so skilled, so perfectly equipped that he seemed almost supernatural. Man had always confronted nature by beating it down. This was going to require something new—the werewolf would have to be accepted. He wasn't likely to submit to a beating.

Becky felt her inner resolve strengthening. She knew the feeling. It often came when they were confronting a particularly rough case, the kind of case where you really *wanted* to find the killer. The ones where a drug pusher was knocked off or some other scum—those you didn't really care about. But when it was an innocent, a child, an old person—you got this feeling, like you were *going* to make that collar. Vengeance, that's what it was. And Ferguson's words had that effect. It damn well *was* an extraordinary moment. Mankind was already in this situation and didn't know it, and had a right to know. There might not be much that could be done about it, not at first, but the victims at least had the right to see the face of their attacker. "Let's call Dick, make sure he's ready. No point in moving through the streets until we have to." She picked up the phone.

"Make sure he's got walkie-talkies," Wilson rumbled. "Civilian models. I don't want them on the police band."

Dick answered on the first ring. He sounded grim. His voice was subdued as he answered Becky's questions. Unspoken was the fact that he also had heard of Evans's death and knew what had killed him. She concluded the brief conversation and put down the phone. "He's got the camera. The radios he'll pick up this afternoon. A couple of hand-held CB's." Becky had felt something new when she heard Dick's voice. There was a strong warmth in her, a sensation of closeness that she never remembered, not even when they were first married. If he had been here she would have embraced him just to feel the solid presence of his body. Too bad for Dick, he was a better human being than he was a cop. Too good to tough out life on the force, that was Dick. God knows it wouldn't make a damn bit of difference to the Board of Inquiry when it came along, but there was a hell of a lot of justice to shaking down organized crime to help an old man in an honest nursing home. His old man. It was going to be hard when he got his Board, Goddamn hard.

Wilson was now staring off into space, vacillating between competent involvement and numbness.

"Come on, George, snap out of it! You're a million miles away. If we're gonna organize a stakeout we'd better get it together. We need to take sightings with that camera, set up observation points that are damn well *covered,* all of that. We'd better go over there and do what's gotta be done before it gets dark."

Becky hadn't allowed herself to think about all that had to be done because it meant leaving the momentary safety of the museum and facing the streets. But it looked like nobody was going to think about it if she didn't. Wilson sure as hell better hold up his end later, when it was going to count.

"I hadn't realized we were so close to leaving," Ferguson said. "There are some things I want to know from you two. A couple of things I don't quite understand. I'd like to get them cleared up before we move. It might be important."

Becky raised her eyebrows. "So OK, shoot."

"Well, I don't quite understand the sequence of events this morning. How exactly did Evans get killed?"

Becky didn't say so, but she would be glad to hear Wilson's explanation as well. The werewolves were obviously superb hunters, but how exactly they had accomplished their feats this morning was still fuzzy in her mind.

Wilson replied, his voice a monotone. "It must have started when we were at Central Park West and Seventy-second investigating one of their homicides. Obviously, they had us under observation at that time." A chill went through Becky, remembering the morning, the crowd of men and cars, the blood-soaked bench. All that had saved them was the presence of so many other cops. Wilson went on. "They knew that they couldn't get to us easily unless we were in a more isolated situation. So they arranged a lure. It's a technique human hunters have used for generations. And it worked beautifully in this instance. They went into the park, found an isolated patrolman beating the bushes for evidence and wounded him. The fact that he died later made no difference to them. In Africa hunters tether wildebeest to lure lions. The wildebeest might think it's unfair, but they aren't expected to survive. Neither was our lure. As soon as our car pulled up, the werewolves must have started creeping toward it. When we returned to it they would have been underneath, jumped out and—two dead detectives. I guess I got it figured just in time." He fumbled in his pockets. Becky handed him a cigarette. Something seemed to be coming over him. For a long moment his face kept getting grayer and grayer, then he took a deep, ragged breath and continued. "I was lucky, but them leaving that guy half-killed just didn't add up. Then I figured it. We were in their trap. That was when I told Becky to take off on the scooter."

"And Evans—"

"The last I saw he was sitting in the car. You'd have thought he would have locked the doors. I guess he didn't think of it in time."

"They opened the doors?" Becky asked.

Wilson shrugged. "What's surprising about that?"

He was right. It was just hard to accept, even with all she had seen. Somehow you just couldn't see animals behaving like that. But then, they weren't animals at all, were they? They had minds, that qualified them as . . . something. You couldn't include them as part of humanity. They were fundamentally our enemy. It was in their blood, and in ours. Although they were intelligent they couldn't be called human. Or could they? Did they have civil rights, duties, obligations? The very question was absurd. Despite their intelligent nature there would be no place for them in human society.

Except as hunter. There was a very definite place for the hyena in wildebeest society, for the leopard in baboon society. Their presence was respected and accommodated because there was *no choice*. No matter how hard they tried, the wildebeest and the baboon were never going to defeat their predators. So the social order reflected their presence. Baboons protected the young, exposed the weak. They hated it but they did it. You would too, in time.

Ferguson was the first to speak after absorbing Wilson's explanation. "It fits," he said. "That's a very clever plan. They must have been amazed that you got away."

"Unless they're playing games."

"Not likely. You're too dangerous. Can you imagine how it must feel, knowing that your way of life is about to be destroyed by just two human beings? Hell, they probably knock off one or two people a day for food. Hunting you down must have seemed easy at first. No, I don't think they're playing games with you. You're damn hard to get, that's all. Like all predators, when they come up against competent members of the prey species they have a hard time. They aren't equipped to deal with determined resistance. Among animals, this nets out to a trial by strength. The young moose kicks hell out of the wolf. With us it's wits—ours against theirs."

Wilson nodded. Becky noticed that what Ferguson was saying was having a good effect on him. And her too, for that matter. It didn't change the fear, but it added some perspective. You began to get the feeling that the werewolves were almost omnipotent and you were like mice in a trap, just waiting there until they got tired of toying with you. But maybe Ferguson

was right. After all they had thus far defeated the
werewolves every time. They could go on defeating
them. But then another thought came to her, an ugly
one that had been hiding in the back of her mind
untouched. "How long," she asked, "will they keep up
the hunt?"

"A long time," Ferguson said. "Until they succeed
—or get talked out of it."

Becky pushed hard at that thought, got rid of it.
They couldn't afford an ambivalent attitude. "OK, kids,
let's hit the road. We have work to do."

Herbert Underwood was troubled. He was sitting
in the Commissioner's outer office. The last cigar of
the day was in his pocket but he resisted the impulse
to smoke it. Commissioner didn't like cigars. Again
Herb went through his mind, touching each point of
the case, weighing it, trying to see how it could be
used to strengthen his position and weaken the Commissioner's. Word from Vince Merillo, the new mayor's
first deputy-to-be, was that the Commissioner still had
an inside track to reappointment. That would mean
that Herbert Underwood would reach retirement before he reached the top job. And he wanted that job
bad. Wanting the next job up the ladder was more
than a habit with him. He deserved the promotion, he
was an excellent cop. A good man too, good adminis-
trator. Hell, he was a better man than the Commissioner. All he needed was a nice, ugly embarrassment for
the Commissioner and Merillo would start mentioning
the Chief of Detectives as successor. He was sure of
Merillo's support. The guy owed him. Merillo was into a bank in a very ugly way and the Chief of Detectives knew it. The DA didn't—and wouldn't as long
as Merillo played on the right side of the net.

"Come in, Herb," the Commissioner said from the

door of the inner office. Underwood got up and went inside. The Commissioner closed the door. "Nobody here but us rats," he said in his singsong voice. "I got two mayors screaming at me. I got reporters hiding in my file cabinet. I got TV crews in the bathroom. Not to mention the Public." He added in a more clipped tone, "Tell me what happened to Evans."

"Oh come on, Bob, you know I'm up against a brick wall."

"Yeah? I'm sorry to hear that, very sorry. Because it may mean I'll have to replace you."

Underwood wanted to laugh out loud. The Commissioner was crashing around like a wounded elephant. The pressure from upstairs must be hell. Bad for him, very bad. "You mean that? It'd be a relief." He chuckled.

The Commissioner glared at him. "You know, our new mayor is a very smart man."

"I know that."

"And so is Vince Merillo, your good buddy."

Underwood nodded.

"Well, here is what the Mayor and his first-deputy-in-waiting think about this case. Want to hear?"

"Sure."

"They have got the Wilson theory on their brains. I mean, essentially the Wilson theory. The DiFalco mess, the Bronx mess, the bloody bench, the gutted patrolmen and Evans—"

"All the work of hybrid wolves. I know. I've talked to Merillo."

"So what's your position?"

"The theory is total bullshit. I've known Wilson since we were kids and I think he's pulling a fast one on us, trying to get us to buy bullshit so we'll look like fools. Especially me. You I don't think he gives a damn about."

"OK. So what else are you working on?"

"I just organized a special squad. They're going to be under Commander Busciglio of the Fifth Homicide Zone. Goddamn good guy. Good cop, lot of smarts. They will be investigating the three incidents that happened today in Central Park. We'll be working on the assumption that these incidents are entirely separate from the Bronx case and the Brooklyn case. I think that makes sense. It's not out of the question that they're all related, but it's very farfetched. That enough to keep me from getting fired?"

"You know I'm not gonna fire you, Herb. Hell, you're the guy slated to kill me off. If I fire you it'll look like sour grapes to the Mayor." He laughed. "Can't let that happen." He had been standing in front of Underwood, the two men in the middle of the office. Now he went over to a leather chair and sat down, motioning the Chief to follow. "Herb, you and I, we've been buddies a long time. I gotta tell you though, I've been hearing some things about you that've made me very sad. Like, you're trying to get me dumped, to put it bluntly. Why are you doing that, Herb?"

The Chief smiled. He had to hand it to the Commissioner, the man didn't play around. "No, sir, I'm not trying anything of the kind. In fact, like on this case, I'm doing everything I can to strengthen your position. I think we'll get a good solution very quickly. It'll help you and because of that it'll help me. That's as far as my ambition goes."

Now it was the Commissioner's turn to smile. He turned on a crinkly, jolly one, wore it for a few seconds, then nodded, seemingly satisfied. He spread his hands in a gesture of meekest assent. "OK," he said, "just keep up the good work. Glad you're still on the team."

Underwood left after further protestations of loyalty, capped by a solemn handshake. The Commissioner watched him go. Hell, with technique like that the guy would make a damn fine commissioner if he won out. Good projection of sincerity. Handles himself well.

But he ain't gonna fuck me. He must think I'm some kind of schoolboy. He closed the door behind Underwood and stood there a long moment. Soon the Chief would be blown so high and wide he wouldn't have a political future of any kind. So the son of a bitch wanted to kill off Bob Righter. Fine, let him try! Now the Commissioner's face set. He leafed through a report on his desk. It was titled "Project Werewolf. Eyes Only." It had been seen only by Merillo, the new mayor, and the current mayor. It had been written by Bob Righter, in longhand.

This was the only copy.

He opened it, reading to review. He had written it three hours ago, had taken it to the Mayor and then to the Mayor-elect. There had been a meeting and it had been agreed that not one word of the report would be made public unless absolutely necessary. The Commissioner started to say his thoughts aloud, then stopped, the words unspoken in his throat. How often do I talk to myself, he wondered. Getting old. But not tired, dammit. Let Herb Underwood realize that once and for all. Not tired. Underwood was going off on a hell of a wild-goose chase. That stinking Wilson had been much closer from the start. Brilliant but a creep. A good cop after his fashion. A good cop with a good partner . . . Becky Neff . . . no matter how old you get, you'd still like to get into something like that. Hell, stay clear. Her husband was bent—maybe she was too for that matter . . .

He dismissed them from his mind and returned to the matter of the report. It was the first time in his career that he had written something so secret, and kept its contents so close to the top. In a position like his a man gets into the habit of using advisers, conferees, administrative assistants. He becomes not an individual but an office. He identifies himself as "we." Not in this case, though. There was too much here to entrust to staff members. It was not only a horrendous crime, it was also a priceless opportunity to completely outdistance Underwood, to crush him. "Herbie's gonna love me," he said, this time without realizing he had spoken aloud. Now that he had the endorsement of both his current and future bosses he would begin to draw together the team that would solve the *real* Werewolf case. He pulled out a yellow legal pad and put it down beside his report. He drew a box at the top, and put the letter *C* in the box. That's me, he thought. Then he drew a dotted line to the Chief of Detectives and put a *U* in that box. And that's as far as he goes. All alone in his box with his God-damn *U*. Now another box, with a full line to the Commissioner. Call him Deputy Assistant for Internal Affairs. DAIA. OK, now give him a staff. Three more boxes under him, all Police Commanders. Now a team. Three squads under the three Commanders. All high power. Now assign a Tactical Patrol Force Group to the Deputy Assistant, the grunt-work department so all these officers don't have to get their hands dirty. Very nice. About two hundred men. The Mad Bomber had commanded a crew of two hundred and fifty. Son of Sam had tied up three hundred. The Werewolf Killers would be more economical with just two hundred.

Now he pulled a small cassette recorder out of his desk drawer. He rewound the cassette and played it again. Voices, confusion, then a whispered word, unintelligible. Then more. "Mama . . . hey look out (a sob) . . . there it is . . . (Voice: what is it, Jack?)

Dog . . . somethin' weird . . . don't don't get it . . . hey . . . oh, wow that was—oh, hey it cut, cut my uniform . . . ouch . . . aaaAAHH! (Voice: Jack, you need more? The doc's gonna give you more pain-killer.) Yeah . . . OK, there was a dog . . . big mother-fucker . . . weird, like a human face . . . a couple of others standing nearby . . . face, not like a person . . . you'll never get it . . ." More whispers. (Second voice: the patient is expiring.) Tape ends.

The patrolman hadn't given them much to go on, but it was more than they had gotten before. Enough for a good start. M.O. was established. This added a rough description. He read the first sentence of his report: "The Werewolf Killers are a group of twisted individuals utilizing an extremely skillful disguise . . ." That was where Underwood was falling down: he didn't realize that there was a whole group, or that they were disguised.

Outside the museum tension was building. The sun had moved far down the sky. The first, faint smells of cooking were coming into the afternoon air. When the subways stopped beneath the street the sound of more and more feet were heard getting off. Man's afternoon ritual of moving back to his nest was under way. And this would also be occurring to the hated ones inside the building. There would be no need to take the risk of going inside after them. Soon they would want their food and their nests, and start their movement. Then the moment would come, not so long from now. Waiting like this made your heart soar, knowing that relief and success lay as the reward for patience. Soon they would come out, very soon.

Garner had returned to the scene of the Evans murder and picked up Rich Fields, the photographer the paper had sent to join him on the story. "We're gonna take some pictures of a couple of cops," he said to Fields.

"What for?"

"Nothin'. Don't even waste film. Just flashes. I want flashes."

"Great. Makes good sense. Keep convincin' me."

"Shut up, Fields, you're too dumb to understand."

They got into Garner's car and rattled out of the park, back up to the Museum of Natural History. Garner felt full of vitamins. There was a Goddamn good story in here and these two detectives were the exact center of the whole little cyclone. Ah, a beautiful story, had to be. Let the *Times* send fifty gentlemen downtown to worry the Police Commissioner, Sam Garner was going to stick right close to these two detectives until he got the story. He parked his car directly in front of the museum and settled back to wait. "Want me to start shootin'?"

"Shut up, Tonto. I'll tell you when. And make it fuckin' good if you don't mind. I mean, run up and flash at 'em. Make 'em mad."

"You payin' my hospital bills, honey?"

"The *Post*'ll take care of you, darlin'. Just do your thing."

He stared at the huge edifice. Sometime soon the two cops would appear in the doorway and start down. Fields would get after them with the camera. No words, no more questions. Those two cops were *scared* already. This would panic them. If they were hiding anything interesting the little picture-taking session would make them think the *Post* was on to it. So next time Sam Garner got to them maybe they'd start trying to save their own asses by doing a little singing.

It had happened before. Pressure breeds information. The first rule of investigative reporting. Make 'em think you know enough to hang 'em, then they'll give you what you need. Visions of delicious headlines went through his head. He didn't know exactly what they said, but they were there. The way it felt, he had a good week of dynamite on his hands. The boss would love it. It must be something really horrible. Whatever was going on, somebody had seen fit to tear the Medical Examiner apart. Not just kill him, but actually tear him apart. The skin had even been pulled down off the skull, the face nearly separated from the body. The throat was gone. The stomach was pulled open and the body severed so completely that the legs fell to the floor of the car when the orderlies tried to move the body. It had been a vicious murder, particularly so, unusually so. A monstrous murder. Hell of a bad thing. All of a sudden he felt kind of chilled, sick inside, like he was going to throw up. "Hurry up," he muttered under his breath. A drink lay just the other side of this little assignment and he needed it very badly.

"I got some good stuff on Evans," Fields said. "I mean—that was some mess."

"I just been thinkin' about it. Doesn't make much sense, does it? Whoever did that must have hated the hell out of the guy. And right in broad daylight, right in the middle of the park. Strange as hell, weird as hell, you ask me."

"Look close, boss. The doll and the old guy?"

"That's them. Get moving."

Fields opened the door of the car and walked forward to the base of the statue of Teddy Roosevelt that stood before the museum entrance. In this position he would be concealed from Neff and Wilson until they came down the steps and were beside him. They were moving quickly. Another man, hunched, tall, his hands folded before him, walked just behind them. There was something familiar in the way they moved. And then Fields realized why: in 'Nam, people under fire had moved like that.

As they came nearer he could hear their footsteps crunching on the snow. He stepped out from his position near the statue and started shooting. The flash popped in the gray afternoon light, and the three figures jumped away startled. Almost before he knew it there was a pistol in the hand of the old guy. The woman was also pointing a pistol at him. This all happened in the same strange slow motion that things had happened in the war, when an attack was going on. The closer you got to action, the more events separated into individual components. Then an end would come, usually violent, the roar of a claymore going up, the black arcing shapes against the sky, the screams and smoke . . . "Goddamn, they have guns and all I got is a camera."

Something else moved and the old guy's pistol roared. "Don't shoot!" But it roared again, sending out sparks. The tall man shrieked. Now the woman's pistol roared, kicking back in her hand, and roared again and again. But there, off in the snow, something black was skittering along—two things. That's what they were firing at, not him. Then the three of them sprinted toward Sam's car. "Come on," the woman shouted over her shoulder, "move or you're dead!"

Rich moved damn fast, diving into the back seat right across the lady cop's knees. She pulled the door closed and extricated herself. "Step on it!" the old guy snarled at Sam, "step on it, Goddammit!"

But Sam wasn't stepping on anything. He turned to face the old detective who was beside him in the front seat. "What the fuck," he said in a high, silly-sounding voice.

The detective leveled his pistol on Sam. "Move this vehicle," he said, "or I'll blow your brains out."

Sam pulled out into traffic very smartly. Neither he nor Rich had a mind to ask any more questions just now.

"We got one," Becky said.

"Not dead," Wilson replied.

Becky turned to Rich, who was sitting beside her, acutely aware of her salty, perfumey odor, of the warm pressure of her hip against his. "Thanks," she said, "you saved our asses just then."

"What the hell happened?" Sam managed to bleat.

"Nothin'," Wilson replied. "Nothin' happened. Your buddy with the camera got us riled."

"Oh, come on, Wilson, tell them," Ferguson said.

"Shut up, Doctor!" Becky said. "I'll handle this. We don't need press, we've talked about that."

Wilson turned around in his seat, his face a twisted, mottled parody of itself. "If this gets out," he said, "we might as well just kiss our asses good-bye right now! We haven't got evidence, baby, and without it we'll come across as a couple of kooks. Lemme tell you what'd happen. Shithead downtown would get us retired disabled. Mental. You know what'd happen then? Damn right you do! Those fuckers'd be on us so Goddamn fast!" He laughed, more of a snarl. Then he turned and faced forward. Ferguson glared at his back.

"Take us to One fifteen East Eighty-eighth Street," Becky said, "and get the hell away from the park. Go down Columbus to Fifty-seventh and over that way "

"And move the Goddamn thing," Wilson said hoarsely. "You're a Goddamn reporter, you can drive!" He chuckled now, a dry, spent noise. "What're you gonna put in your gunfire report?" he asked her.

"Cleaning accident. Fired three shots while cleaning."

Wilson nodded.

"Goddammit, I've got a right to know," Sam said. "I have a right. I was the only reporter in the whole city smart enough to figure you two had the real story. The other fucks are down at Police Headquarters tryin' to get a statement from the Commissioner. Just tell me what happened to Evans. Hell, what was going on just now I won't even ask."

Becky had leaned forward as he spoke. Wilson was in no shape to keep talking.

"Evans got killed. If we knew anything more we'd have a collar."

"Oh. Then I suppose that shootumup was nothin'. I gotta tell you, you are two very funny cops. I ain't never seen a cop pull out a piece and fire it like that just for a dog. Hell, that in itself is news."

"I bet. Just keep your mouth shut and drive, please."

"Is that any way to talk to a citizen?"

"You aren't a citizen, you're a reporter. There's a difference."

"What?"

Becky didn't answer. Through the whole exchange Ferguson had sat motionless, leaning toward Becky Neff in the middle of the back seat, leaning away from the window. Sam noticed that Wilson was also sitting well away from the window, almost in the middle of the front seat. You could almost say that they were afraid something was going to come at them through the windows . . . except the windows were closed.

Chapter 10

This daylight was a curse. The leader of the pack, the one the others called Old Father, waited behind the fence that separated the front staircase of the museum from the surrounding lawn. He had stationed himself here because he knew that the two were most likely to exit the museum by this door. It was going to be dangerous, difficult work, sad work. It was the luck of his race to prey on humanity, but at times like this, when he was forced to kill the young and strong, he wondered very much about his place in the world. His children thought of humanity merely in terms of food, but long years had taught him that man was also a thinking being, that he too enjoyed the beauties of the world. Man also had language, past, and hope. But knowing this did not change the need—call it compulsion—to kill and eat the prey. Every single human being he saw he evaluated at once out of habit. He enjoyed the way the flesh popped between his jaws and the hot blood poured down his throat. Living in human cities he gloried in the heady poetry of the scents. The pack was wealthy, for many humans lived in its territory. He loved his wealth, the wealth he had bought so dearly when the pack had migrated to this city. In his own youth their leader had preferred the isolation of rural life to the harder job of maintaining a city territory. Other packs would never try to take the sparse territory of that old coward. Its inhabitants starved in winter and skulked through summer, always wary, always risking discovery.

When he had grown to his full size he had taken his sister and set out south, toward the storied place where an uncountable human horde dwelled. Often they had been challenged by other packs, and each time they had bested the challengers. There had been fights, daylong, burning with ritual hate under which lay the love of the race. And each time these confrontations had ended with the rival pack leader giving way. Then there would be a celebration, a wonderful howl, and the two of them would be on their way. So it had continued until he and his sister had a beautiful space to themselves. They marked their boundaries and bore their first litter. There had been three, a girl and two boys. The weakest male they killed, feeding his soft flesh to the two strong ones. It was their bad luck not to have a perfect litter of four, but still two were better than none. Two years later they had increased their space again and birthed another litter. This time only one male and female, but both were healthy.

This spring the first pair would mate, as would he and his sister once again. With luck they would gain two pairs of pups. Greater luck would bring three pairs or even four. And next year the second pair would mate and still more would come. Not too many years from now he would lead a goodly pack in a large and wealthy territory. From his wretched beginning in the desolate hills he had come to this and was glad.

The only thing that was wrong was the two humans with their forbidden knowledge. If it became general among the humanity here the size of packs would have to be diminished, and even amid all this wealth they would be forced to scuttle like dumb animals . . . the hunter would be hunted . . . and it would be on his head and on the heads of his children. For ages hence all the race would remember their failure. His name would become a curse. And his line, the line he had created out of courage, would wither and die. Others would say of him, "Better he had stayed in the mountains."

He sighed, turning his attention back to the problem at hand. Bright daylight still and the scent of the hunted was rising. Yes, they were coming to this door. A few moments more and they would be on the stairs. He snapped his jaw, bringing the others to their stations at the main entrance. The second-mated pair crossed the street and hid under parked cars. That way, if the two got past him they would not get far. The youngest, the third-mated pair, came up and waited with him. His own sister, her coat gleaming with the fullness of her womanhood, her beautiful face shining with bravery and anticipation, her every move calm and royal, went into position on the opposite wall.

There would be no escape this time. At last, the hunt was over. And they would get a bonus thrown in—that tall man with whom the two spent so much of their time, he also would be destroyed.

Very well, but it was all an ugly and dirty business. You don't take life from young. Even the beasts of the forest never preyed on young. Practically speaking it was difficult, but there were also greater reasons. For the pack to live other life must be destroyed. And it was repugnant to do this to the young. When one of their own kind grew old the young gave him death, but before his time he felt a fierce desire to continue and have all of his life. So it must also be for the prey. The few times that he had been driven to kill young he had felt their frantic struggles, the fierce beating of a life that was hard to still . . . and had hated himself afterward when his belly was full and his heart heavy.

They appeared at the door, their scent washing powerfully before them. The woman smelled bright and sharp, not like food. And the young man was the same. Only the older one's scent reminded of food; it had that pungency, that sweetness that was the smell of a weakening body. But still it surged and pulsed with life. Taken together their three scents sparkled. He sighed, glanced at the third-mated pair who were with him. Their faces expressed fear. He had made sure they would be with him for this very reason: from this experience they would learn never to kill the young, and also never to allow yourself to be seen. They saw the pain in their father's face, a sight they would never forget. He let them see and hear and smell the full depth of his emotions. And he noted with gratification that what had for them been up to now an exciting hunt became what it ought to be: an occasion of sorrow and defeat.

Now their bodies tensed. Instantly their scents changed. His own heart started beating faster when he smelled their anticipation. The three victims were coming down the steps, their movements and smells broadcasting wariness—yet they came on, oblivious to the trap they were in. Despite his familiarity with humanity the fact that men would *walk* right into the plain scent of danger always amazed him. They had little bumps on their faces for breathing, but these were just blind appendages, useless for anything but passing air in and out of the body.

The three reached the foot of the steps—and the third-mated pair leaped over the fence. Simultaneously a man who had been standing concealed jumped into the path of the three and made flashes. The old father cursed himself—he had known this man was there but had thought nothing of it! Of course, of course—and now his two young ones were stopping—no, go on!—too late, now they were turning away, confused, their faces reflecting a turmoil of questions—what do we do? And guns were rising, everybody running for the park, the crack of the weapons detonating through the air, the pack leaping the stone wall, and each rushing alone into the underbrush.

They regrouped not far away, much closer than was safe. They had all smelled it—somebody in the pack was bleeding.

The youngest male was missing. The father stood with his nose to the noses of his family. They gave him reassurance, all except the youngest female. Her eyes said to him, "Why did you send us?" And she meant, "We were the youngest, the least experienced, and we were so afraid!" In her anger she said that she would not be his daughter if her brother had to die.

Her anger was deep, he knew, and she would not melt to the entreaties of the rest of the pack. Now that such feelings had passed they could never be erased. Even as they trotted toward the place where the young wounded one had hidden himself the father kept shaking his head with grief. "Now look at you," his sister said with her eyes and ears, "you wag your head like a silly wolf! Are you father or child?"

He was humiliated by her scorn, but tried not to let it show. He kept the hair on his neck carefully smooth, fighting the impulse to let it rise. His anus remained closed with a conscious effort: he would not allow his instinct to spread the musk of danger in this place. His tail he let hang straight out, not as a jaunty flag of pride or tucked humbly between his legs. No, straight out and no wags: this was dignified and neutral, indicating solemnity.

For all his effort his sister said, "Loose your musk, show your grief to your children. You have not even the courage for that!"

His musk burst out, he could not withhold it longer. The clinging smell filled the air. He cursed himself even as it spread, great splashes of it, betraying him, revealing the weakness he felt within.

"I am your father," he said, now using his tail to its fullest, flashing it in a proud wag, making his ears rise and his eyes glisten. But the scent was that of fear. Its betrayal was complete. His first son stepped forward. "Let me find my brother," he signaled with the snap of his jaw, and a disrespectful wag of his own tail. The four of them, sister, daughters and son went toward the wounded scent of the youngest male. As soon as they were out of sight their father submitted to an overwhelming impulse and rolled onto his back. He lay there kicking his back legs softly, feeling the warm wave of submission flow over him, relaxing into it, giving up his leadership. But his pack was not there to see, his own son not there to take his father's throat in his mouth. No, he rolled alone to the unseeing sky. Even if his son replaced him, the boy would never see his father roll.

Now a soft howl arose. The sorrow in it made him tremble. His sister had sounded the note of death! Their youngest boy's wounds were mortal. Wagging his head he battled himself for control. He trotted toward his next and terrible duty. Although his elder son or his sister would shortly become leader of the pack he was still the Old Father and still must be the one to do this. He stopped his running and lifted his head. Let the humans hear! He would sound his dirge. He did it fully and proudly. And at once he heard the fearful whimpering of his second son. Now he hurried on again, soon coming to the place near the wall where his family stood around a huddled gray shape. Their faces were torn with grief, their mouths dripping with saliva.

They ignored him, deferring to him only outwardly. As soon as this final duty was done his leadership would end. He went to his son, sniffed him. The boy was trembling, cold, his eyes even now rolling up into his head. The Old Father felt the boy's pain in his very bones. Yet even in his sorrow he felt proud of this boy, who had dragged such painful wounds so far in order to conceal himself from humanity. The young male took a breath and stared a long moment at his father. Then he lifted his muzzle slightly off the ground and closed his eyes.

The Old Father did not hesitate; he killed his son with one fierce bite. The boy's body kicked furiously in response, his mouth opened wide. By the time his father had swallowed the torn-out tissues of the son's throat the boy was dead. Immediately the others surrounded him. At once he saw who would assume leadership; his sister.

Now it came down to confrontation: either he would roll or fight. If he fought they would all fight, four of them against him, and all full of rage. Looking

at them, he knew that he would nevertheless win
such a fight. But at what cost—this pack would become rotten with hate as they followed a father they
despised. For the greater good of what he had built he
therefore rolled to his sister. She disdained his over-
ture, striding away with her tail held high. Instead his
youngest daughter, still quaking with the grief of her
loss, took the roll. When she grabbed his throat he
closed his eyes, waiting for death. Sometimes those
too young for this custom were overwhelmed by their
feelings and killed the ones who gave them rolls.
Eternity seemed to pass before she released him. Now
the whole pack displayed their tails jauntily; his own
he tucked between his legs. Leadership lost, his life
would become one of risk and danger. The least gesture of superiority would bring them snapping at him.
And until his sister, his daughter, and himself had
new mates there would be an unsettled, nasty situation in the pack.

There was still a last task to perform before the
reorganized pack continued on. They turned the body
of their brother on his back and ate him, crushing even
his bones in their jaws, consuming every bit of him
except a few tufts of fur. He was eaten out of necessity
and respect. They would always remember him now,
his brave death and good life. Each of them committed
the taste of his flesh to precious memory. Afterward
they howled, this howl expressing the idea that the
dead are dead, and life continues. Then they stood
in a circle, touching noses, their joy at being together
breaking through all the grief and upset, and finally
they opened their mouths and breathed their heavy
air together, their hearts transported by their intimacy
and nearness.

Still, the old father and his sister were no longer
a pair. She now needed a husband, a surrogate-

brother who would be willing to accept her as leader. Most males running loose, those with some awful sin on their heads, something so serious that they had been driven from their pack, would welcome such a position. And the daughter who had lost her brother, she also must find a male soon. Already the two females were spreading their scent-of-desire, causing the two males' bodies to react, causing the old father to hunger woefully for his beautiful sister. But his days of mating would probably be over unless some female as wretched as himself were to happen along. Let some time pass, he thought, and then I will spread my own scent for a new mate. Let time pass . . . and heal.

His sister watched him as he stood confused, unable to decide what to do with himself now that leadership had been lost. Her heart demanded that she comfort him and share his sorrow, but she kept her tail flashing high and did not look at his face. They had made this pack together but their children could not accept leadership from a father who had planned so badly that one of his own children had been killed. It was just, and they all had to live with it. But she could not stand to see him like this! He cringed back, glancing fearfully from face to face. Gone was his beauty, his boundless pride in this little pack. They had been going to build it together, she could not stand the idea of doing it with another. She could not remember a time when she had not been in love with him. Their own parents had paired them in a litter of four and the pairing was from the first one of love.

Until this curse had come down upon the pack there had been nothing but happiness. They were getting richer and richer. The pack could afford to pass over many possible kills, picking only the best and easiest. They could afford to pass up ten for one!

And their hunting was easy, always easy in this rich territory.

The day the catastrophe happened they had been preparing to hunt again. They had warm shelter and many potential victims. They even had a nice place to litter, the best they had ever found. All were looking forward to an easy winter and a fortunate spring.

Then had come the news. The first scent of it had arrived on a clear morning in autumn. This scent had been laid at the territorial boundary by their neighboring pack. And so Old Father had met with the father of that tribe and had learned of the dreadful mistake committed by two yearlings on their first hunt. They had taken young male humans, the most taboo of all the taboos, had taken them in a moment of heedless excitement. And the humans had noticed; many had come and investigated. Humanity had taken away the remains the very day after the mistake had been made. So man knew something, more than he should. Then had come the pack's terrible misfortune, the incident that had led them to the position they were now in. They had somehow sparked an investigation themselves. It was fantastic and impossible, but nevertheless humanity had come to the very lair itself and taken away the remains of some kills. How they had cursed themselves then for not consuming even the bones! But it was too late. They could only hope that man would be confused, but he was not. The two whom they hunted now had come up into the lair, had been sniffing about and had almost been killed then.

Those two were the bearers of knowledge, that was why they had come into the lair.

And since then this desperate hunt had continued. It had disrupted the life of the pack, forcing them to follow their quarry into the center of the city,

a place of few abandoned buildings, few good lairs.
Now it had destroyed their happiness too. She wanted
to throw her head back and howl out pure grief but
she would not. Could she lead them better than her
brother? She doubted it! The alternative was to give
it to her headstrong first son who certainly could not
equal the exploits of his father.

This son she distrusted. She looked at him, so
happily asserting his newfound status over his father.
And her beloved brother cringed before the boy—he
was that brave, to do even that to preserve the unity
of the pack. But a boy demanding such an act needed
a lesson. She went to him, sniffed him under the tail.
Her hackles rose and she shoved against him. He was
a big, strapping boy of three—his eyes glinted with
humor as his mother disciplined him. Very well, let
him laugh! She demanded that he roll. He did it
willingly enough, too willingly. That was the final
straw—she grabbed the loose flesh of his neck and
bit it hard. He gasped in surprise—he must have
thought that she was killing him. Very good, let him
think that a mother would kill her son. Let him know
just how far his insolent treatment of his father had
driven her! She bade him rise and he scrambled up
contrite. His eyes were wide, his face full of pain.
Blood oozed down his neck. His sister came up beside
him and stood staring at her mother. Very good, she's
loyal. The mother turned and moved off a little way.
The others understood that she wanted to be alone
with her thoughts and did not follow. The hurts in her
heart conflicted with one another for attention. Her
youngest son was dead, her brother, humiliated. She
herself was forced into leadership at a desperate moment. The order of the pack had been seriously strained.

It was hard for her to accept that her boy was
really dead. He had been bright and eager, brimming

over with life. And he had been so fast and strong, the fastest pup they had ever seen! The truth was, though, his mind was not so fast as his body. When the pack gathered together to share the beauties of the world there was a definite confusion in his eyes. And when they hunted, his father sometimes gave him leadership, but it always wound up with his sister. But he was a fine, good male and he loved his life!

There was a sound nearby. She turned to see, completely unafraid. If it was nearby it could not be dangerous or she would have sensed it long before. She saw staring from the brush her brother's eyes. Now why did he do this? It was just like him, flaunting all custom. How dare he stand there staring at her! She tried to raise the hairs on her neck. They would not move. She tried to growl warning but all that came out was a purr.

He came closer, never allowing his eyes to leave hers. Then he shook himself free of the brush and stood there with snow clinging to his fine brown coat. It hurt all the way through her to see him, to smell him so close, to hear the familiar sound of his breathing. Putting her ears back she went to him and rubbed muzzles. She longed to mourn but held herself back with a fierce effort. He sat on his haunches and regarded her. His eyes were full of love and a kind of quiet joyousness that it surprised her to see in so unfortunate a creature. "You take the pack," he said, "our troubles give it to you." And she felt afraid.

He sensed it at once and patted his tail on the ground briskly, a gesture that communicated the thought, "Have confidence." She was fascinated by the way his eyes seemed to sparkle; he didn't even appear sad. As if reading her thoughts, he lifted his eyes and made a low growl. This meant, "A heavy load has been lifted from me." Then he inclined his head toward her, closing his eyes as he did so. "You must take it." The three knocks of the tail and a tongue-lolling smile, replaced instantly by an expression of calm repose. "Have confidence in yourself— I do. I trust you."

These words moved her deeply. She knew that he was relinquishing his pride, his very life, to prevent discord among the members of the pack. And he was communicating confidence to her not only because she needed it but out of real sincerity. His scent had changed subtly as he talked, indicating that behind his words were love and a certain hard-to-define excitement that revealed his real happiness at her accession to leadership.

She made a series of gestures with her right forepaw, clicking her toenails together. He gestured back, nodded. She punctuated her remarks with brief keening sounds of emphasis. She was telling him that the only reason she had accepted his roll was that their firstborn children would have left the pack if he did not step down. He agreed. Then they rubbed muzzles again for a long time, their eyes closed, their breath mingling, their tongues touching gently. There was nothing but this to express their feelings: long years of companionship, puppyhood together, youth, adulthood. This parting would be the first time that they had not shared life totally. And there was no way to know how long it might last. Although he might become her mate again in the future, it would never be as it was, with the sharing of pack leadership that had so increased their pleasure at being together.

Abruptly she turned and trotted away. She could not stay longer with him or she would never turn away again. Full of sadness she returned to the three children. They were standing together in the shadows of the trees, nearly motionless, their dark shapes exuding the smell of fear. Now the truth had begun to insinuate itself into their minds: they dared not trust their father—they did not know if they could trust their mother.

She came up to them exuding an impression of affability and confidence that she did not feel. They rubbed muzzles and the three stood facing her. Just hours ago she had stood thus with them, facing her brother.

Using the language of movements, growls and gestures that communicated so much without the need for articulated words, she outlined the plan of the coming night. It was not an original plan, all it involved was returning to the woman's place and awaiting any chance that might befall. No better plan presented itself, however. The wonderfully canny ideas of her brother had resulted in the death of a member of the pack at no gain. Simple, straightforward plans would be more acceptable to the others now.

She knew that time was running very short for them. Soon they would have to leave the center of man's city, to return again to the outer areas where there were more shadows, more abandoned buildings. Not much more time. The truth was that they were about to lose this hunt. Man would learn about his hunter and the greatest of all taboos would be broken. What were the consequences? Endless trouble for all the race, suffering and hardship and death.

What a monstrous burden for the pack to carry! If only . . . but the past was the past. If it happened failure would have to be accepted. She thought that thought but her heart screamed no, they must not fail. *Must not.*

Sam Garner watched the two detectives and their friends rush into the apartment building. They huddled past the doorman and disappeared. The afternoon had become unseasonably warm, and they had splashed through slush as they ran, not even bothering to step around the puddles.

"Unbelievable. Can you beat that?"

"Splashin' in the puddles?"

Garner closed his eyes. Fields was a nice guy but his was not one of the great intellects. "Let's have some ideas about what's going on with these folks."

"Well, they shot a dog over there at the museum."

"That was a dog out there in the snow? You sure?"

"Looked like a shepherd to me. And it ran like hell even though it musta taken at least a couple of slugs."

"I didn't see it."

"What can I tell you? It was very fast."

Garner pulled back into traffic. He would return to the museum, examine the snow-covered lawn. Surely there would be blood if something had actually been shot.

They drove back through the streets until they reached the area where the encounter had taken place. "Come on, and bring your camera." The two men helped each other across the fence that separated the museum lawn from the sidewalk. There were marks there, perfectly plain to see. The melt had distorted their shape, but it was still clear that they had once been pawprints. And there was an area spotted with blood and little clots of meat. Farther on, toward the street, was another tiny drop of blood. Just over the fence more could be seen. With the photographer cursing, the two newspapermen crossed the fence again. Sam Garner loped across the street and trotted up and down before the stone wall that marked the boundary of Central Park. Then he saw what he was hoping to see, a long bloody scrape on top of the wall. "Over here," he called to Fields, who was busy trying to stomp wet snow off his shoes. On the way across the street he had slipped into a slushy puddle.

"My feet're gonna freeze," he moaned.

"Come on! Help me across this friggin' wall."

He was only too glad to give Garner a leg up. Sam scrambled to his hands and knees atop the wall and then dropped over into the park.

At once everything changed. Central Park in winter is as quiet as a desert. This was true especially up here near the wall, away from the paths, an area choked by snow-covered bushes. Garner turned and looked back. Fields was not following. "Fine," he thought, "I'll get the Goddamn story myself. Better not be any pictures." He pushed bushes aside. It was cold and wet in here and he wasn't dressed for a stroll in the shrubbery. Then he saw it again, the little red trace lying on the snow. And there were more pawprints here, at least three sets. Whatever made them had gone tearing through here not too long ago. A pack of wild dogs running from two trigger-happy detectives? What the hell, this was getting interesting.

He followed the tracks a few more yards, then stopped. Before him was a great smear of blood, and leading away from it were heavy splashes, impossible to miss. This trail led up a low rise and into even deeper brush. Cursing, Garner followed it. Low branches overhung, dropping snow on him every time his bent back brushed against them. He clambered along from splash to splash, and came upon a place where branches had been broken, many paws had ground away the sodden snow, and everything was bloody. "Oh God," he whispered. Bits of meat and fur were scattered all around, lying half-frozen on the ground, stuck in the bent twigs. It was a fearful sight and it made Garner feel suddenly alone and afraid. He peered into the bushes around him. Were shapes moving there beyond the edge of visibility? This place was awfully quiet. It had the sullen atmosphere of a crime scene, a place where violence had been done and gone, and it stank. All around there was a nasty, cloying animal smell. It was musty, reminding him . . . it was a female odor, mixed with the stench of the blood. "What in hell is this?" he said softly. His mind turned to the two detectives, to the strange events of half an hour ago. What in hell was going on here?

He backed away from the area slowly, carefully. Sweat was popping out all over him. He gritted his teeth, fighting an impulse to turn and run wildly through the trees. Instead he walked as softly as he could. Not far off he could hear the rumble of traffic on Central Park West. Yet it seemed an eternity away right now in this savage, inhuman place. That was the word to describe it—inhuman. There was a powerful and monstrous presence about the spot, the blood, the bits of flesh, the horrible odor—it all combined to produce in Sam Garner an overwhelming dread that seemed to rise up out of his dark core and threaten to reduce him to blind, running panic. He moved faster but he did not run.

"Hey, Sam," came a distant voice. "Sam!"

Garner heard it but was afraid to answer, afraid to raise his own voice. Something was near him, he was sure of it, pacing him, keeping just out of sight beyond the bushes. He broke into a trot, then a loping run. Branches lashed at him, scratching his face, knocking off his old fur hat, cutting his hands as he struggled. Then the wall was before him, too high to scale from this side. "Rich," he shouted, *"Rich!"*

The photographer looked down. His eyes opened wide, he let out a high bleat of a scream.

"Help me!" Garner shrieked. He raised his arms, grabbing frantically for the photographer's outstretched hands. Slowly, painfully he clambered up the wall and with Fields' help got over onto a bench.

"Good Christ, what the hell was that thing?" Fields babbled.

"Don't know."

"Come on—gotta get out of here!" Fields ran to the car, causing traffic along Central Park West to screech and skid as he hurried across the street. Weakly Sam Garner followed him. He was sick with fear. Something unspeakable had been going on in that park, and he had been paced by some kind of hellhound as he had left.

He jumped into the car, slammed and locked the door and leaned his badly scratched face against the steering wheel. "What was it?" he whispered. Then he looked up at Fields, blinking tears out of his eyes. "What was it!"

Fields was embarrassed and looked away. "Dunno. Lots bigger'n a dog." Now he mumbled. "Had a sort of . . . face. Good Christ . . ."

"Describe it! I've got to know."

"Can't . . . only saw it for a second." He shook his head slowly. "No wonder those two cops are triggerhappy. That thing came straight from hell, whatever it was."

"Bullshit," Garner replied. His chin was jutting out now, he was regaining himself. He took deep breaths. "Bullshit, whatever it was it was real. A flesh and blood something-or-other. Tasmanian devil, I dunno. But one thing is sure, it's on the loose in New York City and it's damn well gonna be big news."

"So a wild animal escapes. Page two."

"Ha! Think about it. Mutilation killing in the park. Cops scared to bejesus of something that looks like a dog. Then we get a closer look, and it ain't no dog that's spookin' 'em." He stopped, a powerful and withering image of that *thing* in the bushes near him overcoming his pugnacity. He hadn't seen it clearly but he could imagine— "Rich, there was a fuckin' blood-bath in there. I mean, I found a place where there was so damn much blood it looked like a slaughter-house. Something got it bad there, man, not so long ago, and the *smell*, Holy Christ!"

"Smell?"

"It was obscene. All the bushes were covered with it, like something had been sprayed on them. You couldn't see it but you could smell it. It was like—"

"What?"

"I don't know. Never mind."

Out of the corner of his eye he thought he saw a fierce, inhuman face peering over the wall so he put the car in gear and moved out. He got away from there, going downtown into the heart of the city. Their press credentials made it easy to park, so they stopped at the Biltmore for a drink.

"The place is quiet," Sam muttered, "and there ain't any other newshounds hangin' around. I just want to get myself together again."

Fields didn't protest, just followed. "So whad-daya think?" he asked as soon as they had slipped onto a couple of stools at the luxurious mahogany bar.

Sam didn't answer. "Perfect Manhattan, up," he said to the bartender. "They know how to make a Manhattan here," he growled. "That's my definition of a good bar."

"What's going on, Sam?" Fields was insistent now. He wanted to know. This was a good story and there were going to be great pictures. He certainly wasn't going to tell Sam Garner, but he had gotten a good look at the thing that had been following the reporter. It had come out of the brush just as Sam reached the wall and had sat and watched him go. Then its ears had snapped toward Rich Fields and it had simply disappeared. There it was one second, then a flash of gray and it was gone.

There had been a perfect picture there for a second before the thing had taken off. But Rich Fields hadn't taken a picture. For that second he had been frozen, staring at the most horrible living thing that he had ever seen. But it had all happened so fast. You couldn't be sure about moments like that, maybe it was a trick of light on a dog's face. He eyed Garner. "What was it?" he asked.

"How the hell do I know! Quit ridin' me, you ain't an editor. It was somethin' weird. Out of the ordinary."

"Well, that's obvious. Did it kill Evans?"

Garner raised his eyebrows, looked at the photographer. "Sure. And it was responsible for the bloody bench the cops found this A.M. too. It's a monster livin' in the park." He stared a moment at the drink before him. "Monster Stalks Park. It's more a *National Herald* story, ain't it? There's no proof, except what we *might* have seen. That won't work in the *Post.*"

Fields nodded his head slowly. He sipped his Martini. Garner was right about this place; you spent half your life around fifth-rate bars, you forgot how great a skillfully made Beefeater Martini could be. Right now it really hit the spot. "We gonna file?"

"Not yet. There's too many loose ends. I think we might get lucky, wrap it up nice and pretty. Those two detectives, they're scared shitless about this. You know what they did, they shot one of those things on

the museum lawn. They were scared of being attacked.
I'll tell you what's goin' on. We got some kind of a
holy terror loose in this town and the police are
scared to make that fact public."

Fields smiled. "That's gonna be a very beautiful
story, Sam. If we can get it together, that is. It's gonna
be very hard to get together. We sure ain't gonna
trap one of the beasts. And I can't see us workin' it
out of those two cops. I think we got a toughie on our
hands."

"Brilliant insight, Dr. Freud. It's a very tough
story, but we'll break it—if we live through it."

Fields laughed but not very hard.

The human had come snooping along, following
the blood trail of the dead child. As soon as he
dropped down from the wall the old father was aware
of the human interloper. He was a small man with
quick, light movements. His face was tense with
curiosity. His movements were halting and confused
though, as if the trail was hard to follow. And evidently it was; the human was tracking by eye from
blood droplet to blood droplet. Three times the old
father thought that the man would lose the trail but
each time he had regained it once again. And he kept
hurrying along between the branches, oblivious of
the fact that the old father was never more than six
feet away.

The rest of the pack had moved off, getting away
from the scene of this afternoon's disaster. Only the
old father had lingered behind, drawn by his sorrow
to stay near the place where his son had died. He himself had been about to go, to fall into his new place
at the bottom of the pack, when he had heard the
scrape and thud of the human dropping over the wall.
He had scented the man almost immediately; it was

a fresh smell, mostly of the cloth in which the man was wrapped. But even so the flesh beneath the wrapping had a definite odor—a healthy man, one who smoked heavily but did not breathe poorly. He came along, crunching and clattering, his lungs loudly passing air in and out. As he got closer to the spot where the boy had died the old father stifled an intense urge to kill him. Here was another human meddling in the affairs of the pack, further evidence that knowledge of the clan was spreading.

The man clambered up the slope that led to the very spot that was still covered by the young male's blood. And he entered the bush under which the death had taken place. A stifled sound came from the man. The old father rushed up to the bush, then stood very still as the man came out.

The human did not see him but seemed to sense his presence anyway. Fear had come into the man; here was something unknown, and it made the man want to return to his own kind. The man ran along with the old father just behind. He was in a fever to kill this human, so much so that his mouth hung open. It took every ounce of strength for him to let the creature escape. All his instincts screamed at him, kill it, kill it *now*! But he knew in his mind that this would be a mistake. They could not risk so much killing and after all the man had seen only blood. The snowmelt would wash most of it away before more humans could be brought to this place. Also, the pack was not here to help him dispose of a body. It would have to be left here until he could get them back. They were not likely to respond to his signal although his voice carried for miles. He was no longer pack leader, he would have to run and get them if he wanted them. And while he was gone, other humans might discover

the carcass of this one, making the problem faced by
the pack that much worse.

Nevertheless his mind was not his whole being.
Underneath it were the powerful emotional currents
of his race, currents that now tore at him and demanded that he kill the intruder, tear the creature
apart, end the threat.

Then the man was at the wall, screaming for help.
A pale face appeared above the wall. For an instant
the old father met the eyes of this human; looking
into human eyes was a little like looking into the eyes
of an old enemy, or even a beloved sister.

He should not be here—run! And he ran, moving
back into the brush in the wink of an eye. Then he
sniffed the air, located the pack and started off after
them. His mind was spinning with the terrible knowledge that another intruder had come, and he was
alternately relieved and guilty that he had not killed
the thing. This conflict made him feel angry, and his
anger fed his desperation. Wild, mad thoughts began
to roll in his brain. He wanted the danger to be over.
The pack had to prosper. Soon they must win this
battle against humanity. With the appearance of this
new factor—the stranger who sought the lair of the
pack—came proof that the forbidden knowledge was
spreading. It had to be stifled at the source, and soon.
"Tonight," he thought as he trotted, "or it will be too
late."

Chapter 11

With the coming of night the wind rose. It swept down out of the north, freezing and wild, transforming the afternoon melt into a cutting mantle of ice. The warmer air that had lingered over the city became clouds and blew away to the south, and remaining in the sky were the few stars that defied the electric flood below, and a crescent moon rising over the towers. The bitter wind flooded along the avenues of Manhattan, carrying with it an ancient wildness that seldom reached the inner sanctum of the city; it was as if the very soul of the frowning north had swept from its moorings and now ran free in the streets.

Buses crunched along the ice-slick pavements, their tire-chains clattering and their engines wheezing. From steaming grates came the rumble of subways. Here and there a taxicab prowled in search of the few people willing to venture into the cold. Doormen huddled close to the glittering entryways of luxurious apartment buildings or stood in lobbies staring out at the wind. Inside these buildings normally docile radiators hissed and popped as overstrained heating systems fought to maintain comfort against the freeze.

The last light had disappeared from the sky when Becky opened her eyes. Beyond the bedroom door she heard the drone of the evening news. Dick, Wilson, and Ferguson were there watching. She rolled over onto her back and stared out the window at the sky. In her field of vision there were no stars, only the bottom point of the moon slicing the darkness, cut off by the top of the window. She sighed and went into the bathroom. Seven-thirty P.M. She had slept for two hours. Disconnected images from her dreams seemed to rush at her from the air; she splashed water on her face, ran a brush through her hair. She shook her head. Had they been nightmares, or mere dreams? She couldn't quite remember. Her face looked waxy in the mirror; she took out her lipstick and applied a little. She washed her hands. Then she returned to the bedroom and pulled on her thermal underwear, then threw on jeans, a flannel shirt, and added a heavy sweater. The wind moaned around the corner of the building, making the window bulge and strain. Long fingers of frost were appearing on the glass, twinkling softly as they grew.

Becky walked into the living room. "Welcome to the real world," her husband said. "You missed the show."

"Show?"

"The Commissioner announced that Evans was killed by a gang of nuts. Cult murder."

Wordlessly Wilson waved a copy of the *News*.

Becky shook her head, didn't bother to comment. "Werewolf Killers Stalk Park—Two Dead."

So ridiculously confused, so mindless. The Commissioner just couldn't grasp the truth, none of them could. She found her cigarettes and lit one, then flopped down on the couch between her husband and Wilson. Ferguson, slumped in their reclining chair, had not spoken. His face was drawn, the skin seeming to have stretched back over the bones, giving him a cadaverous appearance. His mouth was set, his eyes staring blindly in the general direction of the television set. The only movement he made was to rub his hands slowly along the arms of the chair.

Becky wanted to draw him out of it. "Doctor Ferguson," she said, "what's your opinion of all this?"

He smiled a little and shook his head. "I think we'd better get our proof." He felt his pocket for the rustle of paper. His notes on Beauvoy's hand signals were there, ready for reference in case his memory slipped.

"He means we've run out of time," Wilson said.

"So what else is new. Any of you guys hungry?"

Everybody was very hungry. They wound up ordering two pizzas from a place down the street. Beer and Cokes they had in the refrigerator. Becky was just as glad, she didn't particularly care to cook for four people. She leaned back on the couch crossing her legs, feeling the weight of the two men beside her. "We got everything?" she asked.

"Two radios and the camera. What else is there to get?"

"Nothing I guess. Anybody been upstairs?"

Their plan was to stake out the roof and man it in relays. One would stay there with the camera while the other three waited below. The reason that they didn't go up in pairs was that they hoped it would help to keep the chance of being scented to a minimum. The three in the apartment would keep in touch with the one on the roof via the handheld radios they had bought. Dick had purchased them at an electronics store, two CB walkie-talkies. They could have checked out a couple of police-issue models but they didn't want their traffic overheard on the police band. No sense in attracting attention. By tomorrow morning it wouldn't matter; they would have the pictures they needed. Becky's eyes went to the camera, its black bulk resting on the dining room table. It looked more like a flat-ended football than a camera. Only the shielded lens, reposing like a great animal eye deep in its hood, revealed the thing's function. They had all handled it earlier, getting used to the awkward shape and the overly sensitive controls. You could take pictures almost without realizing you had started the camera, and the focusing mechanism could be very frustrating to work if your depth of field was changing rapidly. How soldiers had ever used it in battle was beyond understanding. And it was terribly delicate, threatening to break at the least jostle or to lose its onboard computer if the batteries weakened too much.

But it worked miraculously well when it worked. "Anybody tried it out yet?" Becky asked.

"You're going to be the first."

She nodded. By mutual agreement she would stand the first watch on the roof, eight to ten-thirty. They had divided the hours of darkness into four two-and-a-half-hour segments and allocated the watches. Becky took the first, Ferguson the second. He had argued that he wanted to take his watch in the alley where he could confront the Wolfen, as he called them, personally. But he had been overruled. The third watch, from one until three-thirty, was to be Dick's. This was the most likely time for the night's attempt. Always when they had come before, it had been during this period. Dick had insisted on this watch, saying that he was the best choice, the strongest and the most fit. Becky couldn't deny it. She and Wilson were exhausted, God knew, and Ferguson was showing signs of cracking. Dick was the strongest, it was right that he go at the most dangerous time.

Still, she did not want him to go. She found herself drawn to him in a strange, dispassionate way that she did not associate with their married love. There was something about his vulnerability that made her want to protect him. Physically there was no real attraction, but there was a quality of spirit that attracted her strongly—he had been willing, after all, to put his whole career on the line to keep his father out of a welfare nursing home. He had always been good and kind to her—but there was something inside him that was growing, a kind of wall that shut her out of his heart, kept her away from his secret thoughts. She wanted to be there but he refused her entry, and maybe not only her but himself as well. He brought tenderness and physical intimacy to the relationship but he did not bring himself. The real Dick Neff was as alien to her now as he had been when they first met. And her spirit, after hungering and trying for his love these many years, had simply given up. She knew now what was missing in their relationship and she had begun to try to do what she could to repair the damage. Mostly, it was going to be up to Dick. She longed for him to open himself to her, to give her more than a thin veneer of himself to go with his urgent sexuality, but she felt that in the end he would fail. Exactly why she felt this way she could not say, but she did feel it. Perhaps it came from the coldness she saw in his eyes, and the lust that filled them when she so desperately wanted to see love. Dick had been scarred in a way that many cops are scarred. He had seen too much of life's miseries to open himself to any other human being, even his wife. When they were first married Dick would come home hollow-eyed with sorrow, unable to articulate his feelings about the horrors he had seen. He would describe them woodenly, all emotion absent from his voice.

There had been a child suicide, a little girl of twelve who had died in his arms of self-inflicted burns. She had pressed herself against a gas stove, then lurched, in flames, through a window into the street.

There had been a mother, pregnant, beheaded by a gang of teenage junkies. He had been first on the scene, witness to the spontaneous abortion and miscarriage delivery of the seven-month fetus.

There had been many others in his years on the street, most of them connected one way or another with drugs. These experiences plus his time in Narcotics had made of him an obsessive, consumed man with only one goal, to destroy the dealers who destroyed the people.

The obsession had to be compromised in so many ways that his hatred of crime had turned into self-loathing, a mockery of his personal worth. Problems, to a man like Dick, caused a slow closing of his heart, a shutting out of life, until there was nothing left but anger and animal lust and a vague, overshadowing sorrow that he could not voice.

Becky knew these things about her husband, and longed to tell him about them. But it was hopeless, and this hopelessness was now driving her away from him. She was rapidly reaching the point where if she could not help him, she would have to leave him.

And there was Wilson. George Wilson, a grumpy, unappealing creature with an open soul. He might grumble and threaten, but you could open Wilson up

and get inside. And he loved her with boyish desperation. When his overtures were accepted he was
amazed and gratified. He wanted her in a raw, urgent
manner that possessed him right down to his core.
She knew that he dreamed about her at night, that
he held an image of her in his mind's eye during his
waking hours. And they fit one another in strange and
satisfying ways.

Such thoughts were dangerous. How could any-
one in her right mind want to trade the young, vital
Dick Neff for a busted-up old man like Wilson? Well,
she was thinking about it more and more lately.

The doorbell rang, and in a few moments they
were eating pizza. "You still sulky, Doc?" Becky asked
Ferguson. He was brooding more than he should; she
was trying to draw him out.

"I'm not sulky. Just contemplative."

"Like a soldier before a big battle," Wilson said.
"Like me this afternoon."

"I wouldn't know, I've never been in a battle.
But let's just say that sitting up there on that roof half
the night isn't my idea of my proper role."

"Your idea is to go down to the alley and get
yourself killed."

"We don't know their capacities, but I think I
have the means to communicate with them. On the
roof, you'll be in danger as soon as they become
aware you're there. You'll be hidden, they'll see it as
a threat."

"And climb all thirty stories after us, I suppose."
Ferguson stared at her. "Obviously."

"Carl, we'll have the Ingram up there. Have you
ever seen what an Ingram M-11 can do?"

"No, and I don't want to. I'm sure it's very lethal.
Naturally all you can think of is kill or be killed. And
what about all the other buildings? A sea of windows.

Will you really start spraying high velocity bullets around? I doubt it." He settled glumly into his chair.

He was right, too. Not one of them would feel free to use that gun on a rooftop in the middle of Manhattan. Hell, you wouldn't want to use any gun in such circumstances, surrounded by so many innocent lives. But the gun was the only real protection they had. Its value lay in the fact that it would provide accurate coverage over a wide area and do it fast. A shotgun could do that too, but they were afraid that buckshot would lack stopping power. One slug from an Ingram would knock a heavy man ten feet. They wanted that kind of punch if they were going to come up against the werewolves.

"How likely are they to spot us?" Wilson asked suddenly. He had been gobbling pizza; it had not seemed as if he was following the conversation at all.

Ferguson considered. "The more senses they can bring to bear, the more likely. If scent was all they had, we'd have a chance. Unfortunately they have hearing and sight too."

"We can be quiet."

"How? Stop breathing? That's more than enough sound to give you away."

"Then we've gotta hope we see them first, don't we? You spot 'em, you take a few pictures, you get the hell inside."

Ferguson nodded. "Assuming we see them first—or at all."

"Look, we've been through that. They aren't going to come up through the building and they aren't going to climb the balconies that overlook Eighty-sixth Street. That leaves these balconies, the ones that overlook the alley, as their only route of attack. So if each person just keeps that camera focused on that alley, we're gonna see them if they come. That's damn well where they'll be."

The disconsolate look on Ferguson's face didn't change. He wasn't buying Wilson's theory, at least not enough to improve his disposition. "Have you imagined what it'll be like up there fooling around with that damn camera while they are swarming up the balconies? I have, and believe me it isn't a very comforting thought."

"You'd have a good thirty seconds before they reached the roof," Becky said.

Ferguson leaned forward in the chair, stared at them with contemptuous eyes. "Assuming you even see them coming."

"That's the whole purpose of the camera, for Chrissakes! It makes it like daylight. We damn well will see them."

"Human senses against Wolfen senses," he replied bitterly. "Technology or no technology, there is absolutely no comparison. Let me tell you something. Whichever one of us is unlucky enough to be up there when they come is going to be in very great danger. Let me repeat, *very great danger*. Unless we all realize that all the time, every second, it is very likely that one or more of us will be killed."

"Jesus Christ, we don't need that!" Dick blurted. "I mean, what a fucking —"

"Dick, he doesn't understand. He's not a cop." You don't look at things that way when you're on the force. Maybe it's true, but brooding on it isn't the kind of thing that increases a man's effectiveness.

"He's doing a cop's job. Oh, no, wait a minute. No cop ever had an assignment like this before. But at least we're prepared for it—this guy obviously isn't."

"I don't have to be here at all, may I remind you. In fact, I ought to be in that alley."

Dick started to speak. Becky knew him well enough to know that he was about to get angry, to lash out—and they needed everybody, even Ferguson.

"Dick's right," she said quickly, "let's not talk about it. I'm due to go up in ten minutes anyway, so enough said."

"OK," Dick said after a long moment. Ferguson glanced nervously at his watch and was silent.

She went into the bedroom and put a cardigan on over her heavy sweater, then wound a thick cashmere scarf around her neck and put on her pea jacket. She drew fur-lined gloves on her hands and dropped an electric pocket warmer into the jacket. She already had on three pair of socks and snow boots. She pulled a knit hat down over her ears and added a fur cap.

"Jesus," Wilson said, "you look like a mountain climber in that outfit."

"I've got two and a half hours in that wind."

"I know, I'm not arguing. Let's test radios."

The concern in his eyes touched her deeply. He turned on one handset, then the other, and when they were both running they squealed. "Good enough," he said. "I'll be over here near the terrace. We oughta get a good signal as long as I don't move too far back in the apartment and you stay near the edge of the roof. You got the signals straight?"

"One dot every five minutes. Two if I want to go to voice. Three if I need help." Instead of talking they planned to signal as much as possible by pressing the mike button. It would keep the noise down.

"Right. But give us a vocal as soon as you get up there and another just before you're ready to come down." He glanced over her shoulder. Dick was adjusting the camera, Ferguson was facing the TV set. "Come closer," Wilson said in an undertone. She stood face to face with him and he kissed her a long moment on the mouth. "I love the hell out of you," he said. She smiled at him, put her finger to her lips, then turned and went into the dining room. She was glad—he seemed to be recovering some of his customary strength.

"Camera's good," Dick said. "Just for God's sake don't drop it over the ledge. They'll have my head six ways from Sunday if I don't bring this thing back intact."

She took it from him, carrying it in both hands. Her thermos of hot coffee was under her arm.

"Wait a minute, kid," he said. "Isn't something missing?"

"If you mean the Ingram, I'm not taking it."

"You damn well are." He went into the living room and lifted it out of the box Wilson had brought it in. "It'll fit right up under your pea jacket, very nice and snug. Take it."

"I've got my thirty-eight. I don't want the Ingram."

"Take the fucking thing, Becky!"

She took it from him. His mouth trembled as he gave it to her. They said nothing; there was nothing more to be said.

The three men accompanied her to the elevator. It seemed unlikely that anybody would be encountered on the way up, but if they were, the presence of four people in the car would draw attention away from Becky's strange outfit and equipment.

The elevator rose smoothly to the thirtieth floor. All four of them got out. They went into the stairwell through the gray-painted exit door. The wind could be heard above, booming against the door that led to the roof. Becky ascended the single flight of stairs, followed by Wilson and Dick. Ferguson remained below.

"OK, kid," Wilson said, opening the door. It faced north, and as soon as he opened it a brutal gust of ice-cold wind poured in on them. Becky barely felt it under her layers of clothing. She tromped out onto the roof—and nearly fell flat. The snow had melted up here and now the melt was a layer of ice. She stood bracing herself against the jamb of the open door, staring down at the two men huddled on the steps behind her. "Icy as hell," she shouted over the wind.

"Can you make it?" Wilson hollered back.

"On all fours."

"What's that?"

"On all fours." And she pushed the door closed. At once she was plunged into a dark and alien world. The wind boomed and every move caused her to lose purchase on the ice. The roof was flat, its expanse broken only by this door and by a shed about ten feet away that housed the elevator motors. The building was large and the roof area was wide, perhaps a hundred feet on a side. This area, roughly square, was covered in gravel which made the layer of ice bumpy and even more difficult to walk across. If she stood still the wind moved her of its own accord, causing her to lean into it and stumble until she was down on all fours. Her eyes were tearing and the tears were freezing on her cheeks. Lights whirled past. She huddled against the door, her back to the wind. She pulled out the pocket warmer and cradled its fitful heat near her face. The Ingram's butt jutted into her left breast, the coffee thermos threatened to roll out from under her arm, the walkie-talkie and camera further impeded her movements. She looked around. Lights glowed up from three sides of the

building. Those were the street sides. The fourth side, which disappeared into a maw of blackness, overlooked the alley.

Putting the pocket warmer away, she braced herself and crawled toward the dark edge of the roof. For safety she finally went down on her stomach and slithered as best she could with all the equipment. The edge loomed closer, the wind rocked her prone body. Cold ripped into her, cutting under the pea jacket, so bitter that it felt like fire against her skin. She kept telling herself that she was crazy, she had to turn back, there was no way to endure this for more than a few minutes.

But she went on, dragging herself closer and closer to the edge of the roof. At least the alley was on the south side of the building and her back would be to the wind.

She reached the edge, touched the concrete lip of the roof with her gloved fingers and paused. The lip was about three inches high, a bare handhold. Methodically she inventoried: thermos, radio, camera, weapon. OK, now pull into position. She dragged herself closer to the edge, pulling with her cold-stiffened fingers until her face was just at the lip of the roof. Before her was an empty expanse that plunged into dark. South of the building was a sea of brownstones and older, lower apartments. Beyond them she could see all of midtown Manhattan, the lights glimmering in the wind, the moon now risen high above the city. In the sky the anti-collision strobes of passing planes stuttered. Far to the west a fitful carmine glow marked the very end of day. But here the night was total, and the alleyway below was unlit except by the faint glow from the windows of apartments low down in the building.

Clumsily she maneuvered the camera before her

face, felt for the button, and turned it on. Immediately the readout jumped into the viewfi ler and she pressed the focusing lever. The alleyway swam into view, uncannily bright and detailed. She could see trashcans, see the frozen snow covering their tops. The brownstone houses across the alley all had gardens, and she could look into their shadows and see the frozen remains of summer flowers, the hard limbs of naked trees. The windows of the brownstones were almost too bright to look at, but when her eye adjusted she could see people inside, most of them sitting like statues before television sets. One young family was eating dinner at a table behind a glass door. There were four of them, two adults and two children. She could make out the faces clearly.

Now she pulled the camera back, cradling it against her chest, and drew the walkie-talkie around to her face. It had been hanging from its strap along her back. Clumsily she turned it on, held it to her ear so that the mouthpiece fit under her lips. This would be the only voice transmission and she didn't want it to last any longer than it had to. For all she knew they were out there somewhere right now watching and waiting. "You there?" she asked quietly. At once there was a reply, Wilson: "Hear you." She reported briefly. "I'm in position, camera operating, cold as hell." "Hell's hot." "Right. Let's test signals." She released the mike button, then pressed it once, holding it down for about three seconds. Downstairs Wilson followed suit. The result was a detectable change in the hiss that came from the speaker. She replied with two presses of her mike button. Wilson responded immediately with the same. The emergency signal, three presses, was not tried. It was reserved only for trouble. If one and two worked, three would also. "OK by me," she said. "OK," came the reply. "You'll get your first signal five minutes from now."

Then there was silence. In five minutes Wilson would press his mike button once and she would reply with the same. So it would go for the next two and a half hours. Every five minutes they would renew contact, thus insuring that the cold would not lull her into sleep. If she ever failed to reply they would be on the roof in a matter of minutes. She thought of them down there together in that apartment and hoped they kept away from each other. Wilson and Dick were not friendly, to say the least. And Ferguson was so nervous the least bit of tension might send him into a panic. The wind rocked her body again, making her cling to the edge of the roof with her free hand. Leaving the walkie-talkie against her ear, she withdrew the pocket warmer and put it on the roof just beneath her chest, making a tiny area of relative warmth that would keep her neck from freezing as the tendrils of Arctic wind curled around her body.

She repositioned the camera and made a sweep of the alley peering through the viewer. Nothing. Closing her eyes she turned her face into the pocket of warmth under her chin. The wind kept pulling at her, kept her body tense, her mind on the ragged edge. It was going to be a long and brutal watch. The first signal came through and she replied, then made another sweep and again bowed her head.

This continued through the first hour. At the end of that time she pushed back from the edge of the roof, put her equipment down, and stood up. Methodically she stomped until she was sure her feet were unfrozen, then jogged in place for a few moments. She blew into her gloves, grateful for the warmth that this produced. She drank a few swallows of coffee. Overall she was in good condition. She struggled across the roof and peered down the three street sides. Each one revealed the same scene: an empty street with the ice glaring yellow-white under the sodium-arc streetlights. Aside from a few parked cars there were no signs of humanity.

Then she noticed one of the cars. It was double-parked and it looked a lot like an NYPD unmarked car. Why the hell would it be here? It could only be a stakeout. But from this height who could be sure? Then the wind hit her and she had to go back to hands and knees, crawling precariously across the roof once more. Let them stake the place out, maybe they would come in handy one way or another. Goddamn them, they were watching Dick. Those were Internal Affairs Division investigators for sure. When you thought about it, it was almost funny. She huddled down and made another sweep.

"You're through, kid," came Wilson's voice. She buzzed back, saying nothing, and immediately retreated to the doorway. It seemed like an eternity had passed up here. Her whole body ached except for her feet, which were ominously numb.

They were waiting for her in the stairwell. Ferguson was bundled up now. She passed the equipment to him and told him about her experience with the wind. He nodded, his face sunken and silent. Dick replaced all batteries—pocket warmer, camera, walkie-talkie and then tucked a hot thermos under Ferguson's arm. The scientist slammed through the door with a bang and a gust of frigid wind.

The brutal conditions hit him harder than he had expected. He struggled to keep his balance, slipped and collapsed against the door. This whole thing was

such a farce. Instead of hiding up here they should
be down in the alley under spotlights making the
open-handed gesture of friendship from Beauvoy's
diagrams. The wind cut into him, making his muscles
convulse. How could those cops possibly take this
punishment? He tried to move out, fell back again.
His eyes were tearing now, the tears freezing and
obscuring his vision. He got to his feet, took a few
staggering steps forward. His legs shot out from under
him and he landed painfully on his side, smashing
the absurd, unwieldy gun into the ice beneath him.
He struggled to his stomach and got out the radio,
began calling them. This roof was beyond his capabilities; despite the others he was going to have to
take his chances with communication—in the alley.

Back in the apartment Becky went to the bedroom and peeled off her clothes. She checked her feet,
found no signs of frostbite. Still shaking, she went
into the bathroom, closed the door, and turned on
the shower. When the warm billows of steam hit
her naked body she actually laughed with delight.
Warmth, delicious warmth was all she could think of
as the water sluiced over her body. It had been a
brutal, killing two and a half hours and she was
bitterly tired. After a thorough shower she toweled
and powdered herself, then once again put on long
johns, jeans, and a heavy sweater. Anything could
happen tonight and she wasn't about to assume that
she wouldn't be going outside again, maybe in a hurry.

When she went into the living room, Wilson was
hunched over the radio and Dick was suiting up. He
was doing it slowly but he was doing it. For a moment she was confused—how long had she been in
the shower—but then she realized what was happening. "Just hang on, buddy," Wilson was saying, "Neff's
gonna be up in a minute and you can come down."

The reply was garbled.

Becky flared with anger. "That little creep! Leave him where he is."

"I ain't hurryin', honey," Dick said mildly. "He's been whinin' ever since he got up there."

"He's by the door," Wilson called from his station at the living room window.

"The hell!" Becky said. "We need that little bastard. The three of us can't take his time."

"We got to. Dick's gonna take an hour, I'll take an hour, then you take a half hour. Then Dick does his full shift and I do mine. That's what we have to do." He said it laconically but his voice was tired. They all knew what hell it was up there.

"It's no surprise. You can't expect an untrained man to withstand that kind of punishment. But I still ain't hurryin'."

"As if we were in any better shape ourselves. Hell, none of us are street cops."

"Speak for yourself, dear. I'm in good shape. You and Wilson're a mess, but—"

"OK, so how's about you take his shift and yours too. Five hours. Sound good?"

"That'd be convenient, wouldn't it, honey?" He spoke in a quiet, level tone. What in the name of God did he mean? He couldn't possibly suspect that there was anything between her and Wilson. There wasn't— at least very little!

She decided not to pick up on it.

Again the three of them took the elevator to the roof, and there was Ferguson sitting in the stairwell looking bleak. Nobody spoke to him, just took the equipment and got Dick checked out. The door to hell opened and closed again and Dick was gone.

The ride down was strained and silent. Once in the apartment Ferguson began silently picking up his things, a book, his wallet and keys which he hadn't wanted to take to the roof. "That roof was too much for me," he muttered. "But I'll make it up to you, I'll do exactly what I should have done in the first place." He slipped out, the door clicking behind him. A last glance revealed a face set with fear and determination, the eyes wide and glazed.

"Don't let him," Wilson murmured.

"Yeah, don't let him."

But neither of them moved. Maybe he was going to die out on the street and maybe he wasn't. It was his risk, he had chosen it. "We should have stopped him."

"How? He's a determined man. Brave, too, even if he couldn't handle the roof. Signal Dick, let's get started." They went to the radio.

"White male about thirty-five exiting building," said one of two plainclothesmen who were sitting in a car in front of the building. "Nah, it ain't Neff." The other plainclothesman hadn't even opened his eyes. Inside the car it was warm and quiet, the two cops barely moving through the long hours of the shift. Another four hours and they would be relieved. Hell, you could get a worse gig on a night like this. Likely Captain Neff wasn't going anywhere anyway until tomorrow. Still, he had that fancy camera, he must be planning to do something with it.

The two plainclothesmen didn't watch Ferguson as he rushed past the front of the building and turned the corner. If they had they would have noticed the furtiveness of his movements, the desperate way his eyes darted around. But they would not have seen what happened when he turned that corner.

They were waiting there under cars. They had placed themselves just inside the alley. This way they could hear both front door and back and at the same time watch the apartment. When they heard familiar footsteps crunching on the snow they were filled with eagerness. The pack was damaged and angry, hungry to kill.

When they came out from under the cars, Ferguson stopped. They could smell fear thickly about him, it would be an easy kill. He spread his hands in the palms-up gesture he had seen in the ancient book. They took their time getting positioned. He looked into their faces. Despite his fear he was fascinated by them—cruel, enigmatic, strangely beautiful. They stepped toward him, stopped again. "I can help you," he said softly.

Three of them executed the attack while the fourth kept watch. He was dead, his body rolled under a car within five seconds. One jumped into his chest to wind him; another collapsed his legs from behind, and a third tore his throat out the moment he hit the ground.

Their race had long ago forgotten its ancient relationship with man. His hand-signals had meant nothing to them, nothing at all. The four of them literally tore him apart in their fury, ripped at him in a kind of frenzy of rage. They were the mother, the second-mated pair and the female of the third. Old Father had disappeared, they weren't sure why. Perhaps he was too ashamed or too hurt to take his new place behind the youngest in the pack.

But he was nearby. Older, cannier and more sensitive than the others, he knew better than they how desperate the situation had become. He was determined to right the wrong he had done his pack—even at the cost of his life. Although he was unable to see them, he heard their attack. "They act from fear," he thought. "They need strength and courage."

And he resolved to help them. He had been

aware for some moments of a human presence on the roof of the building and took care to stay close to the wall, out of the line of sight from above.

He went quickly to the front of the building, slid under a car and waited. A few minutes later a pedestrian came along, opened the door to the lobby. He ran in past her.

"Hey!"

"A dog—damn it, Charlie, I let in a dog!"

"I'll get it—Jesus, it's *moving!*"

He raced for the stairs and went up. He knew exactly where he was going and why. He trusted to luck that these were the right stairs. The shouts of the humans faded below him. Maybe they would rationalize his presence, maybe not. He recognized the danger of what he was doing and he knew how it would probably end.

But he owed this to the pack he loved.

Dick Neff cursed out loud when he felt the cold and was tugged by the wind. Becky was one hell of a girl to have endured this for two Goddamn hours! He was proud of her, there hadn't been a single peep of complaint. A person like that humbled you, hell, awed you. She was a total pro, no question about it.

He was heavier than his wife and the wind didn't force him to slither on his stomach. But he crawled. He crawled slowly and carefully, not liking the way those gusts hit him from behind and made him slide. Thirty stories was a long Goddamn drop. You went over, you'd have time to think about it on the way down. Plenty of time. He hated heights like this. The view from his apartment was beautiful but he hated this. In his nightmares he always fell, and lately he had been falling a lot. His subconscious reached out to him, imparting a strange *déjà vu*. It was as if he had been here before, crawling toward this precipice, shoved and jostled by this same wind. This was going to be a test of every particle of endurance and courage that he had. No wonder Ferguson had caved in so fast, this was a direct confrontation with the wild power of nature—and beyond that there was the even greater danger of what they faced.

He could tell where Becky had been lying by the indentation in the snow. He went to approximately the same place. First the equipment check, then the camera sweep.

Nothing there.

Now the voice check. Wilson came in clear. They punched off with the mike signal and Dick settled in as best he could. He was just making another sweep when he heard a muffled bang behind him. The door? He turned. It stood ten feet away. It was breathing hard, as if it had just run up the stairs.

He jumped to his feet, snapping away with the camera. Then it moved and he hurled the camera at it. The machine bounced against its flank and rolled away. It wasn't attacking, probably because he was so close to the edge that a direct assault would send them both over. It moved quickly, trotting to the edge itself, now parallel with him. He was going for the Ingram when it jumped him. He lurched sideways, slipped on the ice and found himself half over the edge. But so was the werewolf, just a few feet away, so close he could see its face.

They hung there, it with its forepaws dug into the icy edge, he hanging by his arms. Its eyes bored into his with a look of hatred more terrible than he had ever seen before. The eyes darted around, calculating, seeking the crucial advantage that would kill Dick Neff, leaving the werewolf alive.

Carefully, not looking at the emptiness beneath his feet, Dick brought an arm down toward the .38 he had in a pocket. This was his one chance, his only chance. He wanted so desperately to live, not to fall! The inches-high concrete lip was the only thing that held him here, and it held him now by only one arm.

The creature tried to pull itself up, failed, and hung still. It bared its teeth and made a low, horrible noise. Its eyes followed his movements, its face suddenly registered understanding. Now it began to slide along the ledge toward him, inch by inch closing the gap between them. With only one arm hanging on Dick could do no more than stay where he was. And he was having a hard time doing that. He sobbed aloud. Waves of fatigue poured through the arm on which his life was hanging.

Now the thing was so close he could smell its fetid animal odor, see its savage teeth working in its jaw. He grasped the .38, pulled the gun up, fired, felt an agony in his arm, tried to pull the trigger again. But there was nothing to pull. He looked at the arm— his hand was not there. Blood was pouring out and steaming in the cold. And with horror-struck eyes he saw his hand, still clutching the .38, dangling in the creature's mouth. Then his death began.

As his fall started he felt fear, then something else, a vast and overwhelming sadness so great that it was a kind of exaltation. His body bounced on the hard ice off the alley and he died instantly. A few moments later his hand slammed into the ground beside him.

Far above the old father was in a death-struggle of his own. He had barely, barely cut the hand off as the gun fired. There was a searing pain in his head, an eye closed. The bullet had passed there, grazing his eye and forehead. His own forelegs were tiring and he could not lift himself back over the ledge without risking a fall. But he didn't want to lift himself.

He had seen the highest of the balconies not far away; he could work his way over there and drop down to it.

When he landed he stood dazed, shaking his head. The eye was not going to work, it seemed. Very well, he would complete this task with only one eye. He was going to save his family and save the secret of his race. He knew it now, he was going to win.

He climbed down the balconies carefully and painfully, wounded more seriously than he could know, until he had gotten to the one balcony that mattered. He crouched there inhaling the filthy smell of the two that were left alive, just the other side of the glass.

Chapter 12

"Hey, Becky, I got a problem." She came over to him. "He's not picking up on the signal."

"Interference?"

"Don't think so." He pressed the mike button twice. No answer. He went over to voice. "Wake up, Dick. You gotta signal back or I can't tell if you're still there."

Only the whisper of static answered.

"Maybe there is some interference," he said. "I'll go out on the balcony, get a better line."

"We'd better go to the roof. It won't take a minute."

"Look, I'll just go outside and—"

"We're going up right now. Get your coat on."

He complied. Now that she was making their command decisions, he seemed to be returning to a more normal equilibrium. This was fine by her; she'd trade her stripes for his bars any time.

Both of them had moved their pistols to their jacket pockets by the time they reached the roof door. Becky felt ice-cold inside, as cold as the night on the other side of the door. "You cover my back," she said. "Draw your gun. We take no chances." She pushed the door open and stepped out, her eyes going at once to where Dick should be.

But wasn't.

A pang of fear made her heart start to pound. She suppressed it, took a deep breath, called him.

Nothing answered but the wind. Then she saw an object not far away, a dark bulge on the icy roof. "Christ, here's the camera!" Slipping and falling she went and retrieved it.

Part of the housing was knocked off. The lens was cracked. She backed into the stairwell, closed the door against the wind. In the quiet she heard her own ragged breathing. Her insides were churning, she wanted to be sick. "Something's happened to him," she said. "Let's get downstairs."

"To the alley?"

"Hell, no! If they got him that's where he'll be—and they'll be there too, waiting for us to come to him. Remember this morning—the lure? They only get to play that particular trick once a day." She spoke from reason, but her heart screamed at her to go to the alley, to save her husband. If he was there, though, he was most certainly beyond saving. She wanted to weep, but instead she pressed on. "We'll go back to the apartment and look out over the balcony. Maybe this damn camera will work enough to let us see what's on the ground down there."

They returned to an apartment that was already changing for Becky, ceasing to be a home. Everything was the same except Dick was . . . gone. If he had fallen, his body must have sailed right past these windows while they were trying to get him on the CB. She put the camera down on the dining room table, wiped tears angrily from her eyes and examined the damage. All you could see through the viewer was a pearl-white blur. "It's totaled," she said. "At least the film's intact." She tossed Wilson the cassette.

"Six shots. He took six shots."

Talking made her throat constrict. She stood silent, unable to answer, her mind searching for some way to believe that Dick was still alive. She wished that the camera hadn't broken. Then they could use it to look out over the balcony into the alley, and at least confirm the worst. She went over the possibilities: he had been attacked by a werewolf on the roof and had fallen—that was number one. A distant number two was that he had somehow escaped this attack by jumping onto the topmost balcony. Highly unlikely. If he had been able to jump down there, so could the werewolf.

Wilson came to her, put his hand on her arm. "He's had it, baby," he said gruffly. His eyes were wet. He looked furious.

"I wish I knew for sure."

"You know."

"Oh, God, maybe he's down in that alley bleeding to death!" She knew it was irrational, a man surviving a fall like that, but stranger things had happened.

"I'll go look, Becky, but it isn't going to tell us anything we don't know." He went toward the balcony, paused at the door. He pushed the curtains aside. "Just reconnoitering," he said. He failed to notice the shape huddled against the glass almost at his feet. He rolled back the sliding door.

It leaped at him through the curtains, its snarling mouth ripping the cloth. He fell back into the living room, rolled, and headed for the bedroom door. Becky was in motion behind him as the thing pulled the curtains down around itself, shook free, and came on into the apartment.

Becky and Wilson reached the bedroom, and she slammed and locked the door behind them. There was a moment of silence, then the sound of a body pressing against the door. The plywood creaked and popped, but the door held. Suddenly the handle began rattling furiously, almost as if it would be torn out at its roots. Becky put her fist to her mouth. "Did you see?" she whispered as she fought the panic. "It's brains are all out. It's been horribly hurt."

"That must be Dick's doing."

The door groaned. Now the beast began throwing itself against it. The hinges quaked, the damaged doorknob rattled loosely with each impact. "Shoot it. Shoot through the door."

"My gun is in my coat." And his coat was in the kitchen.

She found her own .38 and aimed it about where she estimated the creature's chest would be, flicked off the safety, and pulled the trigger.

There was a deafening blast, and a smoking hole splintered the door. "That's done," she said in a shaky voice. She started toward the door, but Wilson's hand grabbed her arm. "You missed," he said.

"How could I miss—it was right there."

"Look."

Through the two-inch hole in the door she could see something gray—fur. And she could hear a low, deep sound of breathing.

"I didn't even wound it." She raised the gun again. At once there was light shining through the hole. The creature had retreated.

"They're damn smart. It must have heard and moved to avoid the shot. There's no use trying again, it won't be there. And we aren't doing the door much good."

Outside the door the Old Father moved cautiously. He had jumped to avoid the shot just in time and could still feel a hot sensation where it had passed his face. His head throbbed terribly, it was all he could do to keep the pain from making him scream in agony. He fought for control, found it somewhere within him, and forced himself to think about the situation. The most important thing was that he was in. He had heard the man walking over to the balcony door and had hidden just in time. The man had opened the door and—at last.

The next thing was to get the rest of the pack up here. He wasn't sure that they would come if he called them, but he knew that the sounds of a fight would certainly get them climbing up the precarious balconies. Very well—he would create such sounds. He leaped into the living room, letting his hatred for his tormentors be vented in destruction. He pulled down lamps, smashed furniture, did everything he could to create a din. But only for a few moments, not enough to alert the humans in nearby apartments. Then he stopped, stood with his ears cocked. And there it was! The clatter of toes, the grunts of struggle. They were on their way up.

How he loved them! He thought of their future and his own past, and felt hope not only for them but for his whole race. The last of the enemy cowered behind a flimsy door ready for the slaughter. Soon all packs everywhere would again be safe from human interference. They, not he—for their safety he was going to trade his life.

They came rushing in, their faces full of the lust of victory.

When they saw him they stopped. Very well, let them be shocked. He knew a mortal wound when he felt it; their expressions of horror did not surprise him. He was glad to give his life for them; now they knew it.

A curtain of grief descended over them. Very well, that was to be expected. He refused to allow himself to share their grief. Memories clattered at the edge of his mind, but now was not the moment for them. There was much work and little time.

Using their language of movements, tail-wags and sounds, he quickly communicated to his family that the two behind the door had a gun and that the door must be burst. They all knew without its being said that he planned to jump first into the room, to take the impact of the gun.

His mate looked pleadingly at him.

He reminded her that he was already as good as dead. This last act—of jumping into the gunfire—would be useful to the pack. Her sorrow, or his own, must not be allowed to intervene.

Inside the bedroom Becky and Wilson listened closely. They heard a rapid series of growls of varying pitch, then the rattle of claws against the floor.

"Now they're all out there," Wilson whispered. "The rest of them must have come up from the alley. How many shots you have left?"

"Five."

"They better count." His voice was choked. It was obvious to them both that five shots would not be enough.

"The phone!" Becky grabbed it, dialed 911. Nothing. "The receiver in the living room must have been knocked off the hook."

"We won't make it," he said softly.

She whirled and faced him. "We'll make it, you bastard. If we don't give up hope, that is."

"I'm just being realistic, Becky."

"Speak for yourself." She held her gun in both hands, pointed straight at the door. Not even the fact that Wilson was trying to kiss her cheek caused her to move.

"Your timing stinks," she said.

"It's probably my last chance."

"Shut up and watch the door."

The Old Father had gathered the pack well clear of the door but in sight of it. He told them what they would do, assuming his accustomed role. Nobody questioned him, nobody dared. He had gotten them this far, they could not but listen to him.

They would go in low, burst the door. Then he would make his rush. He would do it alone, hoping that the gun would be emptied into him. Then the others could destroy them, consume his body, and leave without a trace of themselves remaining. Man would not understand how these tragedies had occurred, and the secret of the packs would be safe once more.

He snapped his jaw, a sound that brought them all to immediate attention. Now they prepared themselves.

They all quivered with the desire to speak but said nothing. There were no words for what the pack now had to face, for the sorrow that they all felt. Despite his loss of the right to lead, he had nonetheless founded this pack, had built it through his strength and effort. Now in death he received its respect.

"You hear anything?" Becky asked. Wilson was standing near the door.

"They're in the living room. Maybe we could make a break."

"We wouldn't get three feet. Just stay put and think."

The phone lay on the floor, a tiny voice telling them again and again that a receiver had been left off the hook on the line. Becky felt like ripping the damn thing out of the wall and tossing it through the window. "Hey, wait a minute—" She went over to the window and peered down. "Listen, why don't we toss the Goddamn bed out the window. That'll bring somebody up to investigate."

"So the poor soul opens the door and gets torn apart. Meanwhile, we're already dead."

"You got a pen?"

"Yeah, but what—"

"So we write on the sheet. Gimme—" She took the pen, threw the covers off the bed and started scratching big letters on the fitted bottom sheet. In a few moments there was a rough message, "SEND ARMED COPS 16G. MURDER. GREAT DANGER. BREAK IN. CAREFUL OF AMBUSH!"

They pulled open the window, finding that it was not big enough to accommodate the mattress. Becky stationed Wilson at the door with the .38 and wrapped the quilt around her right arm. She looked down to make sure the street below was empty, then smashed the window with her fist. "OK, give me a hand again, let's get this thing out." Together they pushed and struggled until the mattress fell from the window. It tumbled end over end and hit squarely on the sidewalk. It must have made a noise, but the sound was lost in the wind.

Then there came scratching at the door. "They're onto the lock again," Wilson said. His voice was strained. He looked desperately at Becky.

"Get the dresser over there—move it!" He obediently shoved it against the door while she held the pistol. A moment later there was a tremendous bang, and the door sprung on its hinges. A crack appeared down the center. "Lean against that dresser," Becky said to Wilson, who had cringed away toward the bathroom. Now he came forward again, pressing his back against the dresser. The door shook with the onslaught of the strength behind it.

Across the street the two plainclothesmen had heard the thud when the mattress hit the sidewalk. Both of them peered out the closed windows of their car, toward the sound.

"Somethin' hit the sidewalk."

"Yeah."

Silence for a moment. "You wanna take a look?"

"Nah. You go if you're curious."

"I'm not curious."

They settled back to wait out the end of the shift. Another hour and they would be able to hand off to the next crew and get a hot shower. Despite the car heater the cold got to you on these long gigs.

"What do you suppose Neff is doin'?" one of them said to break the monotony.

"Sleeping in his bed like all smart people this time of night."

They said nothing further.

The door smashed into three pieces, which came flying in over the dresser. One of the creatures was there, pulling itself in through the space above the dresser. Becky shot as it leaped at her. The bullet smashed into its head, and it dropped to the floor. Wilson had been thrown aside by the assault on the door and now scrambled to his feet. Despite its head-wound and the blood bubbling out of a new two-inch hole in its chest, the thing jumped on him, clawing into him with its vicious paws. He gasped, his eyes widening, and screamed in agony. She shot again.

It had to be dead now, but still the claws worked, the jaws cut into Wilson's neck and his screams pealed out.

Then the thing slumped away from Wilson.

The only sound in the room was its ragged breathing. Wilson started to stagger away, his whole front ripped and streaming with blood. She stumbled to help him—and a paw grabbed her ankle. Agony pierced her leg as the sharply pointed claws penetrated. She put her hands to her head and shrieked, kicking frantically with her free foot. The blows landed again and again, but the grip would not release.

Becky's whole being wanted to shoot it again, to shoot it and shoot it, but she did not. The bullets must be saved.

Then the grip faded.

She slumped back to a sitting position on the bedframe and pointed her pistol at the broken door, at the apparitions that were gathering there. There were four of them, obviously very unsure about her weapon. She had two shots left. Wilson, now huddled moaning on the floor beside the body of the werewolf, was beyond helping her. She was alone and in agony, fighting unconsciousness.

Downstairs the doorman was staring at a patrol car that had pulled up in front of the building. Two cops, the collars of their heavy winter coats turned up against the wind, got out and entered the lobby.

"Help you?"

"Yeah. We gotta check out a disturbance. You got a disturbance?"

"Nah. It's quiet."

"Sixteenth floor. People been callin' the precinct. Screams, furniture breakin'. You got any complaints?"

"This is a quiet building. You sure you got the right place?"

They nodded, heading for the elevator. This looked like a standard family disturbance situation— no arrests, just a lot of argument and maybe a little fight to break up. You spent half your time on family disturbances, the other half on paperwork. Real crime, forget it.

"Lessee, sixteen." One of the patrolmen punched the button, and the elevator began to ascend. After a few moments the door slid open revealing a long, dimly lit hallway. The two cops looked up and down. Nobody was visible. Aside from the sound of a couple of TVs it was quiet. They proceeded into the hall. Apartment 16-G had been the source of the disturbance. They would ring the bell.

The creatures were watching Becky by lifting their heads briefly above the edge of the dresser that stood in the doorway. Though she kept the gun aimed she wasn't fast enough to get a shot off at one of those darting heads.

Then they became quiet. They could jump right over the dresser and get at her throat, she was sure of that. She hobbled to the window, wishing that she could somehow protect Wilson, who had lapsed into unconsciousness. But she couldn't. If the creatures came at her she planned to jump. Death by falling was to be preferred a thousand times to disembowelment by those monstrosities.

A head appeared above the dresser, paused for a long moment, then was gone. That pause had been longer than the rest. Becky braced herself. Still nothing happened. They were being very careful. They knew what a gun could do.

The doorbell rang.

One of the creatures sailed across the dresser, its teeth bared, its claws extended toward her throat.

It took Becky's last two slugs in the muzzle and dropped at her feet. The claws went to the face and the body hunched, its muscles standing out like twisted ropes. Then it collapsed into a widening pool of blood. Becky watched it with a mixture of horror and sadness. Her ankle was almost useless; she could barely support herself on the windowsill with her hands. The wind was whipping her hair around her face, biting into her back. She looked across the carnage in the room. There were three hideous faces staring at her over the dresser that still blocked the doorway. With trembling hands she lifted her .38 in their direction. Without her hands on the windowsill, balance was precarious. The wind buffeted her, threatening at any moment to make her fall. But the creatures hesitated before the gun. Then one of them made a low, strange sound . . . almost of grief. It closed its eyes, tensed its muscles—and suddenly turned away from the bedroom. Now all three of them disappeared below the edge of the dresser.

Then there came a knock on the door. "Police," said a young voice.

"No! Don't open that door!"

The knock came again, louder. "Police! Open up!"

"Stay out! *Stay—*"

With a crash the door flew open. The two cops who were standing there didn't even have a chance to scream. All Becky heard was a series of thuds.

Then there was a silence.

Becky was crying now. Still with the gun held in both hands she moved forward. But she could not go on. She sank to the bed. Her pistol fell to the floor. Any moment now the werewolves would be back to kill her.

"Hey, what's goin' on in here?"

She looked up through a haze of tears. Two patrolmen were standing on the other side of the dresser with guns drawn. She sat stunned, hardly believing what she saw. "I—I've got a wounded man in here," she heard herself whisper.

The patrolmen pushed the dresser aside. Ignoring the two werewolves, one of them went to Wilson. "Breathin'," he said even as the other was calling for assistance on his radio.

"What's the story, lady?"

"I'm Neff, Detective Sergeant Neff. That's Detective Wilson."

"Yeah, good. But what the hell are those?"

"Werewolves." Becky heard herself say the word from far, far away. Strong arms eased around her, laid her back on the bed. But still she fought unconsciousness. There was more to do, no time to sleep.

In the distance there were sirens, then a few minutes later voices in the hall. Then light, flashbulbs popping as police photographers recorded the scene. She raised her head far enough to see Wilson being carried out on a stretcher. "O-positive blood," she called weakly.

Then somebody was beside her, looking at her, a half smile on his tired face. "Hello, Mrs. Neff." He moved aside as medical orderlies slid her onto a stretcher. "Mrs. Neff, do you want to make a statement to the press?"

"You're the man from the *Post*, aren't you?"

"I'm Garner, ma'am."

She smiled, closed her eyes. They were moving her now, the lights of the hallway passing above her face. Sam Garner hurried along beside her, trying to hold a tape recorder microphone in her face.

"It's a big story, isn't it?" he said breathlessly.

"A big story," she said. Sam Garner smiled again, elbowed his way into the elevator already crowded with medical orderlies and her stretcher. Her leg throbbed with agony, she felt exhausted, she wanted to close her eyes, to forget. But she gave Garner his story.

Epilogue

Their mother jumped as soon as the gun had been emptied into their father. She would make the kill, then the four of them would destroy their father's body.

Then the incredible happened. The gun crashed again and their mother was also killed.

They stood staring at her lifeless form, too stunned to move. All three of them felt aware of grief—and almost overwhelming anger at the monster who had killed their parents.

It sat waving its gun, and the gun smelled hot and deadly.

They watched, not quite sure what to do. Then there was a sound outside the door—more humans approaching, their breath rising and falling, their feet crunching against the carpet in the hallway. And the sharp, nasty scent of guns was upon them also. The three young Wolfen turned to face this new threat.

The door burst open amid shouting human voices, and they prepared to kill whatever appeared there.

But it was two young males, dressed as those in the Dump had been dressed. All of this agony had begun when two such had been killed; they would not repeat the mistake. They ran past the two policemen into the hallway. Now the bodies of their parents would be left behind for men to see—but this could not be helped. They bolted down the hall, pushed through the heavy door there, and began to run down the stairs.

They raced across the lobby of the building, smashing the glass front door with their bodies, and running on, indifferent to the shouts and crashing glass behind them and to the cuts they had received.

They ran through the empty predawn city, moving north past the rows of luxury buildings, through the ruined streets even farther north, past crowds of homeless men huddled around open fires, not stopping until they reached the dark and rat-infested banks of the Harlem river.

The eastern sky was glowing fitfully, the light casting into black relief the girders of the bridges above the river. The three of them stopped. They had come to a well-hidden place, marked safe by the scent of the pack that roamed this area. All felt a terrible sense of loss. Their parents were dead, the pack they knew was ended. Worse was the fact that Wolfen bodies had been left behind in the hands of man.

They felt loss but not defeat. What burned in their hearts was not fear but defiance; hard, determined, unquenchable.

They howled. The sound echoed up and down the banks of the river, crossed the icy muttering waters, echoed again off the distant buildings.

High above them on the Third Avenue Bridge a

repair crew was deploying its equipment. When they heard the sound the men stared wordlessly at one another. One of them went to the railing but could see nothing in the darkness below.

Then the howl was answered, keening on the wind as pack after pack looked up from their haunts in the City's depths and responded to the powerful sense of destiny that the sound awakened in them all.

Novels of Suspense
JAMES ELLROY

CLANDESTINE 81141-3/$2.95 US /$3.75 Can
Nominated for an Edgar Award for Best Original Paperback
Mystery Novel. A compelling thriller about an ambitious
L.A. patrolman caught up in the sex and sleaze of smog city
where murder is the dark side of love.

SILENT TERROR 89934-5/$3.50 US /$4.75 Can
Enter the horrifying world of a killer whose bloody trail of
carnage baffles police from coast to coast and whose only
pleasure is to kill…and kill again.

FEATURING LLOYD HOPKINS

BLOOD ON THE MOON 69851-X/$3.25 US /$4.25 Can
Lloyd Hopkins is an L.A. cop. Hard, driven, brilliant, he's the
man they call in when a murder case looks bad.

"A brilliant detective and a mysterious psychopath come
together in a final dance of death."
The New York Times Book Review

BECAUSE THE NIGHT 70063-8/$3.50 US /$4.95 Can
Detective Sergeant Lloyd Hopkins had a hunch that there
was a connection between three bloody bodies and one
missing cop…a hunch that would take him to the dark heart
of madness…and beyond.

AVON Paperbacks